BLUE TWILIGHT

BLUE MOUNTAIN SERIES - LOGAN BEND, BOOK ONE

TESS THOMPSON

PRAISE FOR TESS THOMPSON

The School Mistress of Emerson Pass:
"Sometimes we all need to step away from our lives and sink into a safe, happy place where family and love are the main ingredients for surviving. You'll find that and more in The School Mistress of Emerson Pass. I delighted in every turn of the story and when away from it found myself eager to return to Emerson Pass. I can't wait for the next book." - *Kay Bratt, Bestselling author of Wish Me Home and True to Me.*
"I frequently found myself getting lost in the characters and forgetting that I was reading a book." - *Camille Di Maio, Bestselling author of The Memory of Us.*
"Highly recommended." - *Christine Nolfi, Award winning author of The Sweet Lake Series.*
"I loved this book!" - *Karen McQuestion, Bestselling author of Hello Love and Good Man, Dalton.*

Traded: Brody and Kara:
"I loved the sweetness of Tess Thompson's writing - the camaraderie and long-lasting friendships make you want to move to Cliffside and become one of the gang! Rated Hallmark for romance!" - *Stephanie Little BookPage*

"This story was well written. You felt what the characters were going through. It's one of those "I got to know what happens next" books. So intriguing you won't want to put it down." - *Lena Loves Books*

"This story has so much going on, but it intertwines within itself. You get second chance, lost loves, and new love. I could not put this book down! I am excited to start this series and have love for this little Bayside town that I am now fond off!" - *Crystal's Book World*

"This is a small town romance story at its best and I look forward to the next book in the series." - *Gillek2, Vine Voice*

"This is one of those books that make you love to be a reader and fan of the author." -*Pamela Lunder, Vine Voice*

Blue Midnight:
"This is a beautiful book with an unexpected twist that takes the story from romance to mystery and back again. I've already started the 2nd book in the series!" - *Mama O*

"This beautiful book captured my attention and never let it go. I did not want it to end and so very much look forward to reading the next book." - *Pris Shartle*

"I enjoyed this new book cover to cover. I read it on my long flight home from Ireland and it helped the time fly by, I wish it had been longer so my whole flight could have been lost to this lovely novel about second chances and finding the truth. Written with wisdom and humor this novel shares the raw emotions a new divorce can leave behind." - *J. Sorenson*

"Tess Thompson is definitely one of my auto-buy authors! I love her writing style. Her characters are so real to life that you just can't put the book down once you start! Blue Midnight makes you believe in second chances. It makes you believe that everyone deserves an HEA. I loved the twists and turns in this book, the mystery and suspense, the family dynamics and the restoration of trust and security." - *Angela MacIntyre*

"Tess writes books with real characters in them, characters with flaws and baggage and gives them a second chance. (Real people, some remind me of myself and my girlfriends.) Then she cleverly and thoroughly develops those characters and makes you feel deeply for them. Characters are complex and multi-faceted, and the plot seems to unfold naturally, and never feels contrived." - *K. Lescinsky*

Caramel and Magnolias:
"Nobody writes characters like Tess Thompson. It's like she looks into our lives and creates her characters based on our best friends, our lovers, and our neighbors. Caramel and Magnolias, and the authors debut novel Riversong, have some of the best characters I've ever had a chance to fall in love with. I don't like leaving spoilers in reviews so just trust me, Nicholas Sparks has nothing on Tess Thompson, her writing flows so smoothly you can't help but to want to read on!" - *T. M. Frazier*

"I love Tess Thompson's books because I love good writing. Her prose is clean and tight, which are increasingly rare qualities, and manages to evoke a full range of emotions with both subtlety and power. Her fiction goes well beyond art imitating life. Thompson's characters are alive and fully-realized, the action is believable, and the story unfolds with the right balance of tension and exuberance. CARAMEL AND MAGNOLIAS is a pleasure to read." - *Tsuruoka*

"The author has an incredible way of painting an image with her words. Her storytelling is beautiful, and leaves you wanting more! I love that the story is about friendship (2 best friends) and love. The characters are richly drawn and I found myself rooting for them from the very beginning. I think you will, too!" - *Fogvision*

"I got swept off my feet, my heartstrings were pulled, I held my breath, and tightened my muscles in suspense. Tess paints stunning scenery with her words and draws you in to the lives of her characters."- *T. Bean*

Duet For Three Hands:

"Tears trickled down the side of my face when I reached the end of this road. Not because the story left me feeling sad or disappointed, no. Rather, because I already missed them. My friends. Though it isn't goodbye, but see you later. And so I will sit impatiently waiting, with desperate eagerness to hear where life has taken you, what burdens have you downtrodden, and what triumphs warm your heart. And in the meantime, I will go out and live, keeping your lessons and friendship and love close, the light to guide me through any darkness. And to the author I say thank you. My heart, my soul -all of me - needed these words, these friends, this love. I am forever changed by the beauty of your talent." *- Lisa M.Gott*

"I am a great fan of Tess Thompson's books and this new one definitely shows her branching out with an engaging enjoyable historical drama/love story. She is a true pro in the way she weaves her storyline, develops true to life characters that you love! The background and setting is so picturesque and visible just from her words. Each book shows her expanding, growing and excelling in her art. Yet another one not to miss. Buy it you won't be disappointed. The ONLY disappointment is when it ends!!!" *- Sparky's Last*

"There are some definite villains in this book. Ohhhh, how I loved to hate them. But I have to give Thompson credit because they never came off as caricatures or one dimensional. They all felt authentic to me and (sadly) I could easily picture them. I loved to love some and loved to hate others." *- The Baking Bookworm*

"I stayed up the entire night reading Duet For Three Hands and unbeknownst to myself, I fell asleep in the middle of reading the book. I literally woke up the next morning with Tyler the Kindle beside me (thankfully, still safe and intact) with no ounce of battery left. I shouldn't have worried about deadlines because, guess what? Duet For Three Hands was the epitome of unputdownable." - *The Bookish Owl*

Miller's Secret
"From the very first page, I was captivated by this wonderful tale. The cast of characters amazing - very fleshed out and multi-dimensional. The descriptions were perfect - just enough to make you feel like you were transported back to the 20's and 40's.... This book was the perfect escape, filled with so many twists and turns I was on the edge of my seat for the entire read." - *Hilary Grossman*

"The sad story of a freezing-cold orphan looking out the window at his rich benefactors on Christmas Eve started me off with Horatio-Alger expectations for this book. But I quickly got pulled into a completely different world--the complex five-character braid that the plot weaves. The three men and two women characters are so alive I felt I could walk up and start talking to any one of them, and I'd love to have lunch with Henry. Then the plot quickly turned sinister enough to keep me turning the pages.
Class is set against class, poor and rich struggle for happiness and security, yet it is love all but one of them are hungry for. ......Where does love come from? What do you do about it? The story kept me going, and gave me hope. For a little bonus, there are Thompson's delightful observations, like: "You'd never know we could make something this good out of the milk from an animal who eats hats." A really good read!" - *Kay in Seattle*

"She paints vivid word pictures such that I could smell the ocean and hear the doves. Then there are the stories within a story that twist and turn until they all come together in the end. I really had a hard time putting it down. Five stars aren't enough!"
- *M.R. Williams*

EMERSON PASS

The School Mistress of Emerson Pass

The Sugar Queen of Emerson Pass

RIVER VALLEY

Riversong

Riverbend

Riverstar

Riversnow

Riverstorm

Tommy's Wish

River Valley Bundle, Books 1-4

LEGLEY BAY

Caramel and Magnolias

Tea and Primroses

STANDALONES

The Santa Trial

Duet for Three Hands

Miller's Secret

BLUE TWILIGHT

For all the small town girls with big dreams. Keep fighting. Your time will come.

PROLOGUE

I n the years afterward, I came to think of that evening of the
Logan County Fair as Blue Twilight. The transition from
the light of day to the dark of night. Awash in the pink-
grapefruit-hued light of the setting sun, I had no idea of what
was to come. Life held only promise to me then. I knew nothing
of the night. My sister and I thrived in the long days of summer
like newly budded roses, dewy with youth and beauty. I
believed the world was good and nothing bad could touch the
people I loved. How wrong I was.

The highlight of summer for Beth and me had always been
the county fair. Since we were small, my father had taken us,
leaving my mother at home for what she referred to as her
Calgon night. Each holding on to one of our father's hands, we'd
weave through crowds to see the 4-H animals, the winning pies,
quilts, and art. Of particular interest for my father was the new
car on display, which we found boring but knew that if we were
patient, the best part of the evening would come. The rides.

He'd buy us each ten tickets and then sit with his friends
while we got our fill. I was too scared to go without Beth, so we
always rode together. Our favorite was the Ferris wheel. It was
the view that we loved, squealing with glee as the magic wheel

lifted us high enough to see the entire fairgrounds, then dipped low only to climb once more to the glorious top. All the while music would play. The kind of music that made you think anything was possible. Our lives were ahead of us, after all. Nothing but promise.

Now, though, we were sixteen and seventeen, and being seen at the fair with our father was absolutely not done. We were here without my father for the first time. He'd fretted, but in the end had agreed that Beth could drive us in the family station wagon to meet the Paisley brothers.

I stood in line at the booster club's burger stand with Beth and the Paisley boys. Smoke from the grilled meat wafted into the warm summer air and intermingled with dust kicked up from the hundreds of people traipsing through the fairgrounds. I loved this scent of summer, along with river water drying on rocks, coconut sunscreen, my mother's roses, and Dad's charcoal grill. These were the staples of my young world.

The line for overly priced and mediocre food was long, and my stomach rumbled with hunger. Beth, me, and the three Paisley brothers huddled together as the line inched forward slowly. I didn't care. I'd stand here next to Cole Paisley the rest of my life if I could.

Cole Paisley. My confidant and best friend. The person I could tell anything to except for the most important thing. Athletic and bronzed with wavy hair that curled just right at the nape of his neck. Eyes the color of the river in the winters, somewhere between green and gray. Lover of books. The object of my undying yet unreciprocated love. Since we were eight years old, Cole and his twin brother, Drew, had been the center of my heart.

"Carlie, what do you want?" Luke Paisley draped an arm around my sister's shoulders. "My treat. I got my paycheck today." Luke and my sister were going to be seniors when school started next week. The high school quarterback and the head cheerleader were the envy of every kid in town. Golden-haired and tanned, they fit together like two genetically blessed bookends.

"I'll have french fries," I said, smiling shyly at Luke. "But Dad sent us with money. He told me to tell you that you're not to blow your hard-earned cash on my sister."

"Your dad's the best." Luke smiled, but there was a hint of sadness in his eyes. Mr. Paisley was not the best or anywhere near it. The bruises on the boys' backs and arms were proof of that.

"What do you want, doll?" Luke asked Beth.

"Nothing. I feel kind of off." Beth glanced at me, then quickly looked away. A jolt of alarm charged through me. Something was wrong. My sister never turned down the chance to have a milkshake and fries. She liked to dip the fries in the blended ice cream. Our mother was the kind who didn't like for us to have desserts. Her idea of a sweet was dates rolled in sesame seeds or carob oatmeal balls. We looked forward to fairground junk food all year.

"Do you feel sick?" I asked my sister.

"My stomach's bothering me." Beth twisted a strand of her hair around one finger. She always did this when she was nervous or upset.

An ominous dread crept up my spine. I shook it off. Mom always said I had too much imagination for my own good. That's why I had to have a lamp on at night even though I was practically grown. In the dark, I could swear there were bugs on the walls. When I turned on the lights, though, it was only the purple flower pattern of the wallpaper.

"You want to sit down?" Luke asked Beth. "I can bring you something."

Beads of perspiration dotted Beth's perfect nose. "No, I'm fine."

"Are you warm?" I asked.

"A little, yeah," Beth said.

"Maybe you're dehydrated," Drew said. Cole's identical twin

brother stuffed his hands into the back pockets of his 501s and squinted at Beth from under his fringe of dark blond hair. "Coach Richards says that can make you feel sick to your stomach."

Not many could tell the twins apart. They were constantly being mistaken for the other. But not by me. Yes, they were unnervingly similar. However, I could tell them apart just like that. I'd been able to from the first day they stumbled into Logan Bend Elementary School in second grade. It wasn't their appearances that differed but their insides. They shared athleticism, but Cole was gentler and quieter than his outgoing, fun-spirited brother. Cole liked to work with wood and assisted his mother in her garden. Drew preferred social activities. In the hallway or lunchroom at school, he was almost always at the center of the sound of laughter. I adored all three of the Paisley brothers. But it was Cole I loved. Until last summer, when I suddenly realized I was in love with him, I'd thought he was just my favorite person. Now, though, I knew. He was the only one I wanted. Probably forever and ever.

"I might be dehydrated," Beth said, faintly. "Luke, will you get me some water when you order for us?"

"You got it, doll." Luke's eyes were the same color as his brothers', but his hair was a lighter shade of yellow and he wasn't as thickly built. He was light on his feet and whip-smart. One day he would be a doctor. I felt certain of it.

"What happened to your glasses?" Cole asked.

"Glasses?" I asked, not understanding the question.

"I mean, why aren't you wearing them? Can you see?" Cole asked as he peered at me. Fringed with dark lashes, his eyes had the power to make my stomach do cartwheels.

I could see all right, and Cole happened to be my favorite sight.

"Did you lose them?" Drew asked. "I lost my retainer, and my mom had a total cow."

"No one wants to hear about your disgusting retainer," Cole said.

Drew grinned and tapped his teeth with his fingers. "But look at these beauties. I have to keep them perfect for the ladies." They were indeed straight and gorgeous, just as Cole's and Luke's were. Their mother worked at the orthodontist's office in town. They'd been able to have braces for no cost. My mom told me that Mr. Paisley had been out of work for as long as she could remember. The burden of the household finances was on Mrs. Paisley.

Cole rolled his eyes. "What ladies are you talking about?"

"Oh, they want the Drewster. Trust me."

I giggled. Drewster. Where did he come up with this stuff?

"Only when they think you are me," Cole said.

"Completely false. Everyone knows I'm the fun one." Drew winked at me. "Right, Carlie?"

"Um, I don't know." I looked away, not wanting to answer any questions about the differences.

Drew was right about the ladies' adoration. Every girl in town wanted one if not all three of the Paisley boys. Boys envied them. Girls wanted them.

"Beth, you're not looking so hot," Luke said. "Should I take you home?"

"No, I'm all right," Beth said, sounding weak. "But if I feel worse, will you guys take Carlie home? I don't want to ruin the night for all of us."

"Totally," Luke said.

"Will Dad be mad?" I asked Beth. Our father hadn't wanted us to ride with the Paisleys in Luke's run-down car, afraid we'd have engine trouble and get stuck on the side of the road.

"If I do go home because I don't feel well, he can't be mad," Beth said. "He'll know you wanted to stay."

Luke pointed to a picnic table where a family was getting up to toss their empty cartons. "You guys, grab the table. I'll order and bring it to you."

"Cool," Drew said. "Don't forget drinks. I'm dying of thirst."

"Got it," Luke said.

Beth handed Luke a five-dollar bill. "For Carlie's dinner."

"What's going on? Are you really sick?" I whispered to Beth as we headed toward the empty table.

"Yeah, I'm okay. It's probably the heat and being on my feet all day." Beth was working at our local gift store and had just finished a shift before we headed out earlier. "I'm going to go to the bathroom. I'll be back in a second."

"All right." I studied her for a second. She looked pale. Not wanting to act like Mom, I had to stop myself from feeling her forehead. She pressed my hand with her own. Clammy and cold despite the warm evening.

I watched her as she walked across the aisle toward one of the fairground's restrooms. She wore shorts and a tank top that showed off her curves and longs legs, but she seemed to be walking weird, as though her body hurt. What was going on with her?

"Seriously, Carlie, what happened to your glasses?" Cole asked. "I've never seen you without them unless we're down at the river. And then you say you can't see a thing. Remember when you fell in that one time?"

"Yeah, I remember." I flushed, embarrassed at the memory of the time I'd tripped over an exposed tree root and fallen into the water with my clothes on.

"I got contacts." My parents had finally relented after I'd begged them for two straight years. Mom was worried about eye infections. She was always worried about stuff that never happened. Bacteria were one of her major concerns. The kitchen counters, the toilet bowl, three-day-old chicken—all had potential to kill us or, at the very least, make us sick.

"You look different without them," Cole said.

"Yeah," Drew said. "You're kind of a babe now."

"I am?" I squeaked out, then blushed again.

"You've always been a babe," Cole said. "With or without glasses."

"Thanks, Cole, but I hated my glasses." I don't know if either of the boys had noticed, but I'd finally gotten breasts. They were small, but at least I wasn't as scrawny as I'd been just six months ago. I knew it would take a lot more than an A-size cup to turn Cole's head. A girl could dream, though.

I was a world-class dreamer. If dreaming were a profession, I'd be rich at only age sixteen. All my fantasies starred Cole Paisley as the hero and myself as the heroine. I'd emerge from my ugly duckling shell beautiful like my sister and mother. Mom blamed my daydreaming on all of the romance novels Beth and I read, but Dad said that someday I'd be a great writer. He claimed the best writers started as daydreamers.

Were my daydreams coming true? The soft way Cole was looking made me feel all fuzzy and warm inside.

"I liked your glasses," Cole said. "But you're Carlie either way."

For a second, I buzzed with pleasure. Until it occurred to me that if I was simply Carlie to him, with or without my transformation, he would never see me as anything but Beth's little sister.

"Hot damn, I see Rhonda over there," Drew said. "I can't get enough of all that red hair. I'm going over to say hello."

"After we eat, you want to go on the Ferris wheel with me?" Cole asked.

"For sure."

One side of his mouth lifted in a half smile. "Do you like Drew? I mean, like—*like* him."

"Wh...what?"

"You're always laughing when he's around." He glanced over at Drew, who was currently making an entire table of girls giggle.

"He's funny. But I don't like him that way."

"Luke told me that Beth said you might like *me*." The tips of his ears turned pink. "Is that true?"

I was going to throttle Beth. How could she have betrayed me? "I guess so."

He grinned. "Really?" Cole swatted away a bee that landed on the table. "Because I like you too. I thought you only thought of me as a friend."

It was like the sky opened and the angels started singing just for me. "You like me back?"

"I've always liked you. Since forever," he said.

My heart beat so hard and fast I felt sure it would leap out of my chest and plop onto the table. Was this one of my fantasies or was it really happening?

"But you could have any girl," I said. "They all like you."

"Nah, that's Drew and Luke. I'm too quiet. For most, anyway."

"Not for me." I gave him a shy smile.

"How come you never said anything?"

"About you?"

"Yeah. Luke told me after Beth told him and swore him to secrecy. How was I supposed to know if you didn't tell me?"

"I could never have told you because I didn't think there was a chance you'd like me. I didn't want to be humiliated."

"Well, I do like you. Actually, I love you."

I blinked, then stared at him.

"So much that it makes me feel a little sick," he said. "I want to go on the Ferris wheel with you and I want to kiss you when we're up there."

Kiss me? The angels sang again.

Luke arrived with a tray filled with food, saving me from having to answer. My stomach had a thousand hummingbirds flying around in there. I'd never be able to eat anything.

Beth returned from the bathroom. Her lips were bare of her pink gloss. Why hadn't she reapplied? She always put it on after she went to the restroom.

"Carlie, can I talk to you for a minute?" Beth asked me.

"Sure." I got up from the table, stealing a quick glance at Cole, who smiled back at me.

I followed Beth to just outside the covered area. Her fair skin seemed a little green. She must really be sick.

"I'm going home," Beth said. "I just threw up in the bathroom. Will you tell Luke for me? I don't want him to smell my breath."

"Yeah, if that's what you want."

"He'll understand. He always understands everything. That's the thing, Carlie, he's so good."

The thing? What did that mean? "Do you not like him anymore?"

"What's not to like?" Beth asked. "He's perfect."

"So are you."

"I'm not. Not anymore." She pulled me into a hug and held me so tightly I could barely breathe. "I love you. No matter what, don't forget that."

I separated from her, then studied her expression. Something was off for sure. "What's going on? You're acting weird."

"Nothing. I'm fine." She wrinkled her nose. "Have you ever noticed how many smells there are at the fair? Foul smells?"

"I think it smells good," I said. "Like summer."

"Have fun, okay?"

"Cole told me he likes me," I said, unable to contain my excitement.

"I knew it. Luke thought he did."

"He said he wants to kiss me. What if I do it wrong?"

"You won't. You'll know it's right if your whole body feels like a magical unicorn sprinkled fairy dust on you."

"Is that how it feels with Luke?"

Her gaze flickered upward, then back to me. "Let's just say I've felt that feeling or I wouldn't be able to tell you what it is."

"Drive home safe."

"I will. I'll see you in the morning. I don't have to work so we can go swimming if you want."

I nodded, then watched as she walked away until she disappeared in a sea of people. As I turned back to join the boys, the sun slipped behind Logan Mountain.

When it was our turn at the Ferris wheel, Cole stepped aside to let me go in first, then slid next to me. The attendant pulled the bar into place, and the carriage swayed back and forth. We sat close enough I could feel the heat from his skin.

Cole and I were quiet as they loaded the entire wheel before we were able to get any speed going. Then, around and around we went with REO Speedwagon's "Keep on Loving You" blaring through the speakers. On the third time around, we lurched to a stop. We were at the very top. The valley spread out before us. Streaks of pink colored the sky in the last light of day. We swayed on top of the world.

"Do you want me to kiss you?" Cole asked. "Luke told me you have to ask, otherwise you're a predator."

My stomach flopped over. *Just stay in your body*, I told myself. "It's nice to be asked." A gust of wind ruffled our hair and brought the scent of popcorn.

He smiled as he brushed his hair out of his eyes. "Are you scared?"

"I kind of am."

He took my hand. "We could start by just holding hands. If you aren't ready."

"I might be ready." I'd only imagined it a thousand times. "But if I'm bad at it, you can't tell anyone."

"I would never say anything bad about you. There's not anything wrong with you as far as I can see."

A warmth started in my stomach and spread to all parts of my body. "I never thought you noticed me at all."

"You're all I notice. Since second grade."

Could this be happening?

"Drew and I used to have fistfights about which of us got to marry you."

I laughed. "Who won?"

"Me. Obviously. Or he would be here with you." Cole looked down to where the attendant was bent over the machine that operated the Ferris wheel. "Do you ever dream about what's after this? Like when we grow up?"

"Sometimes."

"What do you dream of?" Cole asked.

"I want to write books."

"What else?"

"Be married to someone I love and have enough money to order takeout whenever we want."

He laughed. "That sounds pretty good."

"What about you?"

"I want to live on a piece of my own property and build a house and have a small farm with horses and chickens. And a dog." He looked up at the sky. "I want to marry you and have a little girl who looks just like you. I'd like to be a good dad. Like your dad."

Touched, I had to swallow the lump in my throat before speaking. "I'd like that too."

"You won't forget me, will you?" Cole asked. "When we go away to college?"

"I could never forget you. After college, we'll just come back here and find our property and you can look after the animals while I write my book."

From below came the sound of the technician cursing.

"Are we ever getting off this thing?" I asked.

"I wouldn't mind." He paused. "I've never kissed anyone either. I might not do it right."

"I thought you'd probably kissed a million girls by now. Like Julie Smith."

11

He made an impatient sound in the back of his throat. "She went around telling everyone that, and it wasn't true. I don't know why people do that."

"Tell lies?"

"Yeah. Like what did she get out of it?"

I thought for second. How did someone like Cole Paisley understand what it was like to want something you didn't ever think you could have so you invented your own truth? "She wanted it to be true. Maybe she thought it would get your attention."

"It did, but not in a good way." He turned his head to look at me. "Mostly, I hoped you didn't think it was true."

"Oh, well, I wasn't sure." I'd burned with envy when I'd heard the rumor about Cole and Julie. The gossip had started after a party down at the river. Kids like me weren't invited to parties like that. Not that my father would have let me go anyway. "I can't go to those kinds of parties."

"I know. Don't feel like you're missing anything. It's usually a bunch of idiots drinking too much and acting even more idiotic than usual."

"Why do you go to them?"

"I don't know. Something to do, I guess." He wrapped the hand that wasn't holding mine around the metal bar. "Gets us out of the house when my dad's having one of his nights."

"Nights?"

"You know. Whiskey and fists."

My stomach clenched. "Cole, is it bad?" My mother had been right. I'd overheard her tell my father she thought Mr. Paisley was abusive.

He nodded. "Luke gets the worst of it. Any time my dad's going after one of us or our mom, Luke always steps in. He won't ever back down. Gets right in Dad's face. Takes the blows for the rest of us."

"I can't picture him that way." Luke was such a gentle guy. Even on the football field, he seemed more like a dancer than a quarterback. My chest ached thinking of any of them being on the other side of Mr. Paisley's rage.

"Yeah, well, it's true." He turned back to me. "Do you ever wonder how some people are so good and some are so bad?"

"I always think most people are good, but sometimes I've been wrong."

"Do you ever worry about which one you are?"

"No. I know I'm good. Even though sometimes I have mean thoughts about other people. Mostly because I'm jealous of what they have."

"Who are you jealous of?"

"Sometimes I'm jealous of my sister. Even though I love her to pieces."

"What're you jealous about?"

"She's so pretty and popular. I could never be a cheerleader," I said.

"Who cares about that? And she's not prettier than you. No one is. Not in this town or maybe the whole world."

"Right." I poked his chest. "You're just saying that."

"I'm not. I swear." He looked into my eyes. "Wearing glasses didn't make you any less pretty, if that's what you think."

"Tell that to everyone who's called me 'four-eyes.'"

"I've beaten up a few of those jerks. Made sure they'd never call you names again."

"What? You have? Not really?"

"Heck yeah," he said in a soft growl. "I'll keep doing it, too."

"I was jealous of Julie Smith." I said this lightly, as if I hadn't cried into my pillow until I fell asleep.

He chuckled. "You didn't need to be."

"Jealousy is so ugly. I hate myself for it sometimes."

He let go of my hand to twirl a bit of my hair around his finger. "It's only you, Carlie. I've loved you forever. I always will."

"I've loved you forever too." I drew close enough that I could feel his breath on my cheek. "If you still want to, I'd like to be kissed now."

"Okay, here it goes. If you don't like it, just tell me and I'll stop."

I nodded, too afraid to jinx the moment with words.

I held my breath as he leaned close. Then, his mouth was on mine. His lips were warm and soft. Softer than I'd expected. In the romance novels, the hero always crushed her mouth with his. But this was like the flutter of a bird's feather. Too soon, it was over. He drew back to look at me. "Okay?"

"Better than okay. Do it again, please."

This time he appeared to have more confidence. He tilted his head to the left, and our lips came together as if they were made to do so.

The carriage jerked, and we fell apart. Then the wheel began to turn. My heart sank. "I don't want it to be over."

"The ride or the kiss?"

"Both."

"What if I promise to kiss you in every location in Logan County?"

I laughed. "Then it wouldn't seem so bad."

"I promise to kiss you in every location in Logan County." To seal his promise, he kissed me again as we made one more loop.

I wished the night would have gone on forever, but an hour later, having used all our ride tickets and stuffed ourselves with cotton candy, we headed out to the parking lot. Cole hadn't let go of my hand since we exited the wheel.

He and I slipped into the back seat while Luke and Drew took the front. The old lime-green Pinto made a choking sound before firing up.

I was tired in the best way and rested my head against Cole's shoulder as we drove out of the dusty parking lot. Stars sparkled down on us from an inky sky. If only that car ride could have gone on forever. We'd have remained innocent, instead of what waited for us at the end of the drive.

"Carlie, do you think Beth's seeing someone else?" Luke asked.

I jerked upright. "What? No way. Why do you ask that?"

"She's been weird this summer. Distracted." Luke caught my eye in the rearview mirror. "Do you think she was truly sick tonight?"

"Yeah. She didn't look good," I said, hoping to reassure him. "If anything were going on, she would tell me." This wasn't totally true. This summer she'd changed, grown secretive and quiet. Sometimes I caught her staring out the window clearly lost in thought. Did she have a secret? "She's probably just going through a thing. My parents have been pressuring her to figure out where she wants to go to college."

"Maybe she thinks we should break up when we go to college and doesn't want to tell me," Luke said.

That could be the case. I'd be surprised, though. Beth wasn't the type to worry about the past or future. That was me, not her. She always seemed to be centered right where she was in the moment. Well, until recently anyway.

"I could be more romantic," Luke said. "Flowers and stuff."

"Don't spend your money on that," I said. "You have to save for college."

"Ah, Carlie, always so sweet," Luke said.

"Carlie's the salt of the earth," Cole said.

"Luke, you have big dreams," I said. "No one should get in the way of that."

Drew put his boots on the dashboard. "Should we start calling you Dr. Paisley now?"

"If I even get into medical school, it's years and years until I'm a doctor," Luke said.

"You'll get in," Drew said. "You're the brains in the family."

"You could be a brain if you applied yourself," Luke said.

"School's boring. I want to do something physical," Drew said.

Luke turned on the radio. A Willie Nelson song filled the car. We only had one station in Logan County. Enjoyed by all who could deal with the crackling.

"This was the best night," Cole said in my ear.

I closed my eyes and breathed in the salty scent of his neck. How could a person be this happy?

"Don't forget Mom wanted us to stop for milk," Drew said as we passed by the Logan Bend sign, population 4,159.

"Yeah, right. Good thinking," Luke said.

A few minutes later, Luke turned into the parking lot of our only grocery store. "You guys want to come in?"

We all agreed and tumbled out of the car. I walked on air into the store. How had I never noticed how pretty the fruit displays were? Red apples and pink peaches stacked into triangles. Water sprayed over the vegetables.

Bins of bulk food were lined up against one wall. Drew opened the one with pretzels and helped himself to a few.

"Don't do that," Cole said. "They have cameras in here."

"What are they going to do? Arrest me for stealing one pretzel?" Drew shoved his twin's shoulder.

"They might," Cole said.

"Nah, I was born lucky," Drew said.

We followed Luke back to the milk section. He picked out a gallon of low-fat and we all headed to the front. Mrs. Pierson was at the register.

"Hi, Mrs. Pierson," Luke said. "Why're you working the late shift tonight?"

"Filling in for Sheila. She went to see her mother in Peregrine, who's feeling poorly. Plus, I need the money. Willie broke his arm."

"Playing T-ball?" Drew asked.

"Yep. I'm afraid he's not going to be athletic like his dad was," Mrs. Pierson said. "He takes after me." Her husband had drowned in the river a few years back. Since then, Mrs. Pierson had struggled to keep her two young sons fed and clothed. My mother often dropped a load of vegetables from her garden off at the Pierson place.

"You know how Dr. Lancaster is. No discounts for the poor or uninsured," Mrs. Pierson said. "He charged me five hundred dollars. Greedy like the rest of them Lancasters."

The Lancaster family had been early settlers in Logan County. Legend said they'd come out west in the late 1800s and struck gold. They'd built a mansion above town, nestled into Logan Mountain. Every Labor Day weekend the town celebrated with Lancaster Days. The three Lancaster brothers pretty much ran the town these days. Dr. Robert Lancaster had the only medical practice in town. John Lancaster was the sheriff. Stanley Lancaster owned the newspaper. My dad called it the propaganda piece for the Lancaster family. Rumor had it that the good doctor wanted to run for governor. Their sister, Shelley Lancaster Richards, after divorcing her very wealthy husband and moving back to Logan Bend, had single-handedly built a golf course and clubhouse. She made sure no one under a certain income level could become a member. My dad managed one of the two banks in town. Even so, we couldn't afford to join. Not that he would have. My mother teasingly called him a socialist when he started ranting about how everyone in Logan Bend should be able to enjoy the golf course. I think my mother secretly wished she could be a member, but she never said a word about it.

Most recently, Shelley's son, Thom Richards, had moved back to town. He'd been the town football star and had played at the University of Oregon during college. To everyone's surprise, he'd moved back to Logan Bend and taken a teaching position and now coached the high school team. If his good looks and local football hero legacy weren't enough to make him the most popular guy in town, he'd also delivered two winning seasons. Mom had remarked that he was the Lancaster who should pursue politics, not the stingy old doctor.

Mrs. Pierson rang us up. "Two dollars and nine cents," she said.

Luke pulled out a five from his wallet. "Keep the change."

Before she could protest, Luke swept the milk carton from the counter.

"You kids have a good night. Drive safe." Mrs. Pierson crossed her arms over her green apron.

"We're going straight home after we drop my girlfriend, Carlie, at her house," Cole said.

Mrs. Pierson winked at me. "Well done, Carlie."

I grinned and waved to her as we exited into the warm summer evening. The breeze brought the scent of river rocks and wildflowers. Luke turned up the radio when Johnny Cash's "I Walk the Line" started.

Luke started singing along, which prompted both the twins to do the same, followed by me. We sang our hearts out as we headed down Holland Loop Road to my family's home. The last notes of the song faded as we approached our mailbox. *Webster.* Beth had painted it with bright flowers a couple of summers ago. My father said he was the only man in town with flowers on his mailbox.

A cove of trees shielded the house from the road. As we turned the corner, we were met with a scene I couldn't at first comprehend. Red flashing lights. An ambulance. A cop car. My mom sat on the steps of our front porch. She stared straight into the car's headlights as if in a trance. Her arms hung loose at her sides. The front of her white nightgown was stained and clung to her. Blood? Was it blood? I blinked, sure I was seeing things.

"Cole, what is it? What's happening?"

He leaned forward. "I don't know."

I turned to the ambulance. They were lifting a body covered in a sheet into the back. My dad, dressed in his cotton pajamas, was on his knees in the gravel. My gaze returned to the stretcher. A bit of blond hair hung over the side. "Beth." I might have screamed, or it might not have come out at all.

Luke slammed on the brakes and turned off the car. He stumbled toward my mother, then seemed to think better of it and lumbered like a drunk man toward the ambulance.

Drew was out of the car and moving the bucket seat so that I could climb out. But no. I couldn't move. Cole was out of the car by then. I hadn't noticed him leaving my side. He reached in and lifted me out of the back seat. I clung to him, the two of us standing in the middle of the yard. Luke had run to the ambulance and tried to climb in, but the paramedics stopped him. He might have been screaming, but I couldn't hear anything over the heartbeat that pounded between my ears.

My dad must have seen me then, because he got to his feet. Blood covered the front of his pajamas. Beth's blood, I thought.

"Carlie. Carlie. It's Beth. She's gone."

"How?"

"Someone stabbed her. They left her on the grass. In her own yard." Dad spoke through his sobs. I'd never seen my father cry.

"No. We just saw her." My lips and limbs went numb. Dots danced before my eyes. And that was it. Blackness.

I was told later that Cole caught me and carried me up to my bed. I have no recollection of that or anything else that happened over the next few days.

For thirty years I lived that way, not quite alive, part of me having died with my sister. It was only when we finally knew the answer to what happened on a night that smelled of summer that I returned to life.

1

CARLIE

I found my sister's journal hidden in the false bottom of a shelf. Beth had been dead for thirty years by then, the secrets to her past locked away in a bedroom frozen in time. I had no idea how the discovery of her secrets written down during the last months of her life would alter the rest of mine.

I'd come home to help my mother sell the home she'd lived in for almost fifty years. She'd accumulated too much junk, she'd said to me. "Come help me clean everything out and put the house up for sale."

I'd decided in an instant to say yes. I couldn't decide if she needed me or if she knew I needed her. I was adrift. My only child, Brooke, had just finished her second year of college. My cheating ex-husband was in the arms of his new wife. My university position as an English literature professor had become stale. More and more I dwelled in the past. Reliving all the moments of that summer of 1989 as if they would give me answers to the questions that haunted me. What had happened to my sister? Who was responsible for stabbing her seventeen times and leaving her on my parents' lawn? I kept thinking, if I could just see the foreshadowing, the clues along the way that led to Beth's murder, I would know the answer. But the clues and foreshadowing were not easily found as in the English novels I'd spent my career studying.

On the second day after my arrival, I waited until my mother left for her golf game before tackling the first of many purges to come. Beth's room would be first. I wanted to get it over with. I had a cup of strong coffee while sitting in the shade of the oak in the backyard, followed by a bowl of corn flakes before traipsing upstairs. I wasn't sure, but my mother might be the only person left in the world who still bought corn flakes. She used them for everything, including frying up the stinky fish we'd had last night for dinner.

I stood in the doorway of Beth's room. Like my family, the room was stuck in the past. The same ruffled bedspread, rickety desk, and dresser that had witnessed my sister's short life remained untouched. Like me, the vibrancy of the flower wallpaper had faded. Years and cheating husbands had a way of doing that to a surface.

The room smelled faintly of mildew and dried flowers. Any hint of my sister's scent was long gone. She'd always carried the scent of baby powder and shampoo. I'd been jealous of her beautiful thick hair. Before bed sometimes she'd let me brush and braid it for her. I could still feel the silky strands in my fingers.

I went to the window and looked down to the yard. From this second-floor angle, my father's once-impeccable lawn looked patchy and yellow. Roses still bloomed but were as unruly and gangly as awkward middle-school girls. I tugged on the window to let in some fresh air. Birds sang and chirped outside, with no idea of how heavy a human heart could be.

Memories of a thousand moments engulfed me as thick as the air before a thunderstorm. I sat on the empty bed, gathering myself. This was simply a chore that must be done. I played with the ruffle on the peach-colored comforter that my sister had loved so much. Mom periodically washed the sheets and blankets and then made the bed back up as if someone would ever sleep in there again. When my daughter, Brooke, and I had come to visit when she was small, we'd always stayed together in my old bedroom.

Get on with it, I told myself. I had a task to do. I simply needed to shut off my mind and get it done.

I rose from the bed. I'd do the closet first. God only knew what was in there. I opened the closet door and peered inside. It was too dark to see, and my muscle memory clicked in as my fingers found the string that hung from the ceiling light. I tugged on what was essentially kitchen twine, so thin between my fingers I feared it would break off. To my surprise, it didn't. How had the string not disintegrated after all these years? The bulb shed a ghostly light.

The closet was shaped in a triangle, one of the many quirks of a house built in the late seventies. Wooden rods where Beth's clothes had hung were empty. Thank God for small favors. I'd already taken care of the clothes. That had been a hard day. Several years after her death, I'd taken all of Beth's clothes to the Salvation Army. My father had asked me to do it one afternoon when Mom had gone to the hair salon. The first year, Mom had decided not to return to work as a first-grade teacher. She rarely left the house during those months. When I'd come home from school, I'd find her still in her pajamas curled up in bed. I'd learned to cook a few simple meals, and she'd come down for dinner and then return to her room. However, after the first anniversary, it was like something had clicked inside her. The will to live, perhaps? Maybe she needed that year to grieve fully, to let herself fall into the abyss.

Dad and I had a different method, which in hindsight might not have been as effective. We simply soldiered on. As I did after learning of my husband's infidelities. I never gave myself the time to wallow. Brooke needed me. My students needed me.

And now here I was with another project. Help Mom sell the house.

I started with a shelf lined with books. Most were trade paperbacks with a few hardbacks of Beth's favorites: *Black Beauty, Anne of Green Gables, The Swiss Family Robinson*. Dozens of romance novels were hidden behind the hardbacks. We'd devoured those stories as if they were succulent bites of chocolate.

I held my breath as I opened Black Beauty. The inscription read: To Beth. We couldn't get you a horse, so this book will have to do. Love, Mom and Dad. December, 1980.

A lump formed in the back of my throat the size of a baseball. I sat back against the wall and spread my legs out so that my feet were pressed against the opposite wall. What it lacked in shape, the closet made up for in size. Beth and I had spent many rainy afternoons in here as kids and even teenagers, reading together, one on each wall with our legs spread out long as I had them now. How naive I'd been to think we would always be that way, connected by limbs and hearts.

I sniffed the romance with a cover of a scantily dressed hero in the arms of a redheaded heroine, hoping for a hint of Beth. The pages smelled of old paperback. How could they smell of anything else having been in the closet without their owner for decades? Still, the heart hopes without understanding the truth about loss. Grief lasts forever.

I set the book aside and sat on the floor, pulling my knees to my chest. "Beth, I miss you so much," I whispered. What was heaven like? Could she feel me or see me? Did she miss me up there or was all pain removed the moment you entered the pearly gates?

I shook off my sadness and began to pull the rest of the stuff from the shelves and into either a box or a trash bag. A bin of paper dolls went into the trash, but I put some of the books in the box of things I'd keep for myself. The only odd item I found was a butter knife from Mom's silver placed in one of the romances like a bookmark. Curious of what she'd bookmarked, I opened the paperback. I laughed to see that it marked a steamy kissing scene. We were innocent enough that they'd made us blush, but we couldn't get enough. The hero in this one was a hockey player who fell in love with the coach's daughter. A favorite of ours. I hadn't thought about this book or any of them for that matter since I'd read them with Beth over thirty years ago. We'd imagined ourselves as the heroine, swept away by the hero's grand gesture. We'd both been such romantics, debating for hours which of the heroes we would choose if we could. How scandalous the stories had seemed to us. If I'd only known then of what was to come—Beth's murder and then the ultimate betrayal by my husband. Murder. Blackmailed by a prostitute. Those were real scandals. True trials.

I put aside the knife. Mom would chuckle when I told her I'd found it up here. Beth had loved chunky peanut butter from the jar. After school, she'd use a knife to take a small amount. She never used spoons because she didn't want too much. "Too easy to take a lot more with a spoon," she'd said to me when I asked. "I have to fit into my cheerleader uniform."

I closed my eyes for a moment as a wave of heartache enveloped me. Beth and her peanut butter obsession. Hopefully peanut butter had made it into heaven and she got to have a large amount on the biggest spoon ever.

Never mind all that, I told myself. Get back to it.

As I worked, I grew damp from exertion. The upstairs of this house had always been warm in the summer. Still, it didn't take me but thirty minutes to finish the closet. Soon, everything had been emptied and put in either a box or the trash. Rickety and unstable, the shelving unit was something my dad must have put together. After forty years of neglect, who could blame it for giving in to decay? I felt this way some days. Too old and worn out to keep on going.

Last night my mother had asked if I would start dating again. It had been two years since my divorce from Max.

I'd dismissed the idea. Dating? At my age? Forty-six and faced with the prospect of showing my naked body to a man seemed impossible. When I'd married Max I would never have guessed that twenty years later I'd be out there again. Did I even want someone? After living with Max, picking up after him, cooking his meals, coddling his ego, I wasn't sure I wanted a repeat.

I'd thought Max was a good man. Or at least an honest one with flaws. I could deal with flaws. The dishonesty, the deception—that's what I couldn't look past. The betrayal had sliced through me like a dull blade through my middle. When I'd lectured in front of my class, I'd wondered if they could see the hole he'd left.

Anyway, that was all in the past. Now I had the opportunity to reinvent myself. I had enough money to live for years without working. I might not go back to the university. Maybe I would stay here in Logan Bend and grow tomatoes. I could never get a darn tomato to ripen in Seattle's cool climate. But here? Here I could have oodles and oodles of juicy red tomatoes.

These were my thoughts as I emptied the rest of the room. Beth's desk had been emptied at some point, so there was nothing much to do. Under the bed was also clear. I went back in for one last look in the closet to make sure I hadn't missed anything, kneeling once more in front of the shelves. That's when I saw a crack in the bottom shelf. The shelving unit had a false bottom, covered by the decorative front. I looked more closely. Actually, it wasn't a crack but a rectangular incision in the board. A secret hiding place? I needed something like a knife to lift it.

The butter knife. Had she actually kept it up here to open this hiding place? Not peanut butter after all? I grabbed the knife from where I'd set it on the bed, then used it to pry the part from the rest of the shelf.

I gasped at what I saw. Beth's journal. The one with butter-flies on the cover. She'd gotten it as a gift when we were in middle school from an elderly aunt. I'd never seen her write in it when we were small.

She'd hidden it, which meant she must have been writing in it when we were in high school and didn't want me or Mom to find it. Our mother wasn't above snooping. I lifted the journal from its coffin.

I opened to the first page. My heart beat fast as I looked at the date of the first entry, which was roughly six months before she was murdered.

I can't let anyone see this. Not ever. But today we did it for the first time. I won't say his name, not even in here. I'm in love. I feel really guilty about Luke, but I can't seem to stop myself. I'm sick with love. And now I've done the thing I can't even tell Carlie about. Sex. It wasn't good, like I hoped, but he assures me it gets better with time. We're planning to meet in our secret place again tomorrow.

I'm playing with fire. I know that. But he's too irresistible. There's no one like him. Luke seems like a child compared to him.

I stared at the page, unable to comprehend what I was reading. Beth had a boyfriend other than Luke. A boyfriend she couldn't tell even me about? And she'd had sex with him. How could this be?

Shivers ran up my spine. This was a lead. After all these years, something to go on. Information the police hadn't had at the time. There had been another boy in Beth's life. She'd had a secret. One that she kept from even me. But why? Why not just break up with Luke and go out with whoever this was? Had she sensed he was dangerous? Had instincts told her to keep us in the dark so we wouldn't see him for who he was and make her break it off with him? She'd always said I was scared of everything and that Dad was overprotective. I'd been right to be scared. My dad had been right too. Neither of us had the power to stop whoever it was that took Beth from us.

Would this journal hold answers? Was it possible that Mom

and I could finally have closure? We were the only two left of what had been a happy family of four. The Websters. Two beautiful blonde daughters. A bank manager and a beloved teacher. Native sons and daughters of Logan Bend. The rivers and mountains of Idaho ran through our blood. We were Logan Bend. Until we were not.

2

COLE

Summer mornings started early in Logan Bend. The moment the sun rose in the east, my rooster, Willie Nelson, crowed to make sure I wakened. He wasn't the type to let a man sleep in. Not that I wanted to. Since I'd moved back to Logan Bend and the property where I'd spent part of my youth, I leaped into each day with the energy and anticipation of a child. I didn't want to miss anything. Not now, when the life I'd dreamed of for so long was mine.

The hour wasn't yet seven, and I'd already eaten my usual boiled egg and toast. I was sipping a second cup of coffee standing by the French doors that led out to my stone patio. This time of day when the world was not quite awake always seemed sacred to me. The sweet scent of cut grass and wildflowers drifted in through the open windows.

Although the temperatures would reach the mid-eighties today, the night air had cooled the house while I slept. Dew sparkled on the wild grasses in the meadow. The sun hovered above Logan Mountain, shooting rays across my fenced property. Sprinklers came on in my garden patch, telling me it was already seven.

Chores waited for no man. Horses needed feeding. Garden

needed tending. July had brought warmer temperatures, and my vegetables were growing and ripening. Even from here I could see my red tomatoes peeking out from their green hosts.

I called out to Duke and Moonshine. "Time to make the doughnuts, kids." Duke, my yellow Lab, was asleep in a spot of sun with my mad-as-a-hatter tuxedo cat Moonshine curled up against his stomach in their mismatched couple spooning. Duke lifted his head lazily and blinked at me as if to say, "Can't you tell we're sleeping here?"

"Come on, you two. Let's go out to the garden. We got stuff to do."

Moonshine shook awake and leaped to her feet, let out a loud and disgruntled meow, then weaved, as if drunk—thus her name—and flopped back down onto the floor. "One too many, Moonshine?"

She answered by rolling onto her back and showing me her belly. That white stomach got fatter every day. I knelt and rewarded her for being irresistibly cute by petting her belly. "Your abs have disappeared, Moonshine. Outside, pronto. You need the exercise."

She gave me an affronted look before rolling over to look at Duke. Moonshine went nowhere without her best friend. Duke rose to his feet and wagged his tail. That dog. Good-natured to the end.

I'd gotten Duke and Moonshine when I'd moved back to Logan Bend two years ago. Only babies when they met, they never really understood that they weren't the same species. Perhaps missing their mamas, the two quickly became insepara-ble. I guessed Moonshine figured she was a dog. She acted like one, friendly and loyal to Duke and me. Plus, the girl could eat with the best of them. She never met a bowl of food she didn't love. On the other hand, Duke slept as much as a cat.

We were almost out the door when my phone buzzed. I pulled it out of the side pocket of my cargo shorts. "It's Mom," I said to my sidekicks.

They gave me a blank stare.

I went out to the stone patio as I answered. "Hi, Mom. Everything all right?"

"Why do you always start conversations out that way?"

"What way?"

"Like I'd only call if something was wrong."

I could picture my pretty mom on the other end of the phone. Slight and tanned, she'd still be in her tennis clothes this time of the morning and treating herself to a glass of iced coffee, no sugar, on the patio that overlooked the ocean. Her choice of a second husband had been a lot better than the first.

"Sorry, Mom. I'm not sure why I always expect the worst."

"You've been like that since you were in high school."

The comment hung in the air. We both knew why, but the Paisleys didn't mention that night. Not ever. Darned if it didn't pop up every once in a while. "How are you, Mom? How's Dom?"

"He's golfing this morning, enjoying his retirement. We're going to head over to Luke's tomorrow for a cookout to celebrate Sarah's birthday. She'll be sixteen. I can hardly believe it."

"I sent a card with a gift card for the bookstore." Sarah was the bookworm of my three nieces. Jessie was obsessed with surfing and soccer. The baby, Olivia, loved dance. My sister-in-law was always in the car taking them to various activities.

"You spoil those girls," Mom said.

"They're my only nieces. What can I say?"

"They hardly need anything more than they have."

"Sarah says she can never have too many books," I said. "She texted yesterday to say thank you."

"Pamela's done well to teach them good manners." Mom was quiet for a moment. I imagined her looking out to the blue Pacific, gathering her thoughts. She *had* called for a reason.

"What is it, Mom?"

"I ran into Iris at the store yesterday."

31

Iris. My ex-wife. I held my breath, waiting for what Mom would say next.

"She's getting married," Mom said. "To the gun guy."

"Gun teacher. Jeff." The boyfriend she'd gotten before leaving me. In hindsight, I should have known that no one could be that interested in the gun range.

"I thought you'd want to know," Mom said.

"Not really." I didn't care about her any longer; still, it stung. Whatever, I told myself. You have a good life. Your dream life in Logan Bend. The one you wanted. Except there's no Carlie.

"That gorgeous house you built must get lonely. I worry."

"I have Moonshine and Duke. They're great friends and would never cheat on me." I made a joke of my loneliness, but Mom was right. I did yearn for a partner. I'd have loved to share the home I'd poured my heart and soul into with someone special. Someone who made me feel the way I had about Carlie Webster when I was too young to realize how unlikely it was to find that again. No one had ever made my heart ache with love as Carlie had. Not even Iris, whom I'd married. Whenever my brothers or mom were too hard on Iris, I reminded them that she'd deserved someone who loved her beyond measure. I'd loved her. Of course I had. When she left me for Jeff, my ego and heart were bruised, but I knew deep down she wanted and deserved more than I'd given her.

"I believe the right woman is out there," Mom said. "Like Dom was. After I finally got the courage to leave your dad and take my life back, he appeared. She'll just appear one day and you'll know."

"It would take a miracle."

"I pray every night that God will send you your soul mate. You've been such a good son, honey. Even to your father, who didn't deserve it. She has to be special. Someone worthy of you."

"Keep praying, Mom." I said this simply to appease her and change the subject. My marriage and subsequent divorce taught me that it's best to have low expectations. Especially here. This was a small community. Most people who lived in Logan Bend were already married. How many women would be interested in a forty-six-year-old divorced guy whose best friends were an unstable cat and an overly sleepy dog? Logan Bend only had a population of twenty-seven hundred people. The odds were not in my favor.

"Maybe try one of those apps on the phone," Mom said. "Tons of people meet that way these days."

"I've been too busy with the garden and chores to worry about dating. I finally finished the barn—painted it red like a classic Corvette. You and Dom should come visit."

"We will. Maybe this year." This was Mom's typical response. I didn't hold out much hope. She had bitter feelings toward Logan Bend. Considering the way they'd treated us after Beth's murder, who could blame her?

"No pressure," I said.

"All I can recall of our time there was all the snow. Driving in it. Walking through ice or sludge to get to my car, which would then take five minutes to defrost."

"Not this time of year." My land was green and lush because of my access to river water. I settled my gaze on the fenced vegetable garden. I'd built planters and filled them with the finest dirt. "The first of my tomatoes are ripe."

"Goodness, I hated gardening. Constant watering. And the weeds. They grew better than anything else. Your father never lifted a finger to help me. You boys were like garbage disposals, always hungry. Between trying to keep you all fed and my job, I was dead on my feet."

"I don't know how you did it, Mom."

She made a shushing sound. "Why am I going on about all that? I'm glad you're happy there, but I miss you."

"I'll come out in the fall. After the garden's done for the season."

"Have you ever run into the Websters? I've wondered how little Carlie made out."

Hearing her name made my chest ache. "No, but someone in town told me Mr. Webster died about five years ago."

"Around the same time your father died," Mom said. "That's a shame. They went through so much."

"They did." I closed my eyes, seeing that night as clearly as if it had happened yesterday. The sight of Carlie's parents wasn't something I would ever forget.

"Well, if you ever do see Mrs. Webster, you should ask about Carlie," Mom said. "She was such a sweet little thing. It was too cruel, losing her sister that way. And then to lose you too. Only a strong woman could get through all that intact."

"She had grit. I'm sure she's all right." Wherever she was. We'd just gotten started that night. I'd be lying if I said I didn't wonder what might have been had I been able to stay. Over the years I'd looked for her name in bookstores, wondering if she'd fulfilled her dream of writing a novel. All of that was just fantasy. I'd bet she barely remembered me. If she did, I was attached to the worst night of her life. Even if I'd been able to stay in Logan Bend, she would have ended things. My brothers and I had nothing to do with Beth's death, but we were tainted just the same simply by being there.

"Do you ever think about trying to find Carlie?" Mom asked. "You could ask Loretta where she is."

"Carlie Webster wouldn't want to see me. Reaching out would probably cause her pain. I'd bet she wants to forget about anything to do with those days."

As if she didn't hear me, Mom continued. "I never thought Luke and Beth were right for each other but you two—that was a match."

"Luke and Beth were crazy about each other," I said.

"He cared for her much more than she cared for him. They'd never have lasted past high school. A mother knows these things."

"I still think about Carlie," I said. "As embarrassing as that is."

"She might be married. You should prepare yourself for that. Carlie was such a sweet girl. It would be unlikely she's single."

"Well, I'm single."

"That's different."

"How, exactly?" I asked, laughing.

"Never mind." She paused for a moment. "Were you ever resentful of Luke? If not for his involvement with Beth, we might've stayed."

"Resentful of Luke? No way. None of it was his fault. That article in the paper sealed our fate." The rumors and whispers, the certainty that Luke had had something to do with Beth's death, had started to circulate after an article in the *Logan Bend Tribune* had mentioned him as the prime suspect. All of which was a lie. The authorities ruled him out almost immediately. He had a solid alibi, supported by Mrs. Pierson at the store and many others who had seen us all at the fair that evening. Given the time frame, there was no way Luke could have murdered Beth. Yet the paper had irresponsibly and without facts accused an innocent seventeen-year-old of murder. People were only too happy to believe the boyfriend did it. The good people of Logan Bend didn't care about the truth. They wanted a suspect so they could sleep at night, convinced their daughters were safe. It was the first time I understood the power of the press and the written word.

When someone had tossed a flaming Molotov cocktail into our yard, my mother had had enough. We packed up and left town in the middle of the night. With no place to go, we'd headed to LA to live with my maternal grandmother. Soon thereafter, my parents had split up. Mom had gone back to school to get her nursing degree. At her first job as an ER nurse, she'd met Dom. My brothers thrived in LA. I was the only one who wished I could come back to Logan Bend. For the mountains and the girl.

Thinking about all this made my stomach hurt. No wonder

we never talked about the Websters. "Let's not talk about it any longer," I said. "I don't like thinking about all that."

"I'm sorry. Not another word."

"Do you remember Thom Richards?" I asked. "The football coach that all the moms used to swoon over?"

"Yes, I remember. The hunky one with the rich family."

"He's running for governor. They're saying it'll be a landslide after his success as mayor of Boise."

"He has the hair for it." I could almost see my mother rolling her eyes.

I chuckled. "Yeah. I don't remember him that well, but Luke always looked up to him."

"Thom Richards defended Luke. Do you remember that? At Beth's funeral?"

"Not at all." I didn't remember him even being there. All I could think of that day was Carlie.

"Your brother won him a lot of football games," Mom said. "Otherwise I'm sure he would have joined the angry mob. He was only twenty-two when he came home to teach. Grown women twice his age fawned all over him. Frankly, it was a little embarrassing."

"I never thought about how young he was." He'd seemed like a grown-up back then. "When you're sixteen, a man in his twenties seems like an adult."

"I suppose so. When you're in your forties, a man in his twenties seems like a child. It's all relative. Anyway, I should go, honey. It was good to hear your voice."

"You too, Mom. Love you."

"Love you more."

We said our goodbyes and I hung up the phone. Moonshine and Duke had found a new spot in the sun.

"Let's go, gang," I said to them.

They sprang to their feet and charged out to the yard. I grabbed my hat and followed them across the yard toward the barn. The chickens were in their outside pen, pecking in the dirt for bugs. My chestnut horses grazed in the pasture. A humming-bird drank the sugar water from the feeder hanging over the barn doors.

My mother had gotten this property in the divorce. At the time, she thought of the land as a good investment and held on to it, even though she said it would be a cold day in hell before she came back to the town that had betrayed her and her boys. Once she'd married Dom, she'd no longer had to worry about money, so when I begged her to hang on to the property, she'd agreed. I promised to buy it from her as soon as I could put together the money.

I could still see the look she gave me when I asked her, a mixture of concern and horror. However, my mother isn't the type to question motives that are purely emotional. After all, she'd stayed married to my abusive, alcoholic father for almost twenty years when everything on God's green earth had told her to leave. A witch hunt finally woke her to the harsh reality of what had become of her life and family. She and her boys couldn't survive under the drunken dictatorship of Kenneth Paisley. Not when a whole town was against us.

In no hurry, a puffy cloud floated in the blue sky. Bursts of colors from my roses and flower beds contrasted nicely with mountains that looked almost purple this time of day. Countless shades of green grasses swayed gently in the meadow, creating the music I thought of as Idaho. My land. The place where I belonged.

I'd bought the land as soon as I could afford it, just a few years after I'd gotten my contractor license and started flipping houses. Given the property's location by the river and the view of Logan Mountain to the north and Blue Mountain to the south, I'd never have been able to afford it if my mother hadn't insisted on selling it to me for the same amount they'd purchased it for in the late seventies. Five thousand dollars wouldn't buy a used car these days, but it had bought me paradise.

For almost three decades, ten acres sat here empty of life

other than the wild critters and the fish that swam in the river that snaked through the property. When I'd felt financially solvent, I sold my house in LA and moved back to the land that had lived for years in my dreams. The run-down trailer had sunken in upon itself like the cheeks of an elderly, toothless woman. Not a tear was shed as the tow truck hauled away the home my father had made so miserable. I'd bought a plan for a modern farmhouse from an architecture firm and hired a team of guys to help me. Six months later, I moved into the house of my dreams.

Given how everything ended for us here in Logan Bend, neither Drew nor Luke wanted anything to do with the land. I'd offered them both the opportunity to take a parcel, but they had no interest. Luke said he didn't want anything to do with the town or our land and that if I expected to see him for holidays I'd have to come to Malibu.

I still held out hope that at some point in his life Drew might like to move back here. Thus far, he was content working as a stunt double in Hollywood. As had always been the case, he had a bevy of women vying for his attention. He never dated any of them for more than a few weeks.

I gathered eggs from inside the barn where the chickens nested. We had eight today in various hues of brown. "Good girls," I said under my breath. Back outside, I scattered seeds and grains as they gathered round. I'd built the pen as an extension of the barn and encased it in wire mesh so the girls were safe. During warm months, they could go in and out of the barn as they pleased.

As we approached the horse pen, Lila and West raised their heads in greeting. The apple tree that had been here when I was a kid had dropped a few on the ground. I scooped up two of them and leaned over the fence. The horses trotted over to me. Their chestnut coats shone under the morning sun.

I gave them each an apple and some love before heading to the vegetable garden. Deer would have loved to nibble away my entire garden, so I had fenced in the raised vegetable beds. I lifted the metal latch. Moonshine brushed my leg as she sauntered toward the tomatoes. The crazy thing liked to lie under them with her paws in the air. Duke plopped in the middle of the row between the zucchini and the beans and rested his chin on his front paws.

I grabbed a bucket and knelt to pick a dozen of the ripest tomatoes. This time of day, the sun warmed their skin, making their sweet fragrance that much richer. The ground was damp from the morning. I picked a small bucket of beans and a half dozen of the yellow squash and zucchini.

I straightened and pressed a hand into my lower back. Squinting, I gazed out across my property toward the row of aspens that lined the river. Beyond, Logan Mountain rose above us like a protective benefactor. This afternoon, I'd swim in the old water hole where I'd spent so much time during the summers of my youth. First, I needed to head to town. The local food bank needed fresh vegetables, and I was low on the type of groceries I couldn't grow.

For a moment, though, I stood in the stillness of the morning and breathed in the dry, clean air. This was my home. The place I belonged. Nothing could have changed that fact. Not an angry mob or a monster who took Beth from her family. It was hard to believe that anything like that could have happened here in this place of beauty.

I tipped my hat to the mountain and then turned to Blue Mountain and did the same. No reason to dwell in the past. I was here where nature's blessings called my name.

3

CARLIE

A combined scent of scorched coffee and microwave popcorn assaulted me as I walked into the sheriff's department. This was the scent of death. The smell of the days of my sister's murder. Black dots danced before my eyes. I pressed the bridge of my nose between my thumb and index finger. Fainting was not an option. But God help me, this place. These rooms. The Logan Bend police station, built of brick and men's sweat and as old as the town itself, had been host of the worst night of my family's history. I blinked and let the door close behind me.

The place was remarkably unchanged. Tepid light cast from the fluorescent panels shed a depressing yellow hue over a gray-tiled floor and cheaply upholstered chairs. Had they always been army green? I could remember only the color red from that night.

I hadn't planned on this. I'd been walking by and suddenly an urge to go inside had propelled me forward. I had the journal in my purse. Should I tell them about it? So far, it told me nothing. She called the guy Z. She'd been secretly meeting him. Did that mean he killed her? Without any idea who he was, what could the police do with it? I was here now. Too late. The woman at the front desk had already looked up from behind the screen of a computer.

The woman looked to be in her sixties. I didn't recognize her. How foolish would I look, bringing in a journal as if it would tell us anything? The detectives who handled Beth's case were most likely dead or retired. Thirty years was a long time. Would they even entertain the idea of a long-lost journal?

The woman looked up, squinting from behind her glasses as if she were trying to place me. "Can I help you?" A smudge on the right lens of her glasses made me want to reach inside my purse for a tissue. Before she switched to contacts, my daughter had worn glasses. I'd been forever cleaning them.

"I wondered if I could talk to a detective? I have information on a cold case." How did one ask if there were any leads on a cold case from thirty years ago? A murder investigation for which there had been no leads, no answers. The record of my sister's last moments was in a box somewhere, abandoned and forgotten. I knew the contents. I could not forget. The killer had left her with her wallet, which held eight dollars and fifty-three cents, her driver's license, a photograph of Luke, and one of me taken during my sixth-grade year that always made us laugh hysterically. Her heart necklace she wore night and day was in there too. I imagined the white file box as if I'd actually seen it, stored on the shelf with her name and the date of death. Beth's items forever locked away, hoping for someone to pull them back out, to investigate everything again and find the truth this time. No one would. Unless the miracle I prayed for every night finally came true.

"We only have the sheriff here, ma'am. It's lunchtime." She reached for a pad. "But I can take your information and they'll get back to you."

"I can wait." Even as I said this, the urge to flee caused me to turn back to the door.

"Are you sure? They take a long lunch on Fridays. Langley's Bar and Grill has sliders for five dollars."

"They still have those sliders?" I asked as I twisted back around to face her. A mixture of beef and pork sausage, those sliders were famous around here. Once a month my dad used to close the bank for an hour and a half on Slider Fridays so he and the staff could enjoy a lunch together. Did the new manager do that? My dad had been a wildly popular boss. He would have been a hard act to follow, especially since he'd died so suddenly from a heart attack.

"Yes, ma'am. Logan Bend doesn't have much, but we have our sliders."

"I know. I used to live here." Behind the woman, two metal desks held computers and stacks of files. The desks of the missing slider-eating cops, no doubt.

"You look familiar," she said. "I'm Linda O'Brien."

Before I could answer, a man came out of one of the offices and strode toward us, stopping just shy of Linda's desk. His eyes narrowed as he took me in before his brows shot up in obvious surprise. "Carlie Webster? Is that you?"

For a moment I simply stared at him. Who was he? His eyes were familiar. Then the past and present clicked together. This was Deputy Ford. Or he'd been a deputy back then. Hadn't my mother told me he was the sheriff now? Maybe. Half the time I only partly listened when she talked about people in town. It was my way of distancing myself. If I wasn't interested in the present, the memories of the past didn't hurt as much.

"I thought I knew you somehow," Linda said. "You're the other Webster girl."

The other Webster girl. The sister of the murdered teenager. That would be the title of my biography if there were ever to be one. *The Other Webster Girl.* I could see the cover in my mind. A lone girl on a bench built for two. This was why I'd left here and never looked back. I hadn't wanted to spend my life with that as my identifier. The sympathetic, curious look on Linda O'Brien's face was all too familiar.

"I'm Sheriff Ford now." He held out his hand, and we shook.

"Hi, Sheriff Ford," I said. "It's nice to see you."

"And here you are, all grown up." Ford rocked back on the heels of his cowboy boots. "It's been a long time."

"Yes sir," I said.

"You haven't changed much. I knew you right away." He gave me a warm smile.

I smiled back at him. "Thank you. I feel about a hundred."

"I feel you," he said. "I just turned fifty-one."

Fifty-one? How strange. Back then I'd thought of him as old when really he was only five years older than me. "How long have you been the sheriff?" I had a sudden flash of what he'd looked like back then. Chiseled features and bright blue eyes in combination with dark blond curls and a ruddy complexion had made him very popular with the ladies in town. I could remember a photograph in the paper announcing his marriage. My mother had joked that the hearts of half the single women in Logan Bend were surely broken over the news. This was before Beth's murder. Back when my family still had lighthearted conversations about a variety of subjects.

"Couple of years now," Ford said. "Not many choices around here, so they were stuck with me."

"Logan Bend's lucky to have you," I said. Was that true? How would I know? The cops in this town hadn't solved my sister's murder. Maybe they were incompetent and always had been.

"It's good to be a big fish in a small town." He looped his thumbs under his belt. My gaze halted for a second on his large belt buckle. A rose was carved into the silver. Men here and their belt buckles. I'd forgotten that detail.

"What brings you by?" Ford asked. "Is everything all right with your mom?"

"Yes, she's fine. I just wanted to—well, I wondered if you had any updates on my sister's case. And I might have something for you. Something new."

A quick glance in the direction of Linda O'Brien told me she was hanging on every word. It would be all over town by nightfall that the other Webster sister was back in town and asking questions for which there was no answer.

"Come on back." Ford motioned toward his office. "We can chat in there."

I followed him into a small office and sat in one of two metal chairs on the other side of an oak desk. He plopped down in the chair behind his desk, causing it to squeak. For a man in his fifties, he seemed fit and in good health, not in possession of a potbelly like so many men that age, including my ex-husband.

"Are you in town for a visit?" Ford asked. "I can't remember ever seeing you back in these parts."

"I don't come home often. I'm an English professor in Seattle and have to go back in the fall."

"I remember you were quite the bookworm," Ford said. "Makes sense you became a professor."

I blinked, surprised he remembered that about me. Actually, how did he know? My only interaction had been the night we had to come in for questioning. They must have studied our family at the time in an attempt to comb through all possibilities. "My mom needed some help getting her house ready. She's selling and moving to that retirement community."

"I'll bet she's real pleased to have you home." His finger and thumb of his right hand played with his wedding ring.

I assumed she'd have been, but she'd been acting strange, almost secretive. For minutes at a time, she'd stare out into space. The thirtieth anniversary of my sister's death was this coming August. I suspected that was on her mind. However, it didn't explain the way she disappeared for long stretches to talk to someone on the phone. If I didn't know better, I'd have thought she had a boyfriend. She wouldn't even consider dating. Any time I'd brought it up in the last few years, she'd immediately dismissed the idea and scolded me for even thinking she'd cheat on my father. In my defense, he'd been dead for five years.

"I'm not sure she needs my help as much as I needed to come

home. My daughter just finished her second year of college. I got divorced a few years ago. I guess you could say I'm at a crossroads."

"Understandable. Logan Bend's good for a soul."

"I'm enjoying the weather and the clear skies."

Ford put his elbows on the desk and folded his hands under his chin. "Talk to me. What have you found that you think might impact the case?"

I dipped my chin to stare at the purse in my lap. Expensive and pink, I'd bought it online in an attempt to cheer myself up last month after a particularly heinous online date. I pulled the journal from the pouch on the side. "I found this while cleaning out my sister's room. It's Beth's journal, written in the months before her death. I found this in a hiding place. I haven't finished reading it yet but what I've read so far—she had another boyfriend. Someone other than Luke Paisley."

He sat forward. The corners of his mouth twitched. "Are you sure?"

"She talks about him quite a bit. Most of it hasn't been particularly enlightening. She's a wordy writer." In fact, reading through the journal was taking longer than expected. Her terrible handwriting caused me to pause to decipher words, and she tended to ramble. "So far, there's nothing that gives me any ideas about who he is." I swallowed against the ache in my throat before telling him the next part. "She was having sex with him. Not with Luke but whoever Z is. It started me thinking... maybe he's the killer. I mean, isn't that why so many people thought Luke could be the killer? The boyfriend or husband is always looked at first, right?"

"Depends on the case, but yeah."

I could tell by the sympathetic dip of his eyelids that he didn't hold out hope of learning much from a teenage girl's journal.

"Your dad never believed our theory," Ford said. "He made sure I knew that."

45

"I know." Dad hadn't believed their theory that Beth fell victim to the serial killer. During the span of a few years, six girls had been murdered in Colorado and Montana. The authorities had believed Beth was another one his victims. The killer had never been found. But my dad didn't buy it. The other girls had been strangled. Dad felt strongly that the number of Beth's stab wounds were indicative of a crime of a personal nature. She'd been stabbed seventeen times. One for each year of her life. "Why would a serial killer have dropped her off in my parents' yard?"

"He killed her there. There were no gates or fences to keep him out. It's plausible he followed her home and grabbed her when she got out of the car."

Dad had thought their police work was lazy. Ford must have sensed my thoughts, given what he said next.

"None of us here have ever given up hope that we'll find your sister's killer. The detective and sheriff I worked with all those years ago have both passed away. But you should know, right up until their retirement they never stopped trying to solve what happened that night."

"I know you all did your best." As I sat there under the kind gaze of Ford, a vast emptiness seeped into me like ink on absorbent paper. We'd never know what really happened. There just wasn't enough evidence.

What was I doing? Coming to the police station was ridiculous. They might have current cases, and my intrusion kept them from their real work. I gripped the straps of my purse. The hard leather hurt my sweaty palms. "I just wanted to tell you about the journal."

"You be sure to let me know if you find anything. If you're right and it was someone she knew, then we might be able to find him."

I breathed out a sigh of relief. He was open to the idea. "I'll do that."

"I'm here if you ever want to just come by and talk, okay?"

"Thanks. I appreciate the offer." Ford had brought me a cold soda the day I'd come in for questioning. They'd grilled me about the Paisley brothers. "You were nice to me," I blurted out. "I never thanked you for that soda." I tried to control myself, but I started to cry. "They kept grilling me about the Paisley brothers. I kept telling them they were with me all night. It seemed like they didn't believe me."

"I felt real bad about what they did to the Paisleys."

"What do you mean? They who?" I wrapped both arms around my purse.

"The sheriff and the detective—Lancaster and Wright. Do you remember them?"

"Sure, yes." I could remember every detail of their faces as they sat across from me that night. Lancaster had looked like a mountain man. A beard had covered most of his face, leaving only small green eyes that bored through me. Wright had been tall and sloop-shouldered with crooked brown teeth.

"They felt certain Luke Paisley had something to do with it. They're the ones who told the editor at the paper to run with the story on him."

"But why? Why would they do that to an innocent kid?"

"The Paisleys were outsiders," Ford said. "You know how it was around here. Anyone who hadn't had family here since the pioneer days was thought of as an outsider, not to be trusted. Kenneth Paisley had a reputation for being violent. I think they genuinely thought Luke did it until his alibi and what you claimed were substantiated by the gal at the grocery store. But by then it was too late. They'd already run the story."

"And ruined the Paisleys' lives." I spit this out with surprising venom. After thirty years, I still couldn't forgive the men who driven away the boys I'd loved.

He came around the desk to sit next to me in the other guest chair. "I'm sorry we never figured out who did it." He patted my shoulder with his large hand. "The serial killer we suspected must have died or gone to another part of the country. We never had another victim that matched up."

My sister hadn't matched up. We'd already covered that, so I kept quiet.

I wiped under my eyes. "I'm sorry. You'd think after all this time, I could talk about her without crying."

"Being home brings up a lot of memories."

He was so sympathetic I almost started to cry again. "That's right," I said. "Which is why I haven't been home much."

Every time I'd brought Brooke to see her grandparents, the memory of Beth haunted me. We'd talked so many times about how our kids would grow up together right here in Logan Bend. "You'll be a teacher and I'll own a bakery and we'll each have three kids," she'd said.

Best-laid plans and all that, I thought now.

"I was sorry to hear about your dad." Ford patted my shoulder again.

"Thanks. He went fast. No suffering. Heart attack." Ford knew that. He lived here. He was sheriff. He knew everything.

"I'm sorry to say but a cold case like this—well, it's not likely we'll find much of anything at this point. Keep reading the journal. I'll pray for a miracle."

"Maybe there will be something. Anything." The hope in my voice made me inwardly cringe. I stood, thanking him for his time. "I appreciate you listening to me."

"Anytime." He stood as well. "Before you go, I wanted to mention that Cole Paisley moved back here a few years ago. He built a house on the family property. The place is worth a fortune now, what with the river access."

My stomach dropped to the floor. "They still had that property?" I'd assumed they'd sold it years ago. Why would they keep it? An investment, perhaps.

"Rumor has it that the Paisleys divorced after leaving here but she kept the property. Sold it to Cole for next to nothing."

"Okay, well, thanks for telling me. I really have to go." I scurried out of there as fast as I could, knowing if I stayed any longer, I'd start asking a dozen questions about Cole Paisley. I wasn't ready to know the answer to the biggest one of all. Was Cole Paisley married?

Of course he was. He probably had a big family and a bunch of animals. Why else would he have moved back here? The perfect place to raise kids and have a small farm as he'd always wanted.

I'd have to get out of here before I ran into him. Not knowing any details about him allowed me to still have my fantasies. After thirty years, I still had my daydreams. They were still all about Cole Paisley.

Some things never changed.

4

COLE

I'd dropped my load of vegetables at the food bank and headed down the street toward the grocery store. Logan Bend had changed since I was a kid. The brick buildings from the early days remained, but they'd been updated to look quaint and attractive. A park with a gazebo had been put in where the run-down town square had been. Flowerpots hung from business fronts. Cafés and restaurants were packed with summer visitors. I passed by a family with three young children sitting on a bench in front of the ice cream shop happily licking away at their cones. A sliver of sadness threw a shadow over the beauty of the day. I'd wanted that. With Carlie.

That's when I saw her come out of tea shop. I stopped dead and stared. Was it true? Carlie Webster was here in town? Was I truly seeing her, or was it a mirage? I held on to a lamp-post for support. My heart beat between my ears. I couldn't feel my lips.

Fair hair cascaded down her back. Her remarkably high cheekbones were more prevalent than when she was younger. Her face thinner, too. She wore a loose-fitting blue sundress and flat sandals. Not as slight as she'd been in high school, more womanly. Even more beautiful. She had the same straight posture and long, slender neck. She'd always reminded me of a ballerina even though she always insisted it was Beth who had the dancing talent.

As she always had, she took my breath away. I didn't know what to do. Did I call out to her? Would she even recognize me? Remember me? What if I'd built our romance up in my mind? I might have been a blip. Long forgotten. Cole who?

She looked at her wristwatch, then rummaged in a pink purse that dangled from one arm and pulled out a pair of sunglasses. A car came down the street, and I lost sight of her. When it passed by, I thought for sure she'd be gone, having not really been there at all. But no. She remained standing in the exact spot. Her head tilted downward as if she were contemplating something.

Then, abruptly, she headed away from me, toward the grocery store. I'd have known her gait anywhere. The way she walked with the pressure on the toes of her feet was unmistakable.

I'd follow her. That's all there was to do. I couldn't let her slip away. Not after waiting for this moment for the last thirty years.

5

CARLIE

I n aisle six of the grocery store, I knelt down to get a box of pasta. Out of my peripheral vision, a pair of scuffed work boots approached. I used the handle of my cart for stability as I straightened. One knee cracked. I was about to roll my cart away when I heard my name.

"Carlie?"

I turned and almost gasped. Cole Paisley stood before me. Sparks of shock traveled up my spine and raised the hair on the back of my neck. He was taller and broader than the boy he'd once been, but his eyes were the same. I knew those eyes. They'd been in my dreams for as long as I could remember.

"Do you know who I am?" he asked as he stepped closer. Fine lines around his eyes and mouth hinted at his age. Cole Paisley. Now a man. A gorgeous man in his mid-forties. One who apparently still had the ability to make my limbs tingle.

"Cole?" I whispered. "Is it really you?"

"Yeah, it's me." He had the same slight whistle on his *s*'s, but his voice had deepened.

"You look amazing," he said.

I murmured a thank-you as I glanced down at my feet. My polished red toes looked good in my sandals. I wore a sundress the same color as my blue eyes. I'd tied my dark blonde hair back into a ponytail. Did I look different to him? I had fine lines. My face had thinned. The last few years had taken a toll on my already-battered soul. Did it show in my face?

"*Stunning* might be the word," he said.

My heart thumped. *Look at his hand*, I told myself. *Rip the Band-Aid off.* My gaze skipped to his fingers, currently wrapped around a red plastic carrier. Bare of a wedding ring. Had he come here alone? Did he have children? A wife? Maybe a girlfriend?

Of course he had a girlfriend or a wife. A lot of men didn't wear rings. No one who looked like Cole could be single. I didn't think it was possible, but he was even more beautiful than he'd been at sixteen. He'd kept all his fawn-colored hair and wore it short and tidy with a few curls at the nape of his neck. I glanced down at his flat stomach. The blue T-shirt he wore did nothing to hide the muscles underneath.

"You look good too." All the moisture in my mouth had dried up. The years between now and then were written in the lines of his face. I'd missed so much of his life. I wished I could feel his skin under my fingertips. Right now. Forever.

"I didn't know you lived here," I said.

"Yeah, I built a house out on the old property."

"Just you?"

His forehead wrinkled. "You mean, did I build the house myself?"

"No. Is there anyone living with you?" I wanted to die right then and there. Could I have been more obvious?

"Oh, no. Well, yes. My cat, Moonshine, and my dog, Duke. Two horses named Lila and West. There's Willie Nelson and all the girls—that's my rooster and chickens. They all have names but I won't bore you with that." He smiled as he swept his fingers through his hair. "Sorry. I'm nervous."

"Me too." I looked at the floor, afraid to believe he was single. "So, no humans live with you?" I peeked back up at him.

"Oh, no. No humans." His eyes softened, making them appear more green than gray. "I'm divorced. Three years ago. That's when I decided to come back here and start over."

"I'm sorry." I meant it, knowing what a toll a divorce took on a person's soul.

"I'm not." He shook his head. "I can't believe it's you. I've thought about you a million times and wondered how you were. What you ended up doing. If you were married or not."

"I'm divorced too." I blurted this out, feeling a tremendous need to tell him right away. "I have a daughter. She's nineteen, almost twenty. She's at college."

"What's her name?" he asked.

"Brooke."

"That's pretty. Does she look like you?"

I nodded, smiling as an image of my beautiful daughter floated through my mind. "She's taller than me, but she has my skin and eyes and hair. Much smarter, though. She's studying chemistry. What about you? Do you have children?"

"Nah, wasn't blessed that way."

"Really?" My chest ached at the idea of Cole being childless. He'd have been a wonderful father.

He gave me a sad smile. "Dreams don't always come true. But I got my little farm."

Overhead, fluorescent lights blinked. I caught the scent of the fresh parsley in my shopping cart. I'd hoped to tempt my mother with a chicken piccata dish. As far as I could tell she lived on cheese and crackers.

"How come you never contacted my mother?" I asked. "To find out where I was. I mean, since you were curious." From the way I stuttered, no one would believe I'd taught English literature at a private college in Seattle for twenty years. I'd been known for my animated, smooth-as-silk lectures. Cole Paisley always tripped up my tongue.

"She wouldn't want to hear from me." He said the sentence

simply, as if it were fact. "Or want you to have anything to do with me."

"She holds no grudge toward you or your brothers. Why would she?"

"Everyone seemed to believe the lies they told about Luke."

"She knew I was with you guys the whole night," I said. "Plus, she knew Luke. He was at our house every day for a year. She knew he'd never hurt her."

He smiled in that way that made his eyes sparkle, and I was suddenly sixteen years old. "Carlie Webster, you always knew just what to say to make everything better."

I smiled back at him, unable to resist being swept away by his effortless charm. "You did that for me, too."

He dropped his basket next to his feet. For the first time, I noticed it was empty. What had he come for? Did he still like burgers and pizza? When he straightened, I thought for a second he would pull me into his arms. Instead he stuffed his hands into the pockets of his jeans. "We had fun back then, didn't we? Before everything."

"So much fun." The way he'd stretched out across the rock at the swimming hole, his bare torso tanning under the sun right before my eyes, was forever captured in my memory. "Remember how we spent whole afternoons at the river?"

"We could again. The river's still there. I might be older, but the swimming hole's the same." His crow's feet deepened as his mouth lifted into a wide grin. "Sorry, I'm getting ahead of myself. You might not like swimming anymore. Or maybe you have a boyfriend? Someone living at *your* house?"

I laughed. "No. There's no one. Not since my divorce." *There was never anyone like you.*

"I can't say I'm sorry to hear you're single."

Thump, thump went my heart. "I still like to swim, too."

He slapped his chest. "Thank God. I was prepared to sell the property if you didn't still like to swim in the river."

I laughed again. "No need for that."

He cocked his head to the side and seemed to take me in all over again. "Every time I go into a bookstore, I look for your name on a cover."

"Ah well, as you say, not all dreams come true. I'm a college professor. I teach about other people's books."

"It's never too late," he said. "Maybe Idaho will bring you new muses."

"I don't know about that. The years have a way of chipping away at a person's self-confidence. What I was so sure of back then seems pretty far-fetched."

"I hate to hear you say that." He stepped out of the middle of the aisle to let a woman pass by us.

"What made you come back here?" I asked. "I'm surprised."

"It's what I always wanted. You know that. I felt like I belonged here."

"But what about…everything? I didn't think you or your family would ever come back here." How lame. What a way to say it. *Everything.* As if that lone word could capture the pain and wreckage of our two families.

"That property was the only time in my life I felt at ease, like I was home. Nothing could change that. Not even mean-spirited gossip. I asked my mom to hang on to the property for me. She sold it to me for a steal. It took me some time to save enough to leave LA and go into semiretirement, but here I am."

"I thought what happened might have made you bitter about Logan Bend."

"No, not anymore. Anyway, no one remembers any of what happened. It's been too long."

"My mom says only the old-timers even remember," I said. "But I remember. I remember everything. All the ways they took you away from me."

"Carlie." He reached for my hand, and I let him take it. We stared into each other's eyes for a moment. No one but the two of us could understand the exact pain of what we'd endured. "I'm sorry we had to leave. I didn't want to."

"How come you never wrote?"

He shrugged and let go of my hand. "I didn't think you'd want me to. Even if you'd wanted me to, I didn't know what to say. What happened was so horrific. Everything was ruined."

"I know what you mean." He was right. What could we have said to each other after Beth's murder? We couldn't have exactly carried on as if things were still innocent and fine. Not to mention that he'd moved a thousand miles away. "I was completely blissed out one moment and devastated the next."

"I'm sorry. I don't know if I ever said that."

"You didn't have to. I knew." For a second I fell back in time and it was just the two of us under a starry night as we swayed at the very top of the Ferris wheel. Everything had been perfect, because the boy I loved felt the same way. If only we could have stayed in that moment.

I took his hand and turned it over to run my fingers over the calluses. They told me some of the story of his life. "You work with your hands, don't you?"

"I'm a contractor. Flipped houses back in LA. Now I'm semi-retired."

He ran his thumb over the ring finger of my left hand. Would he feel the indentation left from wearing a wedding ring for twenty years? "All this time I figured you were married to a doctor or lawyer or someone rich and lived in a mansion. You were the classiest girl I ever knew."

"My ex-husband was in high tech, so you have the rich part right." It was my only consolation. He'd had to pay for his infidelities.

"Are you here for long?" Cole asked. "In town. Not the grocery store."

I chuckled as I pushed back a strand of hair that had fallen over my eyes. "I'm not sure, actually. For now, I'm here for however long it takes to get my mom settled into her new place. I have to go through the house before I can put it up for sale. There's a lot accumulated after living in a place for forty years.

I'm deciding whether to sell my own house in Seattle. Or whether to go back to my job."

"There's a chance you might stay here?"

"My mom wants me to. Brooke's in college in Boise. They're all I care about now. So it's a possibility."

He nodded, then smiled. "I like the sound of you staying here more than I should say out loud."

"I thought you'd be married too," I said.

"You've thought about me?"

"How many days are in thirty years?"

"Over a hundred thousand. I think."

"Then that's how many times I've thought of you," I said.

He grinned. "Well, shoot. If that's the case, then it's about half the number of times I thought of you. None of this once-a-day stuff. I'm at least a twice-a-day man. Do you want to go to lunch? The pizza place is as good as it ever was."

"Now?"

"Why not? We have thirty years to catch up on," he said.

My stomach fluttered. *Don't get carried away*, I told myself. There was no reason to get all excited over my high school sweetheart just because he asked me for lunch. Our feelings were thirty years old, but they could have been a thousand as far as that goes. A million bad moments between now and then had changed us, and probably not for the better. He wouldn't like me once he got to know me again. I was old and tired, untrusting. I'd forgotten how to have fun. My big dreams were gone. I was only a shell of the girl I'd been.

He must have taken my hesitation for rejection. His eyes bored into me. "You don't want to?"

"What? No, I'd love to have lunch. It's just that, well, I'm… afraid you'll be disappointed. I've changed."

"Not so far as I can see." He brushed his knuckles against my cheek. "You're still the prettiest girl I've ever seen."

My eyes filled. "Oh, Cole."

"Have lunch with me. Please."

"I'm not like I was when we were kids," I said.

"Give me the chance to know the new you, then."

I let out a long breath. *Let yourself have this*, I said to myself. Give life the opportunity to prove not all is lost. There were second acts in life. Or third ones, perhaps? This was the boy I'd loved with all my heart standing before me with every vulnerable part exposed to me. "Yes, all right. I just need to run back to my mom's and put the groceries away. In this weather, they wouldn't last long in the car."

"Great. Good." His eyes were as warm as the touch of his hand as he brushed my bare shoulder with his knuckles. "Carlie Webster. What a good day this is turning out to be."

A surge of anticipation whipped through me. "I agree." So much for keeping my head.

I pointed at his empty basket. "What were you shopping for?"

He laughed. A quiet rumble from inside his chest that reminded me of distant thunder, exciting and soothing all at once. "I have no earthly idea. You've made me forget my own name."

And just like that, Cole Paisley was back in my life.

———

I found Cole sitting on the outside patio under the shade of an oak.

"Hi. I hope you haven't been waiting long?" Perspiration between my breasts made me feel like the girl I'd been when I first fell for him. He could weaken my knees with a glance in my direction.

Cole stood. "Only thirty years."

I laughed. "Well, here I am." All the way here, I'd been thinking only of the questions I wanted to ask him. How was Drew? Had Luke been all right after they left? Did he ever mention Beth?

All that was forgotten as he leaned close to kiss my cheek. "Thanks for agreeing to meet me."

"I'm glad you asked."

He remained standing as I slid into the bench on the opposite side of him. Glasses of water bled onto cardboard coasters. Since I'd worked here in high school, Logan Bend Pizzeria had updated its logo.

"After you left, I worked here." I wrapped my fingers around the glass and then brought it to my mouth to take a quick sip. "Do you know something I used to wish for?"

"What's that?" He placed his hands on the table.

"I used to hope that one day I'd look up from the register or from wiping tables and it would be you who walked through the door. There was this bell back then, and it would ring every time a new customer came in. But it was never you."

"If only I could have," he said.

His green eyes darkened to the color of Logan Mountain. He glanced below the deck where a slender creek ran alongside the building. The gurgle of water over rocks was as familiar to me as the scent of the wood-burning pizza ovens.

"How is Luke?" I reached across the table and placed my hand over his.

He met my gaze. "Luke's really good. He's a doctor now. A surgeon."

"I knew he would be. He always did what he said he'd do." I smiled at an image of Luke's earnest green eyes as he asked my mom for another slice of lasagna. All three of the Paisley boys had eaten at our table more times that I could count. They'd been at ease with my family. We must have been such a haven from the chaos of his house. I really hadn't thought about it at the time, too happy to have Cole sitting across from me gobbling up my mother's meal.

"He's married to a woman he met in college, and they have three gorgeous daughters." He reached into the back pocket of his jeans and pulled out his phone to show me his screen saver.

Three pretty blonde girls wearing Santa hats smiled into the camera. "These are my nieces. Sarah, Jessie, and Olivia. That's from last Christmas. Sarah turns sixteen tomorrow."

I brought his phone closer to get a better look, shielding the screen from the sunlight with my hand. "The middle one looks just like Luke."

"For sure. The other two look more like their mama. She has blue eyes like theirs."

"You're close to them?" I asked, already knowing the answer. The look of pride on his face told me everything I needed to know.

"They put up with me. I worship them."

"Was it hard to move away?"

He hesitated before answering. "Yeah. But I had to come back here. For my sanity."

I put a pin in that to come back to later. "How are your parents?" I held my breath, fearing the answer.

"They divorced after we left here. Mom's remarried to a retired doctor and is super happy. My dad died five years ago."

"I'm sorry. Mine too."

"I'd heard that." He tilted his head and fixed a sympathetic gaze on me. "My heart sank when I learned he was already gone. I know how close you two were."

"I miss him every day." I glanced heavenward. "I know he and Beth are up there together. That gives me comfort."

Cole grimaced. "I'd like to say I miss my dad, but it'd be a lie, and I don't have full confidence he's in heaven."

"He was a hard man to love."

"Yes, he was." He shrugged one shoulder in a dismissive gesture that I suspected wasn't at all how he felt. "I was the only one of the three of us who had a relationship with him. He'd alienated my brothers years before. Drew's hard that way. As kids, he always seemed fine, compared to Luke and me. You remember—he was always the life of the party and had all those girlfriends. But under the surface was a deep anger. An anger that scared me, frankly. I lived in fear of the day the two of them went head-to-head."

"I don't blame him," I said, remembering the bruises I'd seen on all three of them one time or another.

"Luke and Drew refused to see Dad after he and Mom split. As much as I'd wished for a happy family, there was no way it could happen. Too much had gone down. Drew never got over it enough to forgive him, which he was under no obligation to do. If there was ever a guy who didn't deserve forgiveness, it was the old man."

"And you?" I asked softly. "Did you see him?"

"I supported him financially as soon as I started making money. It's not rational behavior, but he was my dad and I couldn't see him starve to death. He'd have been homeless if I didn't pay his rent."

"Why?"

Cole raised a pretend glass. "He drank himself to death eventually. But darned if it wasn't a slow exit."

I reached across the table to touch Cole's hand. "You couldn't desert him. That's not how you're made."

He raised one eyebrow and shook his head. "I've never been too smart."

"It's more important to be kind than smart."

He glanced behind me.

"And Drew?"

Shaking his head, Cole grinned. "He's doing great, actually. He's a stuntman in Hollywood."

"No? That's perfect." I could see it as clearly as if Drew were standing in front of me.

"Right? He makes loads of cash and lives near the beach. He's still working his way through the women of California."

"I can't imagine him ever settling down, can you?"

"I wish he would but no. He's committed to being a bachelor forever." His gaze turned back to the creek. "I worry about him sometimes. He lives too much on the edge."

"What do you mean?"

"I don't know how to explain the feeling. It's probably a twin thing. I get this sense of dread sometimes, like he's in trouble."

"Do you ever ask if he's all right?"

"Often. He always assures me he's living the dream."

I laughed. "That sounds like him."

He quieted as a sadness came to his eyes. I watched him, curious about his thoughts. "What is it?"

"Do you remember how the Ferris wheel stopped for so long?"

"Um, yeah, I remember." Even now, I could feel his mouth pressed against mine. The warmth, the rightness of the two of us together. "I've often wondered what would have happened if…" I trailed off, remembering my vow to stay away from the subject of my sister.

"Me too." He looked down at his hands. "I cried when we left. Like a baby."

"Oh, Cole."

"I begged my parents to let me say goodbye to you but my dad was adamant. The image of you at your sister's memorial was the last thing I had of you."

"I don't remember a single thing from that day."

"After the service, I found you out behind the church." His voice grew husky. "You were crying. I thought my heart would break in two."

I brought my hand to my mouth. A flash of something, like a torn corner of a photograph, danced before my eyes. It was Cole, dressed in black, sitting next to me on the grass. "I remember. Did we talk?"

"I talked. A week had gone by since Beth's death. By then someone had already thrown a torch into our yard. My mom was terrified and my dad enraged. They'd told us before the funeral that we were leaving town."

"Oh, Cole. That must have been so hard."

"You let me put my arms around you. I held you for a few

minutes, and then I had to leave. That was the last image I had of you. Sitting by that tree."

I shook my head. "I don't remember. I wish I did. Did you tell me you were leaving?"

"Yes. Which made you cry harder. I promised I'd come back for you someday. Whatever it took, I'd find you. But I never did. I broke my promise to you."

"We were kids. You couldn't have kept that promise. Nothing was in our control." I wiped tears from my eyes. "I'd have liked to have that memory. Hearing it now comforts me. I can't explain why exactly."

"I've thought about trying to find you so many times. I even went on Facebook one time to see if you were there, but I couldn't find you or your parents."

"I'm not on social media because of my students. College kids don't need any further fuel for ridicule."

"That makes sense." He smiled. "I can imagine you in front of the class. You were always so smart."

"A bookworm, that's all."

"The smartest person I ever knew."

I smiled back at him, a blooming rose under the warm sun instead of a middle-aged woman who had long ago given up on love.

6

COLE

A guy like me hasn't had the best luck with women. As I sat across from Carlie Webster on a July day in the part of the world I loved best, eating pizza that could hold up to the finest eating establishments in Southern California, I understood in a whole new way what the gold standard of women had always been. She was right there, staring back at me with those blue eyes that had haunted my dreams for thirty years. Was this very moment the reason?

"Did you know me right away?" Carlie asked as she put another slice of pepperoni pizza back on her paper napkin. Logan Bend Pizzeria didn't bother with plates. They cut their slices in diamonds small enough to devour in two or three bites, depending on the width of one's mouth. The mouth I was staring at right now was just the right size. I wanted to kiss her more than I'd ever wanted anything in my life.

I nodded as I picked up a wayward piece of pepperoni and stuck it back on my piece. "I have a confession. I spotted you on the street when you came out of the tea shop. I followed you into the store."

"I wondered why there was nothing in your basket."

I laughed. "Actually, I came to town to shop but somehow

that didn't seem as important as taking you to lunch. Did you recognize me right away?"

She dangled her piece of pizza midway between the pan and her mouth. "Wait, are you saying you knew me from across the street?"

"Darlin', I'd know you in the pitch-black."

She rolled her eyes, laughing. "That might be an exaggeration. But I love it."

"Did you know me right away? Please don't tell me you had no idea who the old guy stalking you in the grocery store was."

"You're not an old guy. I'd have known you anywhere. Especially your eyes. Although the rest of you is considerably larger than the last time I saw you."

I grinned. "I'd hope so. I bet I was a hundred pounds soaking wet back then."

"To me, you were the hunkiest guy in Idaho."

"Just Idaho?" I peeked over at her before taking hold of my piece of pizza and taking a large bite. Since my divorce, I'd been on a few online dates. Every time, I'd been astounded at how I suddenly didn't know how to eat without making a tremendous amount of chewing noise. With Carlie, though, it was as natural as if we broke bread every day of the week.

"If only we'd been able to stay in that moment forever." A shadow crossed her face. She reached for her water. Her hair fell over her cheeks and for a split second, thirty years vanished and I could see her exactly as she'd been at sixteen. Freckles scattered across her nose and a smile that lit up every room. Eyes that were both soulful and sweet. No makeup to speak of, other than some mascara and lip gloss. "I've thought about that a lot over the years. How could I have been so happy one moment and the next so utterly gutted?"

I didn't say anything, simply reached across the table and covered her hand with mine for a few seconds.

She set aside her drink and fixed her gaze on me. No longer a girl, here was a woman in her prime. I'm sure she would disagree. Women in their forties and fifties seemed to have no idea how the years they'd lived and loved had made them even more beautiful. There was no use telling them, either.

"What?" She reached over and placed her fingertips briefly on my bare forearm. "What are you thinking about?"

"You're beautiful. That's what I'm thinking."

Her brows knit together as she dabbed at the condensation on the outside of her water glass. "Do you have any idea how nice that is to hear?"

"I'll say it again if you want."

"Tell me what happened with your marriage," she said.

"Short story, she fell in love with her gun instructor. Long story, we were unsuited from the start. There are no innocents when it comes to relationships. I'd withdrawn from her. She was lonely."

She pursed her lips in a decisive way. "If you have problems, you should talk about them and try to work through them. Not cheat."

I studied her as she crumpled the napkin into a ball. Something in our conversation had made her uncomfortable. "What is it? Did your husband cheat too?" I asked this as gently as I could, hoping to coax her to talk.

"He made what your ex-wife did look like a minor offense." She tossed the crumpled napkin toward the end of the table, where it landed near the hot pepper shaker. "He'd been using call girls for years. It all came out in the wash, as my mother would say, when one of his prostitutes decided to blackmail him to keep quiet. She was one of many." She brushed a stray hair from her cheek with the back of her hand. "He's a high-tech executive. His reputation was important enough that he paid her a hundred thousand dollars before he came to me. He told me everything. It had all been going on for years."

"Oh, God, Carlie, I'm so sorry." Sweet, smart Carlie? How could any man do that to her?

"He said it was my fault. My coldness or something like that."

"Wow, that takes a certain type of person."

"I gave him the best twenty years of my life. We'd had a child together. And then, this. The ultimate humiliation."

"I've never wished I had ties to a paid killer before."

She threw her head back, laughing. When she sobered, she looked back at me. "It's been a long time now. I've moved on. I'm sad about what it did to my daughter. Since she found out what happened, she hasn't spoken to her father. That's the only part that still keeps me up at night."

"Even though I don't have kids, I can understand how much that would hurt."

"I worry about her. Will she be able to have a good relationship with a man, or will she be afraid the same thing will happen to her?"

"She has a great mom, so I think she'll be all right."

"I'd like to think so. It was such a blow to her. She's changed since then. I used to call her my Babbling Brooke because she never stopped talking. These days she's quiet. Introspective. I can see the distrust in her eyes when she meets new people."

"The right man will be able to get through her walls."

"You think so?"

"I do. If I recall, I had to work pretty hard to break down your tough exterior," I said.

"What're you talking about? I was completely head over heels for you. I just couldn't believe a boy like you wanted me. Do you remember my glasses?"

"You were cute in those glasses."

She reached down to the bench and pulled her phone out of her wallet. "Would you like to see a photo of Brooke?"

"Absolutely."

She slid the phone across the table.

I picked it up and looked at the photo of a young woman with a wide, bright smile and shiny brown hair. Although she wasn't as fair as her mother, there was no mistaking that she was Carlie's daughter. "She looks like you."

"Do you think? I've always thought so but I'm never sure."

"Her smile especially."

"She's coming to visit for a few weeks later in the summer. Maybe you'd like to meet her? She knows about you."

"Knows what?"

"That you were my first love." She flushed and dipped her chin to stare into her lap. "My first kiss."

Could I be her last, too? I made a promise then and there that I'd do whatever I needed to. If there was a chance to win her love, I'd do it. "Okay, full confession. My niece Sarah knows about you too."

"Knows what?" she asked, repeating my question.

"That you were my first love. My first kiss." The one to whom I compared every woman I met.

"Is it wrong that I find that incredibly sweet?"

"Not at all," I said. "I love that Brooke knows about me."

She chuckled as she looked over my shoulder. "When she was in high school, I told her she needed to wait for the fluttery feeling that Cole Paisley gave me."

"Fluttery feeling? Is that what it was called?"

"Butterflies," she said.

"I had those for sure. Only every time I saw you."

We grinned at each other for a moment, lost in each other's eyes.

"Can I take you to dinner tomorrow?" I asked. "Then dancing at the Rooster? They have a live band every weekend. The cover band only plays country, though. Do you still like country?"

"What else is there?"

"REO Speedwagon," I said.

"Right, how could I forget?" She tugged on one of her earrings. She'd done that when she was nervous as a kid.

"What is it?" I asked softly. "Your mother? Would she not want you to see me?"

She dipped her chin, staring into her lap. "Oh no, nothing like that. Mom would be thrilled. She thinks I've given up on men. It's just there's something I haven't told you yet."

"You can tell me anything."

She returned her gaze to me. "I found a journal of Beth's. Written the summer she was killed. She'd hidden it in her closet. In it, she talks about another boy. She was cheating on Luke."

I flinched. "You're kidding. With who?"

"I don't know. She calls him Z."

"Do you think he could be the killer?" My stomach hollowed at the thought. "Was he someone we went to high school with?"

"He has to be. Where else would she meet anyone? It's not like there were any neighboring high schools. Which means we might have known him. Beth goes on and on about him. They were sleeping together." A lone tear escaped from her left eye. "I'm sorry. I'm so sorry for what happened to Luke."

"Please, don't cry. Luke's all right, I promise."

"Knowing what Beth was doing—it seems like my family ruined yours," she said.

"What happened to her or Luke wasn't anyone's fault but the killer. Even if this guy she was sleeping with killed her. She didn't ask to be murdered. Anyway, she was a kid."

She hung her head. "I'm mad at her. I know it's wrong, but I am."

"That's understandable. But you have to remember she was seventeen years old."

"Luke would never have done anything like that," she said.

"Regardless, Beth didn't ask to be killed. Cheating on your high school boyfriend isn't the worst crime in the world. She was a kid."

"I'd never have done that to you. And because of her, we never had a chance."

"Because of the killer, not Beth," I said. "Maybe we could see about that chance."

"A second chance?" She folded her hands together on the table. "Is that really possible?"

"I mean, we're both here. Both single."

"For years, this town was the place where Beth was killed and sent you away from me. I was the other Webster girl. The one still alive. Everywhere I went, people looked at me with pity and curiosity. I couldn't wait to get out of here."

"And now?"

She laid her hands flat and leaned closer to the edge of the tabletop. "And now you're here. Plus, the stars. The river on a warm afternoon. The way the air smells in the morning. All the things I used to love."

"Could you love them again?" I asked gently.

"I think I might be able to."

"It's worth exploring, at least."

"We owe it to ourselves to just see, right?" She inched her hands across the table. I grabbed them with my own. "What would your family think if they knew we were sitting here together after all this time?"

I thought about that for a moment. Would they care? If my fantasies were to come to life and I finally had a chance to be with the girl of my dreams, would they approve? They would. I felt certain. They knew how hard I'd taken it when we had to leave. "They'd love it, actually."

"Really?"

"They want me to be happy."

I glanced through the branches of the tall oak that grew next to the patio as a town car pulled into the parking lot. Town car? Someone fancy must be in town.

"I got tested for everything. All the diseases. I'm clean."

Her words drew me back to her. "What?" Clean? I wasn't following.

"My husband slept with prostitutes."

Right. Her husband could have brought something home to her. I'd love to get my hands on her ex-husband. Teach him a little about humiliation. "Good to know."

"I wanted you to know, just in case you wanted to kiss me."

"I'd do just about anything to kiss you," I said.

A middle-aged couple were coming up the steps of the patio. They looked vaguely familiar. It took me a moment to place them. Take thirty years and twenty pounds and I suddenly knew who they were. Thom and Sharon Richards. He was running for governor. His signs were everywhere.

"Isn't that Thom Richards?" Carlie whispered.

I nodded, hoping they wouldn't notice us. No such luck.

"They're coming over here," Carlie said under her breath.

I turned as they approached.

"Now you two sure do look familiar," Richards said. "Were you students of mine?" He snapped his fingers. "Wait a minute now." He pointed at me. "You're one of the Paisley boys, isn't that right? One of the twins."

"Cole Paisley, sir." I rose to my feet to shake his hand. "Nice to see you."

"This is my wife, Sharon."

"Sure, I remember you at practices," I said.

"Yes, I loved watching my man in action back in the day." Sharon shook my hand.

"Now, this young lady must not be from around here," Richards said.

"I am," Carlie said as the corners of her mouth twitched in a nervous smile. "I'm Carlie Webster." She straightened her shoulders, waiting for the moment when he realized who she was. The murdered girl's sister. This was what had driven her away from here.

Richards hesitated and paled under his perfect tan, perhaps as the truth of Carlie's identity hit him. His wife recovered faster. "Carlie Webster. Of course. It's good to see you back in town. Are you visiting your mother?"

"I am," Carlie said.

"What a gift she's been to our local campaign," Sharon said.

"What?" Carlie's gaze fluttered over to me for a second before returning to the pillars of the community who stood before us.

"Didn't you know she's working on our campaign?" Sharon asked.

"Doing what?" Carlie asked.

"Whatever needs doing. That's your mom," Sharon said. "Salt of the earth."

"She's been tremendous." Richards cleared his throat. "A real go-getter."

Sharon smiled as she touched Carlie's shoulder in a disarming manner, the way people did when trying to create a sense of kinship and intimacy. "My goodness, after what she's been through. She just soldiers on." With her medically enhanced tightened skin, precision-cut blonde bob, and studied casual wear, Sharon Richards looked more Beverly Hills than Logan Bend, Idaho.

I scratched the back of my neck, wondering how this would go over with Carlie. The stoic set of her jaw and flash of annoyance in her eyes told me she didn't care for Sharon or her patronizing account of Mrs. Webster's soldiering on. Carlie had never been one to suffer fools.

"How's your family doing?" Richards asked me. "We sure missed you boys on the football field."

"Darling, don't be insensitive," Sharon said in a teasing tone. "No one cares about football games from thirty years ago."

Richards gave his wife an indulgent smile. "My wife doesn't understand why coaching the high school football team made me happy."

"Not when I know what good you've done since joining politics." Sharon put her hand on Richard's upper arm. "Football seems silly compared to solving homelessness."

"True enough," Richards said. "I hope your brothers are well?"

"Luke's a surgeon, and Drew's a stuntman," I said. "They're both doing great."

"Wonderful to hear," Richards said. "I didn't care for how things were handled back then. I'm sorry for how it hurt your family."

No one said anything for a moment. I sensed genuine kindness and remorse coming from my former coach. "Luke thought a lot of you," I said. "Our father had some issues, and you were a good role model for us."

Richards looked out to the trees before answering. "Luke talked to me about your dad one time. I'm sorry I wasn't able to do anything to help. Things were different back then. We weren't able to protect kids like we wanted."

The old shame of our family secrets swarmed me. All I could do was nod.

"It's nice to see you both," Richards said. "We'll let you get back to your lunch."

"Two old friends catching up?" Sharon asked.

"For the first time," Carlie said with an edge to her voice, "since the Paisleys were run out of town."

"Well, have fun," Sharon said. "We'll hope to see you at our fundraiser. Your mother has all the details."

"Sure, thanks," Carlie said.

"Bye now." Richards tucked his wife's arm into the crook of his arm and they walked across the patio and into the dining room.

"How strange. My mother always hated politics." Carlie's brow wrinkled as she returned her gaze to mine. "But if it keeps her busy, I guess it's fine."

"What was bothering you about Sharon Richards?"

She raised one brow and glanced toward the door they'd just walked through. "She's fake."

"You hate that."

Her eyes widened. "Yes. Always have."

"I remember. People don't change. Not their core values, anyway."

She considered me for a moment. "It feels good to be known."

"Agreed."

We smiled at each other for longer than was normal for two people who'd only just found each other after three decades. Finally, she broke away, bringing me back to reality. "I should probably go. Mom needs me to pick up something from the pharmacy."

"Let me walk you to your car." I tossed a five-dollar bill on the table for a tip.

Carlie slipped out of the booth. "I'd like that." She picked up her purse and gestured toward the back parking lot. "I'm out there."

I followed her down the stairs. The driver of the town car leaned against the trunk while smoking a cigarette.

"Don't see that too often in Logan Bend," I said. "We're more of a truck kind of town."

"Speaking of things that don't fit in, I'm the red Lexus."

I opened the door for her and let her slip behind the wheel. Before I could close her in, she put up a hand. "Thanks for lunch. This is the best time I've had in a long time."

I leaned over and before I knew what I was doing, I kissed her softly on the mouth. "I'm sorry, but it had to be done."

She touched the side of my face. "I'd like to go to dinner sometime, if the offer still stands."

"How about I cook for you?"

"You cook?"

"I don't mean to brag, but I'm pretty spectacular in the kitchen. Do you like risotto?"

"Almost as much as pizza."

I handed her my phone. "Would you put your number in here?"

She nodded as she reached into her purse to give me hers. "Do the same?"

"If you insist."

I added my name to her contacts.

"Should I put myself in your favorite list?" she asked with a sassy lilt in her voice.

"Obviously," I said.

"Done." She held out my phone. I took it and gave her back her own.

She settled behind the wheel.

"Are we on for dinner?" I asked.

"Count on it."

"Great." I shut the car door.

She rolled down the window and peered up at me. "This is real, right? You're not my imagination?"

I placed my hands on the window frame. "I'm as real as they come."

"Good. Because I don't like fake people." She gave me one more smile before starting the car. I watched as she exited out of the parking lot onto Fourth Street. For a second, I stood there, marveling at the day's events. Was this truly a second chance? My second chance to make Carlie Webster mine forever? God willing.

7

CARLIE

W hen I arrived home, my mother was on her covered back patio shelling peas. Sitting on the old porch swing we'd had since I was a child, she tapped one foot to country radio playing from the Bluetooth device I'd gotten her for Christmas. Her silvery hair framed her small face, pink from the heat. She wore a pair of cream-colored overall shorts that a woman almost seventy shouldn't be able to pull off, but her trim, tanned frame made it so. As a child, I'd thought she was the prettiest mom in town, and I still thought so.

"Mom, isn't it kind of warm out here?"

"Feels good to my old bones."

"Where did this massive bowl of peas come from?" I asked.

"Nora brought them over. She's overrun with them and knows I don't have a garden any longer."

I looked out to the empty pen overrun with weeds where my dad had grown vegetables. Another thing I would need to tidy up before we put the house on the market.

"Do you miss the vegetables in the summer?" I sat next to her on the swing and gathered a dozen unshelled peas onto my lap.

"A little, I suppose. But it's no fun without your dad. Who would eat it all, anyway?" She touched the cross she wore around her neck. Whenever she talked about my dad, her fingers seemed to subconsciously find it. "I prefer to be on the golf course these days."

"Who do you golf with? Any of your old crowd?"

"Sometimes."

I studied her. This evasiveness was new. She was hiding something from me. Maybe she didn't want me to know she was helping with the Richards campaign? I had no idea why. "Mom, I ran into the Richardses. They said you're working on his governor run."

"That's right."

"Why didn't you mention it?"

She shrugged. "I didn't think about it. Why? Do you not approve?"

"It's surprising, that's all. I didn't think you cared about politics."

"I care about Richards. He's a fine man with policy I agree with."

"Like what?"

She set aside the bowl of shelled peas and turned toward me. "He wants to make laws that protect young women from online predators. Do you have any idea how dangerous the internet is? These men lure information out of these naive girls and then stalk them or worse. It's horrible."

I hid a smile. "I have a daughter I raised in this crazy age, so yes, I do know."

"Right. It was more of a rhetorical question. Thom Richards is an advocate for young women. I can't help but think Beth's death had something to do with it."

"What do you mean?"

"He's never said, but I think having one of his students killed affected his outlook on women's safety."

Interesting. I didn't follow up with more questions, but I could see now that my mother felt a connection with him. One that included Beth. No wonder she was devoting so much time to the election.

"Did you have a nice outing?" Mom asked. "Who did you meet for lunch? You didn't say."

I'd said only that it was a friend from high school. At the mention of the words *friend* and *high school*, she'd turned away, busying herself at the sink. I knew from past experience that she clammed up at the mention of those days. The time when Beth was the queen of the school, homecoming and otherwise. I was never certain if talking about Beth was too painful or if she thought avoiding the subject would help me.

"You won't believe it."

"Who?"

"Cole Paisley. I ran into him at the grocery store, and he asked if I wanted to have lunch. He built a house out on his family's old property."

"You're kidding. He came back here?"

"I was surprised too." I explained how his mother had held on to the property so that Cole could buy it from her when he was ready. "He wanted to be back here and have his little farm. That was his dream back in high school." I told her what I'd learned of the Paisley brothers, including Luke's and Drew's successful careers.

"That's good to hear. I always felt bad about what happened."

I sliced open the pea with my thumb and let the peas plop into the bowl between Mom and me. "Their parents divorced after they left here."

"Is that right? What a shame. That poor woman."

"She married a doctor after the divorce and is doing well."

"That's good. I often wondered about their marriage. In all the years I knew them, I can only think of a handful of times they were ever anywhere together. She was the sweetest lady. Him, though." Mom scowled. "I never liked him. I once saw him dress down Luke in front of God and everybody after they lost a football game."

Mom stared out to the yard, a pea held between her fingers as if it were a cigarette. "All three of those boys were sweet. There was something off about their father. Did the boys ever say anything about him being violent? I could swear he was a wife beater."

"Yes, Cole talked about it with me one time. Luke got the brunt of it, but he hurt all of them pretty regularly."

"I figured as much. Not that I could do anything about it at the time. I didn't like you and Beth going over there when he was home. Beth said Mr. Paisley stared at her sometimes. That's why they hung out here so often."

"Really? You never told me that." I gaped at her as a spark of shock traveled through me. "You don't think he could have had anything to do with her death, do you?" The words were out of my mouth before I could think better of it and keep them to myself.

"I mentioned him as a possible suspect to Lancaster and Wright at the time. Mr. Paisley had a solid alibi. He'd been in the bar all night, sitting in his usual spot."

"Why did the paper peg it on Luke and not him?" I asked out loud, more to myself than Mom.

"Poor journalism. That's all that was." Mom spit this out with enough venom to kill a grown man with her tongue. "Poor Luke. What's Cole say about it now?"

"He says that Luke's fine and not to worry about him."

"I still believe it was someone she knew," Mom said.

"The detectives didn't think so." I said this as if this were new information. Mom and I had been over this dozens of times over the years. I'd come to think of it as her very own loop. Instead of the same day played over and over, it was her endless sorting through the facts of the case. A loop that would not end until we found out the truth. Which we most likely never would. Unless the journal revealed something that led us to the answers we wanted. As much as I'd wanted to tell her what I'd found, I needed more time to read through all the passages. There was no reason to get her upset until I knew more.

"Yes, I know, sweetie. But, as *you* know, I disagree. The way she died, well, it indicates someone enraged in a very personal way." Mom pushed her glasses farther up her nose. She'd recently gotten new ones with large blue frames that matched the color of her eyes.

"Cole asked me out on a date," I said. "For dinner."

"He did? How funny."

"Funny?"

"Not funny in a bad way. It's simply that after all these years, it would seem you're to finally have your wish. Cole Paisley has returned to Logan Bend."

I made a sound between a laugh and scoff. "What're you talking about?"

"I know you've thought about him a lot over the years. You haven't exactly kept that a secret."

I didn't deny it. There was no use pretending otherwise with my mother. She knew my secret longings. Mothers always do. Or did they? Beth had kept a large secret from both of us.

"Did you say yes to the dinner date?" Mom peered at me. The twinkle in her eyes surprised me.

"I did." I smiled, thinking of his hard mouth on mine. "And when he walked me to my car just now, he kissed me."

She plucked three peas out of a pod. "My, oh my. He moves fast."

"Mom, it won't hurt you if I get involved with him, will it?"

She didn't say anything as she picked another pea from the pile between us. "Honey, I appreciate you worrying about my feelings. But whether or not you date someone from high school doesn't make me think more or less about Beth. People are always so worried to bring her up—afraid to make me remember she's gone, as if I'd ever forget."

"Do I do that?"

"A little."

"I'm sorry. I just worry about you."

"And I worry a lot about you."

The breeze brought the scent of roses. "I've felt, sometimes, that it was wrong to ever feel happy because Beth couldn't."

"She wouldn't want that. She'd want you to have a joyful life, full of love and adventure."

"I wonder what she'd say about Cole and me." I smiled thinking of how she'd teased me about Cole. "She used to make fun of me about my secret crush on him." My throat constricted. "I never got to tell her how we finally admitted our feelings and kissed on the Ferris wheel."

"I'm sorry, sweetie." She took off her glasses to wipe under her eyes with the backs of her fingers. "She would've been delighted for you."

"I'm going over to his house tonight. He's cooking for me. I feel like a teenager all over again."

She put her glasses back on and picked up another peapod. "Was it strange to see him?"

"Yes and no. Very quickly it seemed as if no time had passed. He and I were close friends for years and years. I never felt like I had to pretend to be dumber than I was just to get him to like me. It was like that today too. Maybe it's spending time with someone who knew you when you were young. Like a shared language or something."

She patted my knee. "Don't overthink it. If you like him, see where it goes."

I tilted my head to rest my cheek against her shoulder. "Thanks, Mom."

"Love you, sweetie."

"I love you, Mom."

We finished the last of the peas without speaking, enjoying our easy companionship.

"Well, we made quick work of that." Mom brushed her

hands and looked out to the garden. "How will we ever get this place ready for sale?"

"Cole's a retired contractor. He made a lot of money flipping houses in California. We could have him come out and give us some estimates."

"Maybe we should wait and see how the date goes." She smiled, looking impish.

"Speaking of which, I think I'll text him." I flushed, as if I were still in high school and about to call him. "Just to confirm our plans."

Laughing, Mom rose to her feet. "You do that. I'm going inside for a glass of water."

I handed her the bowl of peas. "I'll get rid of the shells for you."

She nodded and walked to the screen door. Before she went inside, she looked back at me. "Don't hesitate to snatch up happiness if it comes your way. You just never know how long you have on this earth."

"I will, Mom."

"If not for yourself, do it to honor Beth's memory."

I returned my gaze to the yard where we'd run in the sprinkler as little girls. Beth had been so full of life. And then she was gone, leaving only me to chase dreams for both of us.

I went upstairs to read more of Beth's journal. *Please, God, let there be something of use,* I prayed silently as I trudged up our creaky stairs to my room.

On my bed, I opened Beth's journal to the entry dated May thirtieth.

School is almost out. I don't know what I'll do when I can't see him every day. I wish I could talk to Carlie about all of this, but she'd be devastated to know the truth. For one thing, she loves Luke. She has such a rich fantasy life that I'm sure she thinks we're both going to marry the Paisley brothers and live happily ever after. If she knew what I've been doing all these months... I don't even know what she'd do. Something like this is not even on her list of possibilities. She's so much simpler than me. I could see her marrying Cole and living here the rest of her life. Cole would take good care of her so she could write books and become famous. I love her so much. She's my best friend. But this? This she wouldn't understand. Carlie's like the rest of this town. She believes in the fairy tale of Luke and Beth, homecoming king and queen. We're supposed to belong together. But he's not who I want. I wish I did. I thought I did until Z came along.

I stopped reading. *The fairy tale of Luke and Beth?* Had she felt trapped by that expectation? The town sweetheart and the quarterback? Had the pressure of being Beth Webster driven her into a bad boy's arms? I'd had no idea she felt that way. She always seemed to soak up the attention. I'd often wondered how she could stand everyone looking at her all the time when I'd preferred the shadows where I could be myself. Maybe she'd been more like me than I'd thought.

I'm a bad, selfish person. I never thought I was before. Mom always told me I'd been given so much in life that it meant I had to be kind and good. I was. Before this. Before I fell in love with the wrong boy. Now all I want is what I want and forget all the people it'll hurt.

Who was he? This wrong boy? This bad boy?

I searched my memory, conjuring up faces of classmates, but no one came to mind. There had been an area behind the school known as the smoking area. The rebels hung out there, smoking, chewing tobacco, and smoking weed. I hadn't gone back there, too afraid and shy. Sometimes, though, I'd smelled marijuana smoke on the jackets of boys as I passed by them in the hallway. Had Beth somehow fallen in with that crowd?

No, I would have known. Or would I?

She'd hung out with her cheerleader friends and with Luke. I was often with them, tagging along, happy to be in the wake of my sister's glow. Not once had she complained about having her nerdy little sister following her everywhere. Wouldn't I have known if she'd gotten a different set of friends? A boy from the wrong social group? Back in high school all that had mattered, especially to someone like Beth. If we'd only known then how much more there was to life than what group you fell into during high school. Beth might have thought it was impossible to go public with a boy outside of her normal and accepted circle. My parents would not have wanted her to go out with someone who smoked or drank. Maybe that in combination with what the kids in school would think was enough to make her keep him a secret. Had that caused Z to become violent? Had her insistence they keep their relationship private caused him to kill her?

I went back to the journal.

I'm not even conflicted or unsure. Guilty, yes. I can barely look at Luke without cringing. He's so trusting and unsuspecting. I'd have thought I'd question myself—like are my feelings real or am I just flattered that he's chosen me—do I actually love Luke like I thought I did and this is all just a mistake because I was bored? But I don't have any of those feelings. I want only one thing. I want to run away with Z and never look back. I've always thought it was only Carlie who lived half the time in her daydreams because she didn't have the stuff she wanted. Now it's me, living only when I'm with him or when I'm dreaming of him.

This wasn't my Beth who went out of her way to be kind to everyone. Whoever this boy had been, he'd bewitched her.

I know I should break it off with Luke. It's not fair to string him along when I'm in love with someone else. I thought I loved Luke, but now that I'm with Z I can see that was nothing but puppy love. I'm a woman now, not a little girl. I can't go back to being innocent, virgin Beth. But if I break it off with Luke, everyone will know that I've changed. I want to keep it to myself.

I read a few more passages. She didn't want school to end because she wouldn't be able to see him. She hated lying to Luke. The next interesting bit was from June fourth. The night of her junior prom.

I went with Luke. I mean, what else could I do? I'm his girl-friend, after all. Mom made a big deal about my dress and even had me get my hair done at the salon. All I could think about was how I wished I could just have the evening with Z and skip the whole stupid thing.

Of course Z was there with her. I hate her so much. I don't even know what he sees in her. She's fat! I know that's mean but it's true. He says it's like me and Luke—he can't break it off with her because it would hurt her too much and then what would people think of him. Plus, it's not like we could ever be together in public. My dad would have a conniption if he knew.

Dad? Have a conniption? He'd been the most mild-mannered, easygoing man. I'd never seen him lose his cool until Beth was killed. Who would be someone my dad wouldn't have liked?

I lay back on the bed and stared up at the popcorn ceiling. What I needed was my yearbook. If I could look through photos maybe it would jog my memory. I had no idea where it was now. I sat upright. Yearbook. Where was Beth's? It hadn't been in the closet. She'd loved having that thing signed by all her friends. Were there secrets scrawled there too, and she'd hidden it some-where else in this house? Or had it been misplaced and had nothing to do with her death? I closed the journal, frustrated. It was getting late, and I needed to get a few more closets emptied before I went to Cole's for dinner. Maybe I'd find something in my cleaning and purging that would help me figure out Z's identity, but I wasn't holding out much hope.

8

COLE

I checked my phone about a thousand times that afternoon. Like a lovesick teenager, I kept hoping for a flirty text. To distract myself, I changed into shorts and a T-shirt and went out to weed the garden. Hot and dusty, I took off my shirt. As I knelt in the dirt to pull out the stubborn weeds, sweating under the afternoon sun, I smiled to myself. Carlie Webster was coming to my house for dinner. I still couldn't believe she was here and that I'd actually spent time with her. I'd only been dreaming about that for thirty years. How was it possible I never forgot her? I don't know. But I'd convinced myself that she was just a fantasy. She wouldn't be as I remembered her. That theory disappeared the moment I set eyes on her. Carlie had grown even lovelier since school. As far as her personality, it was as sweet and interesting as it had always been.

I picked some tomatoes and squash for my risotto and dropped them on the patio, then called for Moonshine and Duke.

"Come on, guys, let's go swimming."

They got up from where they'd been sleeping under the shade of the patio and trotted ahead. A few minutes later, I walked down the skinny trail to my swimming hole. The water was still and deep at this section of the river. Coarse sand created a narrow beach. At its deepest, the hole was about seven feet with a rock in the middle perfect for lying in the sun like a happy lizard. We'd spent some of the best moments of our childhood right here.

Duke jumped right into the water, barking happily, and swam out to the middle of the pool, his golden head bobbing along the surface. The river was where he and his best friend parted ways. Moonshine, with a disdainful flick of her tail, curled up under the shade of a maple. She might think herself a dog, but the cat side of her did not like water.

I slipped my feet out of my flip-flops and dived into the water. No matter how prepared I was, the chill shocked my scorched skin.

I hadn't thought it possible that the girl of my dreams would actually appear right before my eyes. I cautioned myself to take it slow with her. She had been hurt by her ex-husband. If I were to make any headway, I had to establish the kind of trust we'd shared when we were kids.

What did she see when she looked at me now? Did she think I was merely a flirtation from the past? A summer fling? Fun while it lasted but not something she would ever take seriously? Maybe she thought I was a loser, divorced and living out here in the country like a hermit. She was probably used to intellectuals. Professors, not retired contractors. Childless even. What if she thought we had nothing in common anymore? Did we? Other than our ties to this place, was the deep connection we'd shared when we were young still there? I needed to keep myself in check. In the fall, she'd return to her university job. I'd still be here. Pining for the one who got away.

I called to Duke and Moonshine, and the three of us walked back up the trail to the house. The sun toasted the top of my head. My hair was nearly dry by the time I reached the patio. I grabbed my vegetables and went inside.

As I entered the kitchen, my phone buzzed. I placed my

bounty in the sink and reached into my back pocket. Carlie's name showed on the screen. Was she canceling?

"Hiya." *Hiya? Who said that in their forties? I sounded like an idiot, as if I were trying to sound cool and nonchalant.*

"Hi, it's Carlie."

"Hi, Carlie." *Better. I sounded like an adult now.*

"I wondered if you needed me to pick up anything before I head out."

I breathed a sigh of relief. "I thought you were going to cancel."

"Why would I do that?" Carlie asked.

"I don't know. When it comes to love, I'm not really used to things going my way."

"I can relate."

I hesitated, moved by the soft, intimate tone of her voice. "When will you be here?" *Real cool, buddy. Way to act totally needy. I'd been hopeless at dating back when I was young and slightly cool. Now? I was doomed. No, this is Carlie, I told myself. She likes you just as you are. At least she used to.*

"I'm leaving in a few minutes," she said. "Unless that's too early? I couldn't remember if you said a time, and I've been pacing around wondering when I should show up."

"I'm sorry. I can't remember if I said a time either." *I'd been too wrapped up in her.* "As far as I'm concerned, the sooner the better."

"I'm glad I called. I'm making all this way too difficult on myself. I don't want to make a mistake, so I overthink everything."

I chuckled. "Me too. We have to remember this isn't like a real first date. We've skipped all that already, so there's no reason to be nervous."

"I'll be there in thirty minutes. I need to make a stop in town."

"I'll see you soon. Drive safe."

Thirty minutes until she arrived. "Thirty minutes," I said to the animals. "And the most special woman in the world is coming to our house."

Moonshine flopped on the floor, completely disinterested in my love life.

"Should I shave again?" I'd shaved once already, but I wanted to kiss her again. Scratching her alabaster skin was out of the question.

Duke wagged his tail and then came over to lick my hand.

"I can't trust you, Duke. You lick your private parts. What do you know about grooming for a lady?"

9

CARLIE

I could have found the Paisley property in my sleep. Like all the roads and streets of Logan Bend, I knew it as I knew the details of my own face. However, as I drove down the gravel driveway, I began to doubt the intelligence of my decision to go to his home. Having him cook for me seemed intimate and too soon given our recent reconnection. What if I disappointed him after a second meeting? Had it been simply fantasy and nostalgia that we'd felt at lunch? Would all that be replaced tonight with awkwardness?

Were there expectations when one went to a man's house for dinner? Since my divorce, I'd gone on exactly two online coffee dates. Neither led anywhere. After that, I'd decided to give it more time. I hadn't felt ready. Also, I didn't mind being alone. I could read when I wanted, eat what I wanted. Even the television, which had been entirely in my husband's control, had a new owner. Me.

Cole Paisley, though? He was an entirely different situation. He had the power to hurt me. I'd given my heart to my husband only to suffer humiliation after humiliation.

My phone rang as I came upon the Paisley driveway. A metal gate and fence surrounded what I could see of the property. He'd left the gate open for me, but I could see a lockbox that required a code. Did he ever worry about his safety as I did? It wouldn't surprise me. We'd seen evil up close thirty years ago. It was impossible not to be changed.

I stopped before the open gate and picked up my phone. To my delight, the call was from Brooke. "Hi, honey," I said.

"Hey, Mom. Just checking on you. I called the house and Gram said you had a date with Cole Paisley. Oh my God, is it true?"

I had to laugh at the excitement in Brooke's voice. Despite how my ex-husband's behavior had hurt her, my daughter was romantic. "Yes. I'm at his gate now and was just thinking about running away."

"Mom, don't you dare. Is he still cute?"

"Better than ever, I'm afraid. We had lunch earlier."

"And? Well, it must have gone well if you're seeing him tonight too. Mom, I'm super psyched for you."

"I hope I'm not setting myself up to get hurt."

"Not Cole, Mom. Not if he's like you described him."

"He lives here, Brooke, and loves it."

"You once loved Logan Bend too. You're not even sure you want to keep working. Mom, you can't limit yourself just because you're scared."

"When did you get so bossy?"

She giggled. "I want you to be happy. You deserve it. More than anyone. You're always taking care of everyone else. Maybe it's your turn."

"Thanks, sweetie."

"Now, go through the gate. Call me later. Or tomorrow, if you're busy tonight."

"Brooke!"

"I'm just kidding, Mom. Have fun, okay?"

"Okay. Love you."

"Me too."

I hung up, still smiling. My baby girl was a remarkable

young woman. All the struggles of the teen years were as faded as childbirth.

I put the car in Drive and went through the gate. The long driveway that had once been dirt and uneven with potholes was now even and covered with gravel. I rounded the corner expecting to see the Paisleys' run-down trailer. Instead, a charming modern farmhouse stood in its predecessor's place. A study in the contrast of black and white, the house had a white exterior of both painted brick and wood siding paired with a black roof and shutters. The front porch had black herringbone trim that told me what love and care he'd put into every detail. If all his work was like his own house, no wonder he'd been able to retire early.

I parked in front of the two-door detached garage, admiring its traditional crisscross design before reaching over to grab the bottle of wine I'd stopped in town for. As I approached the front door, Cole stepped out to the porch to greet me. My stomach fluttered at the sight of him. He wore loose jeans and a T-shirt that clung to his muscular torso. This was a man who obviously had spent his adulthood doing physical work. Behind him, the yellow face of a Labrador peeked around his legs. A black-and-white tuxedo cat shot between Cole's legs, then, as if dizzy, plopped at his feet.

"Welcome to my home." He smiled before giving me a quick kiss on the cheek. "Did you remember how to get here?"

"Not much had changed until I turned into your driveway. Your place is breathtaking."

"Thanks. I'm partial to it myself." He brushed a few damp curls from his forehead.

I'd have gladly melted right into his arms and let him have his way with me. Instead, I handed him the bottle of wine. "I hope you like red."

"Sure. You look gorgeous." He didn't even glance at the bottle, too busy looking at me. "I love your hair that way."

"Thank you." I flushed with heat. If he only knew how many

times I'd changed, finally settling on a denim shirtdress that made me feel young and carefree. I'd blown out my hair to give it more volume and taken special care with my makeup.

"These two must be Duke and Moonshine," I said.

"Yes. Moonshine thinks she's a dog and also has an equilibrium problem."

I knelt to give them both a good stroke or two. Duke wagged his tail. Moonshine purred. So far, so good. I had a feeling Cole took the opinions of his pets seriously. As he should, of course.

"Did you design the house?" I asked as I straightened.

"God no. I'm not that smart." He held the door open for me. "Come on in. I've already opened some wine."

As I passed by him to step inside the entryway, I caught a drift of his spicy aftershave. Good Lord, a man shouldn't smell that good.

I distracted myself by taking in the decor. A gray rug lay on light wood floors. The walls were covered in a patterned white-and-gray paper. I glanced down at his feet. He wore a pair of leather flip-flops. Given that we only had two months of good weather, we hardly ever wore such things in Seattle. "Should I take my sandals off?"

"Only if you want to."

I decided to keep them on. They were flats and comfortable. Plus, bare feet made me feel too vulnerable.

We walked through the entryway to a light and airy kitchen. "Cole, your kitchen is wonderful." From the risotto dish on the cooktop came the scent of garlic and onions. Fresh vegetables had been chopped and set aside in quaint wooden bowls on the light counter. Windows faced a covered stone patio and grass. Beyond, a fenced vegetable garden appeared lush and green. Farther still was the view of Logan Mountain I remembered so well from childhood. Although not visible from here, I knew the river ran between the mountain and the cluster of trees at the edge of the meadow.

"Why didn't you build closer to the river?" I asked.

"I would have, but the ground was too uneven and rocky. Also, the well and electrical were here where the trailer had been. Easier to do it this way."

"Is the swimming hole the same?"

"Exactly the same. I'll take you down there if you want. I hacked out a trail earlier in the year so it's easier to get down there now. Before then, grass and shrubs had overgrown the path we made with our feet."

Duke and Moonshine settled together into a large dog bed. I gasped in surprise when they snuggled close. "They sleep together?" I asked.

"Strange, right? They don't know they're different."

"Yes, but sweet."

"They're my first pets, so I didn't know what to expect. I didn't plan to get Moonshine, but she was at the same shelter and was such a hot mess I was afraid no one would choose her. She's named Moonshine for a reason." He imitated a drunk person by swaying and stumbling.

"Really?"

He held up a hand. "Scout's honor. Every so often she stumbles and falls, like she's drunk. The vet thinks there's something off in her inner ear."

"Poor baby."

"She has Duke to help her get around. Would you like a glass of wine?" He gestured toward the decanter on the counter. "I brought up something good from the cellar."

"You have a cellar?"

"I know. Pretentious."

"Not pretentious. Surprising. I would have figured you for a beer man."

He patted his flat stomach. "I like beer, but I try to limit my intake. As I get older, the harder it gets to stay fit."

"You seem to be doing a good job of it so far." I took a sip. Smooth and fruit forward. "This is good."

"Thanks. I wasn't sure if you liked Syrah, so I brought up a cabernet. Less risky."

I glanced around the room. Like many modern homes, the kitchen and sitting area were one, separated only by an island. A couch faced a fireplace with a large-screen television above. Had he decorated himself? "Is the entire house your handiwork?"

"The building part, yes. A professional designer did the interiors. She was one of my favorites in LA. Back when I flipped houses, she was part of my team." He set aside his glass and scuttled over to the cooktop to stir the risotto.

"I've never tried risotto. Is it hard?"

"Not really. Requires patience, that's all."

"I don't cook much these days. Most nights I have a sandwich or cheese and crackers. I had enough cooking during my marriage."

"You were the primary cook, I take it?"

"And bottle washer. He wasn't home much when Brooke was little. I did most everything around the house. I felt like a single parent."

"Where was he?"

"Work. At least that's what I assumed. He went from one high-tech start-up to the next." I took another sip from my glass. "Later, after everything came out, I wondered how much of the time away from us was actually at work."

Cole dumped a pile of the chopped vegetables into a steamer. "When Iris told me she was in love with someone else and had been for a year, I started going through every moment of the past months, trying to see where I went wrong. The clues were there, but I sure didn't see them at the time."

"It's an awful feeling," I said. "Thinking your whole life was a lie."

Cole came around the island to stand next to me. "I hate hearing that tone in your voice." He took my empty hand and brought it to his chest. "I wanted you to have the best life."

Touched, I fought against the scratchy feeling that came right before tears. "There was a lot of good, too. My daughter's pretty great, and we have a close relationship. I've had a satisfying career. Right now feels good, too."

He leaned closer and brushed my mouth with his. "If it were up to me, the rest of your life would be with a man who worships you."

"Cole," I whispered as I rested my forehead against his shoulder, too shy to look at him.

"Yeah?"

"You melt me."

He lifted me off my feet and placed me on the island. The skirt of my dress hiked up around my thighs. My breath caught when he kissed me again. He pulled me against him. Instinctively my legs wrapped around him. We kissed as if we wanted to make up for all the years apart. Finally, he pulled away. Grimacing, he ran both hands through his hair and backed away. "Carlie, I'm sorry. That was way out of line."

I laughed, throaty and breathless. "I disagree."

"You do?"

"Yes, we're adults," I said, teasing. "Why shouldn't we kiss?"

"I'm trying not to scare you off."

"Keep kissing me like that and I may never leave."

Before he could respond, the pot on the stove boiled over. He ran over to turn down the burner. "You're so distracting I may burn our dinner," he said.

I jumped from the counter and wandered over to the patio doors. They were open, letting in a breeze. I caught a whiff of jasmine.

"Is that jasmine I smell?" I turned back to look at him.

He was at the sink transferring vegetables into a bowl. Steam rose up from the pot and swirled around his face. "Yes, I had to baby them all winter with a humidifier. They don't like the cold, so I had to make it seem like the tropics."

I almost swooned. Imagining him here with Duke and Moonshine making risotto and babying his plants was too much for my middle-aged heart.

He wrapped tinfoil around a loaf of French bread. "This will take a few minutes to warm and then we're ready." With a quick movement, he had the loaf inside the oven. "I set the outside table, but if you prefer to eat inside, that's fine too. Your wish is my command."

"Outside sounds perfect." I picked up my glass of wine to take with us.

He grabbed the decanter and his glass before ushering me out to the patio. A table had been set for two, including a vase with pink and white roses. I walked to the edge of the pavers and looked out to the pasture where two chestnut horses grazed on grass. The sun hovered just above the mountain, shedding an orange hue of twilight. "When we were young, I took for granted how pretty it was here."

He came to stand beside me. "I missed this every single day I spent in LA."

"You made all your dreams come true. This place is just how you described it to me."

"Not all. There's been something missing." He put his arm around my shoulders and kissed the top of my head.

I leaned into him and sighed. How could this feel so right?

"I didn't think I could ever live here again after Beth," I said.

"And now?"

"I'm not sure. Everything feels different with you here."

"Come sit with me for a few minutes. We can enjoy the last of the light while the bread warms." He gestured toward four chairs placed around a gas firepit.

I took the seat he offered and set my glass on the wide arm of the chair. "I read more of the journal this afternoon."

"Anything telling?" He settled back into the chair next to mine. His eyes shone in the last of the sunlight.

I told him about how she seemed to feel pressure about being part of the "it" couple. "Whoever Z was, he wasn't the type to bring home to Mother. I'm wondering if he was one of the wild boys. A bad boy, so to speak." A hummingbird arrived at the feeder that hung from an awning of the pergola. "He had a girlfriend of his own. Someone he was unwilling to break up with. I spent all afternoon trying to remember other couples from her class."

He crossed his ankles as he looked up toward the sky. "I wish I could remember more high school. Mostly I remember only you and how crazy I was about you. Maybe I should see if Luke remembers any other couples."

"I'd hate to drag him into all this again."

"Good point." From inside, the timer for the bread sounded. "Have a seat at the table. I'll bring out our dinners."

I did as he asked, watching the sun disappear behind Logan Mountain. A few minutes later, he came out with two plates with risotto, steamed vegetables, and buttery bread.

He put mine in front of me, then sat in his own place. "Dig in."

"Wait, we should toast." I raised my glass. "To us. Finding each other again."

"To us."

We ate in silence for a few minutes, other than my murmurings of delight over the complex flavors of the risotto and freshness of the vegetables.

When I'd eaten enough, I set aside my fork and concentrated on him. "How come you never told me much about what was really going on at your house?"

He set his fork down and picked up his wine. "I was ashamed."

"It wasn't your fault."

"Didn't always feel that way. Luke and I were always trying to figure out ways to stay on his good side. Drew, on the other hand, went head-to-head with him."

"I wish I'd done something to help you guys," I said. "I loved you all so much, but I didn't really understand. My dad would've helped you guys get out of there."

"There's nothing anyone could have done. As hard as it was to leave here, in hindsight it was the best thing for my mom. Once her mother figured out what was really happening...and saw the bruises, she gave us enough money to move out and for Mom to go back to school. Everything changed once we were away from him."

"I'm comforted knowing that."

"When he died, none of us went to his funeral. Isn't that sad?" He picked up his fork and stabbed a piece of zucchini. "Of the three of us, I was the only who went by to check on him. I found him. Dead in his chair with a beer can in his hand. Can you beat that?"

I didn't know what to say. "I'm sorry."

"Boy, we sure know how to bring down the mood, don't we?" He shook his head as if to dispel the bad thoughts. "Tell me more about Brooke. I bet she's awesome."

I smiled at the thought of my daughter. "I just talked to her before I got here. She's excited for me—finding you."

"That's sweet." His voice sounded wistful.

"She's studying chemistry at college. The English professor's daughter is a math and science genius. She gets that from her father."

"How is it between them?"

"About like your brothers and your dad. I don't know if she'll ever really accept him back into her life. Everything she thought about her world shattered."

"How could it not?"

"I worry about her, not having a good relationship with her father. Will that spill over to how she sees men? Will she be able to trust?"

"What about you? Can you trust again?"

"I want to," I said softly. "But it'll take someone special."

"Someone who truly gets you?"

"Yes. Someone like you." I smiled, remembering the first time I'd ever laid eyes on him.

"What's so funny?" he asked.

"Do you remember the day you came to school for the first time? Second grade. It was a few weeks after school had started."

"Not really. I can remember my mom telling me were moving back here and being super excited."

We'd already begun our day when the principal escorted them into our second-grade classroom. Two sweet, hapless little boys who more tripped than walked into the room. They'd both been adorable, but Cole captured my heart. "You looked right at me," I said, "and winked."

"No way."

"You did." I laughed at the look of shock on his face. "I swear. My stomach dropped to the floor, and then I flushed from head to toe."

"What was I thinking? Winking at the prettiest girl in class."

"I don't know, but I fell head over heels for you. From then on, it was all about Cole Paisley."

"So what you're telling me is that Drew never had a chance?"

"Correct."

"I can't wait to call and tell him that."

I let my eyes sparkle back at him, enjoying myself. "Then it took you another eight years or so to get up the nerve to wink again."

He groaned. "I pined for you for years and years, suffering in silence."

"As I did you."

He gestured toward his house. "You see that? Black and white? That's how I've always been. I was sure as anything in my life that you were the girl for me."

"We were so young, though. Do you think it was real?"

"It was for me."

"You don't think part of it was pure teenage fantasy?" I

shook my head. "Beth used to tease me about how much I daydreamed about you."

"Are you telling me you fantasized about me?" He rubbed the slight indentation in his chin with the pad of his thumb.

"A daydream. Not a fantasy." My voice came out huskier and sexier than I wished.

His eyes flickered. "What kind of daydreams?"

"Kissing you."

His eyebrows lifted. "That's it?"

I laughed. "Don't look so disappointed. What other daydreams would I have had?"

"I was hoping for ones more on the naughty side."

"I was much too innocent to go any further in my mind. Then, not now." I was baiting him, teasing him, like a woman accustomed to flirting. Who was I?

"We're no longer sixteen, this is true." He gave me a wolfish grin.

"Did you ever think about me? Wonder where I was? If I was married?"

"Every day of my life. I felt sure you were married. How could you not be? I told myself to leave your memory alone, but I didn't listen."

"I was married, but I'm not now," I said.

His eyes glittered, no longer playful. The pull of his gaze reached across the table and took hold of me. "I've carried a torch for you my entire life. Nothing's changed. I doubt it ever will."

My pulse quickened. "Is that true? For real?"

"As real as it can be. What about you? Did you ever think about me?"

"More times than once a day. So I win."

"No, if you thought of me even once in all those years, then I'm the winner."

COLE

Carlie dipped her chin the way she had when we were young. Her dark lashes decorated her cheekbones. Those cheekbones. Age had only made them more pronounced. The angles of her face seemed carved from the finest marble, including her pointed chin and strong jawline. My fingers itched to caress the space between her cheekbone and jawline.

"What is it?" I asked. "Have I scared you?"

"Not at all." She looked at me, her eyes wide. "I'm amazed at your honesty."

"I'm too old to pretend like this isn't a damn miracle. You're here, sitting at my table. I have nothing to gain by acting coy. God's given us a second chance. Unless you tell me you don't want me, I intend on making the most of our time together."

"How can you be so bold after your wife's betrayal?"

"Fate's brought us back together. Her betrayal has nothing to do with us. Or so it seems to me." I settled back into my chair and crossed one leg over the other. I hardly recognized myself. This was not the bitter version of myself who'd clobbered the romantic, trusting one. Or life had, anyway. This was the man she brought out in me. Glorious and bold. Willing to risk my ego for the chance at love.

"I don't do this kind of thing," she said. "Whirlwind romances."

I chuckled. "Thirty years in the making."

A pink flush crept into her cheeks. "I haven't been with anyone but my husband in a very long time. This is new territory for me."

"Except it's me. You know me."

Her mouth curved up in a gentle smile. "I do."

"Make no mistake. I'd love to haul you upstairs to my bedroom right now, but we'll go at your pace. Whatever you want, I'll follow."

"And risk getting hurt again?" she asked huskily.

"That's right," I said. "A chance with you is worth the risk."

"I can't believe this is happening." Her flush deepened. She shifted her gaze toward the horizon as the last of the sun drifted below the mountain. "This will sound strange, but I feel like myself tonight. Like the person I used to be. Before Beth died. Before you left."

"Pleased to be of service."

"I don't know why I said all that."

"I'm glad you did." I picked up the decanter and poured each of us another half glass. The automatic lights I had strung overhead switched on.

She glanced up at the lights. "Those are nice. Romantic for a single guy."

"I hung them for you."

Carlie laughed as she cocked her head to one side. "I know that's not true. Wouldn't it be a good story? A man hangs lights hoping his girl will see them and return to him?"

"It obviously worked." Her laugh brought back a sudden memory of chasing her on the playground when we were eight or so. She'd been small and freckle-faced and adorable. "Do you remember how I used to chase you around the playground? What was I hoping to accomplish?"

"I don't know, but I loved it."

"Did I ever catch you?"

"I think so. Do you remember when you punched Ralphie Truman because he pushed me and I fell and hit my head?"

"I remember, trust me. I wanted to hurt him, bad." To this day I could see Carlie on the ground. Her head had hit a rock and started bleeding.

"Then you picked me up and practically carried me into the nurse's office. My hero. If I hadn't been in love with you yet, I sure was after that."

"That rat Ralphie had the nerve to report me to the principal. My mom got a phone call and everything."

"Did you get in trouble? I never asked you."

"The typical stuff. Nothing I couldn't handle." My dad had taken me outside and beaten my backside, then made me stay outside in the cold until dark. I'd sat under a tree with my knees drawn up shaking with cold. But every moment of pain was worth it. Carlie had needed me, and I'd been there for her. That was all I ever wanted. "I was locked outside for a good portion of the night."

She made a sound at the back of her throat that sounded both angry and sad. "No. All for me?"

I grinned at her, lighting up inside when she smiled back at me. "I didn't even feel the cold. Okay, that's a lie. But I sat there thinking about you. How you looked at me when I escorted you safely to the nurse. I lived to see that look in your eyes."

Now her eyes filled with tears.

"What's wrong? I didn't mean to make you cry," I said.

She dabbed at her eyes with her napkin. "Losing you and Beth at the same time—there were days I wished it had been me. So many days. I always thought that God took the wrong sister."

"Carlie, no. You can't think that way."

"I stayed with you instead of going home with her. Would things have ended differently?"

"She didn't feel well. You wanted to stay. What happened was not your fault."

She wiped her eyes once more. "I'm sorry. I don't know what's gotten into me. Being home and that journal—all of it comes rushing back."

I got up and offered her my hand. "Don't ever apologize for how you feel. You never have to pretend with me." She let me help her to her feet. We stood for a moment under the sparkling lights. I didn't touch her, but my hands were inches from her upper arms. My self-control was being tested harder than ever before. "All that said, I hate it when you cry. If I could, I'd spend every waking moment making you smile."

She reached up with both hands and placed them gently on my face. "How are you still so good?"

"I'm not. Not really. But you make me want to be better."

She shivered.

"Are you cold?" I asked. "I can get you a sweater."

"It's not the cold. It's you. You make me feel things I've never felt."

"I see." I brushed my finger against the hollow of her cheek. "You're beautiful."

"I thought you'd think I looked old."

"Not older. Better."

"Are you going to kiss me again?" she asked.

I didn't hesitate, pulling her into my arms and devouring her mouth. She tasted of wine and smelled of flowers. Her slender frame against my bulk made me want to take her inside and share with her exactly how I felt. I pulled away from her, worried I was losing control. I'd told her she would set the pace, and I was dangerously close to setting it myself.

"What's wrong?" Carlie asked. "Why did you stop?"

Breathless, I smoothed her hair with my hands. "I've never

wanted a woman more, but I don't want to rush. This is too important."

She wrapped her arms around my neck. "Where have you been all my life?"

"Waiting here with the lights on."

Later, we lay under a flannel blanket on the chaise looking up at the vast sky with its billion stars. I had her nestled in the crook of my arm. My chin rested on the top of her silky head. A cricket chirped from somewhere in the yard. Moonshine and Duke were curled together on top of the other chaise.

"I didn't expect for the night to go this way," she said. "Not this easy or exciting or wonderful."

"I was nervous for no reason."

"You were nervous?" she asked. "You didn't seem like it."

"Only for a few minutes."

She reached up to touch my face with her fingertips. "I still can't believe it's you."

"Me either." Here she was in my arms. Here on my land. All this time, I'd hoped and prayed that somehow she would come back into my life, and now here she was.

"Do you remember those yellow folders we used in school?" she asked.

"Pee Chees?"

"Yes, the ones with the athletes on them, which I always thought was odd. When we were in fifth grade, I wrote my first name and your last name on the inside flap to see what they looked like together. Mrs. Carlie Paisley. Hearts over each *i*, of course."

"That's adorable."

"My sister found it and teased me for months," Carlie said. "I'd come down to breakfast and she'd call, 'Good morning, Mrs. Paisley.' I was mortified. My dad laughed every time."

"Carlie Paisley has a nice ring to it." I smiled as I played with strands of her shiny hair that dangled over my shoulder. "And who doesn't dot their *i*'s with hearts?"

"You're very kind."

I breathed in the sweet scent of her hair. "Your hair smells so good. It always has."

She laughed. "You can remember what I smelled like?"

"How could I not? You have an extraordinarily nice-smelling head."

We were quiet for a moment. The cricket kept up his racket. A rustle in the bushes came from the direction of the pasture. Duke lifted his head but didn't seem to hear or smell anything alarming and went back to sleep.

"What's that noise?" Carlie asked, stiffening.

"Probably a rabbit or little fox," I said. "Maybe a raccoon. Nothing that will hurt us."

"Are you sure?"

"Yes, there's a lot of critters who come out at night," I said.

She relaxed and a second later said, "I wish I'd tried harder to get your address."

My heart stopped beating for an instant. The idea of what could have been had we stayed in touch pressed against my chest in the way only regret can do. But it hadn't been up to us. We were kids, without power or influence over our own destinies. "Even if you had, my dad wouldn't have let me see letters from you."

"Because of what happened?"

"It's irrational, but he blamed your family, as if you were the cause of us having to leave town. He was the king of misplaced anger."

"He wasn't the only one who had emotional reactions to what happened. My parents went crazy with grief."

I was quiet, knowing she would continue.

"That whole year afterward it was like free-falling into blackness," she said. "I watched my parents trying desperately to find a reason to keep going. Ironically, the very thing that caused them so much pain was the same thing that ultimately allowed them to continue going. Their love for my sister and the love for me. In equal measures the love they felt for me, knowing I still needed them, kept them putting one foot in front of the other. It's like this new layer of yourself, this part that can never see the world as a good place. Even during the darkest moments, love is still a gift. The only thing that can save a soul. There's beauty in the dark."

"I haven't thought about it that way. My feelings for my dad are complicated, and I certainly can't find the good in the relationship he had with me or my brothers."

"But hasn't it made you a better man? More sensitive? More compassionate?"

"I don't know if I'm either of those things."

"You are. Trials make us stronger," Carlie said. "Even my louse of an ex-husband gave me something. My daughter, obviously, but other things too."

"Like what?"

"A better understanding about who to give my heart to," she said softly. "There were clues all along, too, which I ignored."

"That sounds familiar," I said. "My wife was sleeping with our neighbor for a year. Right under my nose. This is weird to say, but that was almost the worst part. Being duped, so to speak."

"I totally understand. Pride is a terrible beast."

We were quiet for a few minutes. My eyes had started to droop, and the air had chilled. "Do you want to go in now?"

"I'm a little cold."

"It's midnight. You don't want to drive home now, do you? I have a guest room."

"Yes, I'll stay."

"We can have breakfast in the morning," I said. What a thing to look forward to.

"I'll text my mom that I'm not coming back tonight in case

she wakes up and is worried." She giggled. "Mom will be scandalized that we stayed together the first night we went out."

I rose up from the chaise and offered my hand to help her up. As we walked through the doors that led into the house, she slipped her hand into mine. Once inside, I closed and locked the doors. "Wait here while I check that I locked the front door. Would you like a little herbal tea before bed? I always end the day with a cup of chamomile."

"I'll start the kettle," she said.

"Great. I'll just check the lock and turn the security system on."

"Don't forget about the gate. You left it open."

"Right." I'd completely forgotten. She hadn't. A woman who had lost her sister to a violent crime would notice. I had to be more careful to always lock up and reassure her by having the security system on when she came to visit. Maybe I should get some cameras?

I hurried down the hallway to the entryway and locked the door. That's when I saw a shadow. A man, running across the lawn. My outside lights sensed the movement and turned on, making it possible for me to get a better view of him. He appeared to be about six feet and wore all black and a knit cap. How long had he been here? Had he just arrived, or had he been out back while we were there? Was the rustle we heard not an animal but a man?

The night absorbed him. Seconds later, headlights from just outside my gate sparked to life. I went out to the front porch and squinted into the darkness but couldn't make out the make or model through the bank of trees that separated the road from my property. My stomach churned. An electric fence surrounded my land. Unless the gate was left open, no one could enter. He'd taken advantage of the open gate. He'd sneakily parked on the side of the road and come in on foot.

How could I be so careless? Normally, I kept the gate locked, but the moment I set eyes on Carlie, I'd forgotten everything but her. Consequently, I'd allowed someone dangerous onto my property.

Using the app on my phone, I closed and locked the gate, then turned on my security system. I should have splurged and gotten the camera when I had the security installed, but I hadn't been worried. That was before Carlie had returned.

Was he a random burglar? Someone who saw my open gate and came in to case the place for later? Or was it no coincidence that he'd come the night Carlie was here? Could he be Beth's killer, nervous that Carlie was back in town? Did he know of her intention to solve her sister's murder? Was it possible he knew Carlie had found Beth's journal? No, that seemed unlikely. She hadn't told anyone but me. Not even her mother knew yet.

Regardless, my gut told me this had something to do with Carlie. He'd followed her and taken advantage of my open gate. The question was this. What had he intended to do here? Did he want to silence Carlie before she learned too much? Had my presence thwarted an attempt or was the man only gathering information? Whatever the answer, Carlie was in danger.

11

CARLIE

When Cole returned to the kitchen, the color had faded from his face. He flinched when the teakettle whistled. I turned the burner down. "What's wrong?"

A muscle in his face twitched. He stuffed his hands into the pockets of his jeans.

"Just tell me." I walked around the island. "Would you rather have me go back to my mom's?"

Cole let out a breath. "No, no. Nothing like that. I want you to stay." He leaned his backside against the counter. "When I went to check the door, there was a man in my yard. Just as I spotted him, he ran down my driveway to a car or truck parked on the side of the road and sped away."

"Oh." My limbs tingled. I sank onto one of the stools.

"I can't believe I left the gate open."

"Do you think it was a burglar? Or someone looking for you? Or me?"

"I don't know. It could have been random."

"Or it could be someone purposely following me." I placed my hands under the backs of my legs to stop them from shaking. "Someone who doesn't want me poking around about Beth's murder. I went to see Sheriff Ford this morning—to tell him about the journal. Besides you, that's the only other person I told."

"This is still a small town. He may have seen you coming or going from the police station and gotten worried. Even without the knowledge that you found something that might identify him."

"Maybe he came here to spy on us? See if I knew anything." I pressed my feet into the rung of the stool. "He might have been the rustle we heard."

"My thought too. It's not like people just happen upon my property. One night I leave the gate open and someone gets in. This can't be a coincidence."

I felt like my dinner might come up. "This means the killer is still here in Logan Bend. He's here, Cole."

"And he doesn't want you poking around."

His words terrified me. I started trembling. "Do you think I'm in danger?"

"I hate to say it but I do. I'm worried. I don't want you out of my sight."

"I don't want you involved in this mess, Cole. I've already caused you enough harm."

"None of this is your fault," he said. "The only guilty party is Beth's killer."

"But it was Beth's behavior that set this in motion. She was sleeping with some other guy while pretending to be in love with Luke. Her deceit caused this."

"You can't blame the victim. She didn't deserve to die just because she was cheating on her high school boyfriend."

"I still can't believe she was involved with someone else," I said. "She was always chaste and innocent. How could she have changed that much? What power did this guy have over her that she lied to her entire family and the boy she supposedly loved?"

"Teenagers have a lot of hormones and feelings. They're not

known for making the best choices. She was young. That's all she was guilty of."

My chest hurt. "It's just that I'm so—" I cut myself off. What was I exactly? "I'm angry at her. She was lying to us all those months. Did I even know her at all? Before I found the journal, I thought her murder was random, like the cops believed. She just happened to be in the wrong place at the wrong time. Now I don't know what to believe, other than me poking around about it all is putting my life in danger. And possibly yours. I couldn't bear it if anything happened to you."

He placed his hands on each side of my face. "Listen to me. I'm not going to let you or me get hurt. Not after we finally found each other again."

I pulled my hands out from under my legs and wrapped them around his neck. As he pulled me closer, my anger deflated. His touch softened me and calmed my restless mind. "I just want to be with you and enjoy this, and just like thirty years ago, everything's wrecked because of what my sister did."

"Nothing's wrecked. This time we get to choose to stay together. Nothing and no one's going to pull us apart again. Do you understand me?"

"Yes, I understand." I placed my fingers into his thick hair. "Can I sleep with you tonight? I don't want to be alone."

"Of course you can. Come on, let's get ready for bed. It's late."

I followed him out of the kitchen, knowing that from this day onward, I would follow him wherever he asked me to go.

After I came home from Cole's the next morning, I spent several hours sorting through the den. During lunch I read through the rest of Beth's journal. More of the same and no information whatsoever. The only thing of note? At the very end, there was evidence of three pages that had been ripped out.

Around five, hungry, I wandered into the kitchen to grab a snack before showering for my dinner date with Cole. When I'd come home around eight, Mom's car had been missing from the garage. I figured she'd been at the gym. However, when I saw her dart past the doorway of the den around nine, she'd been wearing jeans and a blouse. Wherever she'd been, it was not the gym.

Now I found her in the kitchen wearing her apron and in the process of putting together a tuna casserole for our dinner. For some reason she thought it was my favorite. I didn't have the heart to tell her I hated most casseroles, and especially ones with tuna. The dish had been Beth's favorite, not mine. Having a few bites and hiding the rest under a napkin was a small price to pay for my mother's contentment.

"Hey, Mom."

She raised her head to look at me. "Look what the cat dragged in. How was your night?"

I blushed and immediately started sweating. I was forty-five years old and the mother of an adult and still embarrassed that my mother assumed I'd had sex.

"It was nice. I'd had some wine and didn't want to drive home." I would omit the part about the stranger running across Cole's lawn.

Mom raised one eyebrow. "Very responsible of you."

I went to the refrigerator to hide my flushed face and pulled out a diet soda, then sat at the table.

"You must have had a nice time then?" Mom sprinkled breadcrumbs over the top of her casserole.

"Yes, I did. He made risotto with vegetables from his garden, which was delicious. We sat on his patio. So peaceful. You should see what he did with the property. His house is fabulous." I was babbling and sounded about fourteen.

"A man who cooks. My generation wasn't that way. Or at least your father wasn't." Mom smiled as she brushed her hands on the front of her apron. "Will you be seeing him again? Or was it one of those casual things that happens after wine?"

To hide my embarrassment, I rolled my eyes. "Mom, really? Nothing like that happened."

She shrugged her shoulders. "You don't have to explain it to me. I know how young people are these days."

"We didn't sleep together."

"Sure, whatever you say. What *did* you two do all night?" She spoke with a casual lilt in her voice. The same tone she'd used when I was a kid when attempting to manipulate me into confessing something she already knew I'd done.

"Talked." Kissed. Talked some more. Had more wine. "Had dinner and wine."

"Right, the wine."

"Why the interrogation? I'm forty-five years old." I slid the saltshaker to the other side of the table.

"No interrogation whatsoever. I expected you home around nine p.m. with a definite decision that the crush you had as a kid didn't withstand the test of time. Eight in the morning indicates something else."

"He gives me butterflies. Just like he always did." I returned the saltshaker to its mate. "It's the best evening I've had in a long time. I'm crazy about him." *I'm in love with him, just as I'd always been.* I kept that to myself too. Best to break Mom in slowly.

"Has he asked you out again?"

"Yes, he asked me out to dinner for tonight, but if you'd like me to stay in, I can cancel."

"Don't you dare. We can have this tomorrow or whenever." She folded her arms over her chest. "Two nights in a row. You two kids are awful cute."

"We're not really kids," I said. "Even though it feels like it when I'm with him."

She smiled, rather smugly. "I'm all for it. You need something to liven you back up."

"I'm not lively enough?"

"You know what I mean, dearest. I always liked Cole, but he was intense. He's not the type to do anything casually. You be careful with his feelings."

"It's not like I'm some kind of heartbreaker."

Mom chuckled. "You might be. You don't know. Maybe you grew into it. If you're enjoying a summer fling only to return to Seattle, you'd best tell him that."

"I'm not the casual type of person, either."

Her head jerked up. "What do you mean? Like you might move back here to be with him?"

"Maybe. And to be closer to you, obviously."

"I have a feeling I'm not nearly as hunky as Cole Paisley," Mom said. "Whatever gets you back here is fine with me."

"Where were you this morning?" I asked casually, hoping to lure her into an honest answer as I sat at the table.

She smoothed imaginary crumbs off the counter with the flat of her hand. "What do you mean?"

"I saw you roll in around nine, acting very sneaky."

"I went out for groceries."

"You didn't have any in your arms when you came in. I saw you."

"For heaven's sake, you should've been an attorney. I went for a drive. Is that a crime?"

I laughed. "You're so defensive, which tells me you're hiding something."

"You're not funny. Not even a little."

"Mom, do you have a boyfriend?"

She gasped as if I'd suggested she rob a bank. "Carlie, don't be ridiculous."

"You've been acting secretive. The whole time I've been home."

"I have most certainly not."

I left it at that. My intention was not to have my mom feeling bad. Although my curiosity about what she was up to grew by the day.

I suppose I was keeping secrets from her as well. Telling her about the journal before I understood what all of it really meant would just cause her unnecessary fretting. I was of two minds about whether to tell her about it at all if it yielded no information. Did she really need to know that Beth had another boyfriend and that she was sleeping with him? Some things might be better left unsaid. At least for now, I'd keep it to myself.

"Mom, do you know what happened to Beth's yearbook? It wasn't in her stuff."

"No idea. Why do you ask?" Mom picked up an apple from the fruit bowl and took a bite.

"No reason, really. I figured it would be in the closet, but I didn't find it. It would've been fun to read what people wrote to her."

"She had a lot of friends. There wasn't a blank spot in that thing. It *is* odd that it wasn't in the closet." Her brow wrinkled. "But she probably left it somewhere or it dropped out of her backpack. She was always losing things."

"That's true." Or maybe hiding them, as she had the journal.

"On another subject—"

Before she could finish, the doorbell rang. Mom dropped her apple on the table, which then fell to the floor. Instead of picking it up, she leaped to her feet and hustled over to peer out the window that faced the driveway. A nervous-sounding giggle came out of her as she whipped around to face me. "It's my friend."

"Friend?"

"Joseph. I met him at the gym. Yoga." She smoothed her hair. "I should've put on lipstick."

She *did* have a boyfriend. One she stayed overnight with. One who was about to knock on our door.

Mom scurried out of the kitchen. I followed her to the front door, delighted at the turn of events.

Mom yanked open the door. Standing on the porch was a tall man with a salt-and-pepper beard that matched his thick hair.

He wore a nice pair of jeans and a loose-fitting button-down shirt. He held a bouquet of roses in one hand and a bottle of champagne in the other.

"Joseph, what're you doing here?"

"It's our six-month anniversary, so I thought I'd drop by and say hello." Deep voice. Pretty dark eyes framed in dark lashes. "I wanted to bring these by." He peered around her small frame to look at me. "And meet Carlie."

Mom didn't budge. "Now's not a great time."

"Mom, don't be silly." I scooted next to her, practically pushing her to one side so I could offer my hand. "I'm Carlie. It's nice to meet you. Come inside."

"I don't want to intrude," Joseph said as he glanced nervously at my mother.

"Nonsense. We weren't doing anything," I said. "Mom was making tuna casserole."

"I love Loretta's tuna casserole." He winked at her. "One of my favorites."

I moved aside to usher him into the living room. He handed the champagne to me and the flowers to my mother. "Six months," I said. "Mom, you've been holding out on me. I had no idea of your existence, Joseph."

"Well, I...I hadn't had time to mention it." Mom's eyes darted from me to Joseph.

"I'm insulted," Joseph said, not sounding a bit affronted, then let out a hearty belly laugh. "Your mother thinks you wouldn't understand about us."

"Joseph," Mom said. "Don't."

"Mom, why would you think such a thing? I'm thrilled."

Mom had her hand pressed against her mouth the way she did when was worried. "Well, it's just that I haven't really dated, and I thought you might be upset."

"It's been five years since we lost Dad," I said. "You don't have to live like a nun. Which, seeing as how you didn't come home last night, you're not. Living like a nun, that is." I was enjoying this a little too much.

"Carlie Jane Webster, enough." Mom's face was flushed red, either from anger or embarrassment. I really should have been ashamed of myself, but I simply couldn't bring myself to be.

"Obviously, you two will want to celebrate together tonight, but I'd love to get to know you better, Joseph. You should come to dinner tomorrow."

Joseph grinned and rocked back on his heels. "I have a better idea. Let me take you both out. The new steak place by the river is very good. Your mother loves their Caesar salad."

"That sounds wonderful," I said. "My friend is coming by in about a half hour to take me to dinner." I emphasized the word *friend* to tease my poor mother. "We could have a glass of champagne to celebrate your anniversary before we go?"

"Lovely," Joseph said. "Do you have a beau?"

"Carlie, this isn't a good time for Joseph," Mom said tersely.

"I have absolutely nowhere I'd rather be." Joseph splayed his hands over his broad chest. "I didn't want to intrude on your mother-and-daughter time or I would've been by sooner."

"That's so thoughtful of you," I said. "But I'll be here all summer. We have plenty of time together."

"I'll look forward to it," Joseph said.

"Me too," I said. "By the way, I probably won't be home tonight at all. You two lovebirds feel free to enjoy yourselves."

Mom sent a scathing look my way. "We always stay at Joseph's, if you must know."

"I live out near the golf course," Joseph said.

"Wait, the retirement community?" I asked. "The very one where Mom wants to move? What a coincidence."

"Very funny, Carlie," Mom said. "Now go take a shower. You smell terrible."

I left Mom and Joseph downstairs and went up to shower and change for my date with Cole. As the suds of the shampoo ran down my body I thought about Cole. What would it feel like to have his hands on my bare skin? I'd have liked to have waited a little longer, but I had the feeling tonight would be the night. I only hoped he wouldn't find me disappointing. It had been a long time since I was naked in front of a man. I sure as heck wasn't sixteen any longer.

Could I see myself living here?

Beth's murder had shattered that idea. I'd run off to college wondering if I'd ever want to return. Everything about Logan Bend had reminded me of the heinous way Beth's life had been taken. Everyone became a suspect in my mind. Being at college in Seattle had been a relief. Not everyone who walked past me on the sidewalk made me wonder if he or she were Beth's killer. I didn't have to be the other Webster girl.

But now? Enough time had passed that I could see Logan Bend with fresh eyes. I liked what I saw. Not just the quaint, gentrified town of Logan Bend but one of its finest citizens, Cole Paisley.

I finished putting on my makeup and took a look at myself in the full-length mirror that hung on the back of my door. How many times had I looked at myself in this mirror? If it were one of those tablets that cascaded photographs, I'd be able to see myself in every stage of my life. Now, a woman who had lived a lot of life stared back at me.

A few minutes before six, I heard the doorbell ring. I scurried down the stairs to answer. My stomach did the usual flutter at the sight of him standing on the porch holding two bouquets of pink tulips. "Hi, come on in."

He stooped to give me a peck on the cheek before handing me one of the bouquets wrapped in brown paper. "This one is for you. The other is for your mom."

I rose to my tiptoes to peck his mouth. "Thank you." Then, whispering, I said, "My mom's boyfriend's here."

He raised his eyebrows in surprise but didn't have time to ask me any questions because Mom barreled out of the kitchen. She'd taken off her apron and changed into a nice pair of jeans and a cotton top.

"Cole Paisley, let me look at you." Mom held out her hands. "What a handsome young man you are."

"Thank you, Mrs. Webster. It's nice to see you again."

"You as well."

From the kitchen came the sound of a champagne cork being popped. "Mom and Joseph have invited us to have a glass of champagne before we go," I said. "They've been dating for six months."

Mom made an impatient noise in her throat. "It's the silliest thing. Celebrating a six-month anniversary."

"I think it's romantic," I said.

"You would," Mom said.

12

COLE

We had the champagne out on the back patio under the shade of an umbrella that had seen better days. The yard, too, was in a state of disarray. What had once been tidy planting containers were now filled with weeds. Flowerpots lay empty on the edge of the patio. Grass, which had once been precisely manicured and always green even in the summer, had yellowed and grew in patches. Mr. Webster had been the gardener of the family if I remembered correctly.

The house with its tan shag carpet and oak furniture was just as I remembered. Even the scent of bacon and maple syrup was the same. Mrs. Webster had aged well and was as hospitable as she'd always been.

We sat on either side of a metal table that had once been painted green but was now partially rusted. My chair was the kind that was supposed to rock gently, but this one seemed about to collapse like a lame horse.

"How did you two meet?" I asked.

"At the gym," Joseph said.

"Joseph bought one of the condos where I'm moving," Loretta said. "It's a retirement community just outside of town."

"Broadhurst?" I asked.

"Correct. You been out there?" Joseph asked.

"Just driven past, but it looks like they did a great job," I said. "I'm a contractor, so I notice the details."

"It's such a treat to have you here," Mrs. Webster said.

"I always loved coming here," I said. "My mother used to worry that you'd get sick of Drew and me always tagging along when Luke came to visit Beth."

Loretta smiled, but her eyes were sad. "Those were the best days. The house full of young people. I used to stand just outside the kitchen to hear all you kids talking while you were having a snack. I loved every minute of it."

"I was sorry to hear about Mr. Webster," I said. As soon as it was out of my mouth, I realized my blunder. Talking about a woman's dead husband in front of the new boyfriend? *Good one, Cole.*

"I'm sorry to hear of your father's passing," Loretta said.

"Thank you."

"Look at us, Joseph," Carlie said. "We're going on and on about the past. You must be bored to tears."

"Not at all," Joseph said. "I'm pleased as punch to be here. Loretta has told me so much about Carlie, and now to meet her is what I call a red-letter day."

"What brought you to Logan Bend?" I asked. "You're not from here, are you?" His Southern accent gave that away.

"Heck no. I'm an Oklahoma boy. Born and raised. I retired a few years back and wanted to live in a place where I could fish and enjoy the great outdoors. This place has it all."

"Do you fly-fish?" I asked.

"You bet your sweet bippy I do. You want to go sometime?" Joseph asked. "No pressure. I get a little excited sometimes. Loretta says I scare people."

"His voice carries," Mrs. Webster said.

"You haven't scared me," I said, amused. "Any afternoon you want to go is great with me."

"I'd be happier than a pig in mud." Joseph smacked his two

giant hands together. "Hear that, Loretta? I'm making a new fishing buddy." He turned to Carlie. "Your mother doesn't take too kindly to fishing."

Mrs. Webster smiled. "It would be nice for you to have someone else to partake in that particular sport. It's as boring as watching paint dry. I prefer golf."

"Your mother's becoming quite the golfer. The other women are starting to talk behind her back. A sure sign they think she's dangerous."

"Who's talking behind my back?" Mrs. Webster asked. "Wait, don't tell me. Shelley Lancaster."

"The very one," Joseph said.

"She's always so nice to my face," Mrs. Webster said. "Thanking me for volunteering on her son's campaign. However, on the golf course, she's out for blood."

"Is Shelley Lancaster Thom Richards's mom?" I asked, as an image of a muscular blonde woman came to me.

"Correct," Mrs. Webster said. "She and her brothers were heirs to the sawmill. The money wasn't what it had once been, so the brothers all had jobs. Stanley owned the newspaper, Bob became a doctor, and of course, John was the sheriff. Carlie, you remember him?"

"I do. He scared me." Carlie shot me a glance, obviously worried that her mother had brought up the newspaper. Stanley Lancaster had been the one who'd written the article accusing Luke.

I squeezed her knee to let her know I was all right.

"Shelley married Dirk Richards, who was very rich. Heir to something or other." Mrs. Webster waved her fingers as if to conjure the answer.

"Oil money," Joseph said.

"That's right," Mrs. Webster said. "They ended up divorced but apparently she made out well because all I've ever seen her do is golf and drink chardonnay."

"Mom, be kind," Carlie said, laughing.

"I'm sorry, you're right," Mrs. Webster said. "But she irks me. How she raised such a fine son, I'll never know."

"Are any of them still alive?" I asked. "I'd love to pay a visit to the newspaper owner."

"You and me both," Mrs. Webster said. "He was completely irresponsible. Of the four of them, Shelley's the only one still here riding her broomstick. Back in the day, that woman ran this town. I wanted to become a member of the country club but never got an invite. I'd have loved to whoop her butt at golf back then. Before we lost Beth, I cared about those things." She paused for a moment to take a sip from her glass. "Actually, when they were younger, Stanley was known as quite the playboy. As a matter of fact, he hit on me once."

"After you were married?" Carlie asked.

"No, no, before that. I was only sixteen at the time. We were at a dance out at the grange. They used to have them once a month back then. I'd gone out there to look for your father, Carlie. I was terribly jealous because this girl named Idabel was fawning all over him and I wanted to give him a piece of my mind. We weren't going steady then, but we'd already told each other how we felt. Anyway, I couldn't find Ben but Stanley Lancaster was out there smoking a cigarette and drinking out of a flask. Both disgusting habits. And you won't believe what he did. He made a pass at me. I was sixteen at the time, and he was at least ten years older than me. Your father, Carlie, wanted to fight him. It was a mess of a night." She grinned, clearly enjoying her story. "Logan Bend was rougher back then."

"Mom, I never heard that story."

"I didn't like to talk about it front of your father. He didn't find it as amusing as I did."

"He got the last laugh," I said. "Married to one of the prettiest girls in town."

"You're too sweet." Mrs. Webster gestured toward me with her glass. "I'm so sorry. This drink has gone completely to my head. No one wants to hear my stories from the old days."

"I could listen to you all night," Joseph said.

"Oh, you." Mrs. Webster slapped his shoulder. "You're the silliest man."

"I'm crazy about you, that's all," Joseph said.

"Joseph, no one wants to hear you gush," Mrs. Webster said.

"I do." Carlie grinned. "I'm crazy about her too."

"Stop it. Both of you. You're embarrassing me." Mrs. Webster's cheeks flamed pink, but I could see they'd pleased her.

"I can clearly see you make her happy," Carlie said to Joseph. "For which I'm thankful."

"Goodness me, isn't that nice to hear?" Joseph raised his champagne glass. "To family."

I was struck in that moment about how love could change the course of your life. What had been an empty space for Mrs. Webster was now filled by this boisterous giant of a man. As for me? The very woman I longed for all these years had returned to me.

"To second chances," I said, raising my glass. "And to new beginnings."

We all clinked glasses as the late-afternoon light washed the patio in warmth.

Carlie and I sat outside on the terrace of Logan Bend Lodge restaurant. The rustic outside area ran along the entire back side of the restaurant area with a view of Logan Mountain. Tourist season brought in people who enjoyed outdoor activities, filling the lodge and restaurant. Tonight, the terrace hosted a half dozen vacationing families with small children, two tables of four retirees, a group of ten young women celebrating a birthday, and a scattering of couples out for a romantic dinner. The rise and fall of voices and laughter portrayed the joy of summer weather and vacations.

"I'm glad I made reservations," I said. "This place is really busy."

"Me too. It's strange how so many things have changed here. When I think of Logan Bend, I think of the way it was when we were young. Most everything in the downtown area is different."

"Gentrified," I said. "From rundown and depressing to new and quaint."

"I hope my mother didn't bother you back at the house," Carlie said. "All that talk about Stanley Lancaster."

"No, what's done is done."

"I guess the truth doesn't matter if you're rich," Carlie said. "My mom couldn't understand why he did it. Sheriff Lancaster was his brother. Wouldn't you think he'd have had access to the truth?"

"Maybe he cared more about selling papers," I said.

"Salacious gossip should be left to the rags, not a town paper."

"I used to ride my bicycle by their mansion up on the top of Strawberry Hill. I'd stare at it, thinking how someday I might have a house that pretty and bring you to live in it with me." The Lancaster mansion had been built in the colonial style. Now, through the eyes of an adult and contractor, the place looked stuffy and out of place in the shadow of Logan Mountain. Back then I thought it was the most beautiful home I'd ever seen.

"Beth was obsessed with that house too." Carlie's eyes glazed over as the past took her from me for a moment. "I'd forgotten that until just now. She said she wanted a house just like that."

"I thought the same thing."

"I prefer the house you built," she said. "It's perfect."

"Thanks." I smiled, pleased. "My ego's wrapped up in my place, as I'm sure you've figured out."

"You're proud of what you built. There's nothing wrong with that." Her blue eyes softened as she looked across the table at me. "I'm proud of you."

We paused our conversation when the server brought starter salads. After he'd gone, I waited for her to start before picking up my own fork.

"You look pretty tonight," I said. "That color suits you." She wore a silky dress the color of a ripe peach, which complemented her fair complexion.

"Thank you. I only brought two dresses with me. I might have to go shopping if you keep taking me out."

"Does that imply we can have a third date?"

"Technically, if you count lunch, this *is* our third date."

"Is there anything magic about the number three?" I raised both eyebrows in what I hoped was suggestive but not creepy.

Her eyes twinkled back at me. "Three *is* a nice number."

"A date for each decade we missed?"

Carlie winced as the table of women burst into riotous laughter. "They're a bit piercing," she said.

"Maybe we should have gone someplace quieter."

"No, no, it's such a nice evening. I love the patio." She ran a finger down her water glass. "Especially here with you."

"What's the plan for your mom's house?" I asked, changing the subject. On the way over to the restaurant it had occurred to me that Loretta's house was perfect for flipping. The house would have to be gutted, but the neighborhood was good and the yard bigger than a lot of the modern lots. "Are you going to do anything besides clean it up before you put it on sale?"

"Unfortunately, I think we have to put it on the market as is," Carlie said. "She doesn't have the funds to fix it up and be able to buy the condo she wants. My dad left her a little nest egg, but given how expensive that retirement place is, it's going to be tight. She refuses to take any money from me."

"Do you think she's serious about Joseph? Maybe they'll want to move in together."

"I didn't even know there was a Joseph until today, so I'm not sure." She picked up a piece of bread from the basket and then offered it to me.

"They'd save a lot of money." I took a slice and set it on the bread plate. "Not that it's the only reason to cohabitate."

"Maybe they want to keep their own places but still spend time together." She made a face. "I don't want to think about them in bed together."

"I'd like to make her an offer," I said.

"Really? To fix it up and sell it?"

"Yes. If I bought it, your mom could sell it to me without any Realtor fees, which would save us all a lot of money. I know how to put together a contract."

"Would it be weird for us? Doing business together?"

"There's an us?" I asked, teasing.

She flushed. I loved the way her cheeks pinkened when she was embarrassed.

"There's the little issue of whether you're staying or going." I buttered my piece of bread, avoiding her gaze. "Let's just say for the sake of argument that it's good between us. Can you see yourself living here?"

She gazed at me with those gorgeous eyes and nodded. "I think so."

We were interrupted when a woman approached. She looked familiar, but I couldn't place where I knew her from.

"Carlie Webster? Is that you?" The woman was around our age, but seemed older and so thin it seemed as if no flesh existed between skin and bone. Bags under her eyes and blotchy skin made me suspect drug use. If not now, in the past.

Carlie nodded. "Yes?"

"I'm Thea. Thea Moore. I was friends with your sister."

Carlie's eyes widened. "Oh my gosh, yes. It's been a long time."

"Yes, it has." Thea smiled, and her skin stretched like plastic wrap over the sharp edges of her face.

"Did you move for your last year of high school?" Carlie asked. "I can't remember."

Thea's brown eyes flickered. "Yes. I went to live with my grandparents after Beth...after she passed away."

"Was there a reason?" Carlie asked. I glanced at her, surprised by the boldness of her question, which bordered on rudeness. Was this what she meant about suspecting everyone in Logan Bend of murder?

"What happened to Beth changed everything for me." Thea's eyes filled as she glanced toward the rafters.

"I'm sorry." Carlie peered up at her. "I didn't know you were that close." A slight tremor in her tone couldn't hide the deep hurt that still existed.

"All the girls on the squad were close," Thea said with an edge of defensiveness in her voice. "Why? Did she tell you otherwise?"

Carlie wrapped her hand around her water glass as if to calm herself. "Not that I can remember. I was younger, so Beth didn't always tell me everything."

"That's how it is with siblings. Especially at that age." A definite hint of relief crossed over Thea's face. She was hiding something. I felt sure of it. Did she have knowledge about Beth's murder that she hadn't told the authorities?

"Do you live here now?" Carlie asked.

"No, I'm only in town to see my mother. You?"

"I'm here helping my mom put her house up for sale," Carlie said. "I live in Seattle. How about you?"

"I'm in Eureka," she said. "My husband's family was from there. Ex-husband now."

"I have one of those too," Carlie said, more kindly than before. "And a grown daughter."

"No kids for me." Thea turned to look at me, seeming to notice me for the first time. "You look familiar."

"Cole Paisley. Luke's younger brother."

"Right, yes. One of the twins. I never could tell you two apart."

"You're not the only one," I said.

"You always looked different to me," Carlie said.

Thea's gaze darted between us. "Where do you live, Cole?"

"Here. I built a house on my family's old property."

"How's Luke?" Thea asked.

"He's well," I said. "He's a doctor. Lives in LA."

"He was supersmart," Thea said. "I'm not surprised. Tell him I say hello." She turned back to Carlie. "I'd love to get your number so we can catch up over drinks."

"Sure." She waited for Thea to pull out her phone, then rattled off her number.

"I'll let you two get back to your dinner," Thea said. "My mother's expecting me home."

"It was nice to see you," Carlie said.

"You too."

"I'll call you tomorrow." Thea gave us a nod before scuttling away.

Carlie's gaze followed her until she disappeared through the double doors into the dining room. She turned back to me. Leaning closer, she spoke quietly. "Is it just me or did she seem like she was hiding something?"

"It's not just you." I kept my voice low also, worried about eavesdroppers. "Do you remember much about her?"

"I remember her as being small and annoyingly perky. My sister didn't like her. I remember that too. She was always talking about how Thea would copy what she did, like everything was a competition. When Beth was voted head cheerleader by the squad, Thea had a fit. One time Thea made a move on Luke. Do you think she could have killed Beth?"

"Jealousy as a motive?" I asked. "That's pretty thin."

"You don't know teenage girls."

"I got the feeling that the whole thing had a very negative effect on her life. She looks like someone who's had a checkered past."

"I thought the same thing. The question is—did she go to her grandparents' because she was sad or because she had something to do with the murder and wanted to get out of town?"

"Possibly. But don't you think she's too small to have been able to tackle Beth to the ground and stab her?"

"Probably. The cops thought without question the killer was a man." Carlie closed her eyes for a second as a wave of pain pinched her features.

"Hey, are you okay?" I asked.

"I hate thinking about her last moments." Her eyes filled. "I try never to think of them. It's such a disservice to the dead when we think only of how they went out as opposed to how they lived."

I should not have been talking about the case as if we were merely detached, as if it were a murder mystery in some movie. This was real. Both our families had been torn apart because of it. All these years later the repercussions from Beth's death were still reverberating through those of us who were involved. I reached across the table to stroke her cheek. "What can I do?"

"You're already doing it by not insisting that I get over it. My husband did that all the time. I think he thought he was giving me tough love by shaming me—telling me that all my sister would want was for me to move on and stop dwelling on the past."

"You don't have to pretend to be anything but yourself with me. I was there with you when it happened. I'm going to be here when you finally learn the truth."

"Everywhere I go in this town, the ghosts of the past appear, yet I still don't know the truth." She reached across the table for my hands. "Thanks for being here. Now and then."

If I had anything to say about it, I'd be here for all the rest of the days of her life.

13

CARLIE

The next afternoon, I sat in a corner booth with Thea at Misty's Bar. I ordered an overpriced white wine. Thea asked for the house vodka with soda. Neither of us said anything after the server walked away. Feeling awkward, I asked after her mother.

"She's the same. Still lives in the house I grew up in."

"The one by the church?"

"That's right. How's your mother?"

"My mother's moving to the retirement community south of town," I said. "She's taken up golfing with her new boyfriend."

"That's nice." Thea's thinly plucked eyebrows drew together. "My mom's had boyfriends over the years. Quite a few, actually. None ever last. She knows how to pick a loser. Like mother, like daughter."

"I didn't pick too well the first time either," I said, hoping to make her feel better.

"I'm surprised. You and Beth were always perfect at everything."

"We may have seemed that way, but my mother would tell you differently."

"You and Cole together now?" Thea asked.

"We've only recently reconnected."

"You seemed pretty chummy last night."

"We were in love when we were kids. Old habits die hard, I guess." I purposely underplayed my relationship with Cole. It was none of her business, and I didn't feel the need to explain my deep feelings about Cole to a stranger.

"That's cool. Good for you."

The server brought our drinks. We both sipped greedily. This might go down as one of the most awkward afternoons of my life.

"How long are you in town?" I asked. She might have already told me, but I couldn't remember.

"I'm not sure."

"Was there another reason for your visit, or was it just to see your mom?" I took another sip from my wine. Crisp like a green apple. The wine was good but not enough for the price. My ex-husband had always commented on my cheapness. If I hadn't been, how would he have had enough to pay off his prostitute?

But the bitterness didn't surface as it used to. Nor did the pain. I almost chuckled to myself. I didn't care anymore. Cole Paisley was back in my life. My heart fluttered. For heaven's sake, I was acting like a teenager. I needed to focus on Thea and not how anxious I was to get out of here and drive out to his house. Our dinner with Joseph had been postponed by my mother. She'd come up with a sudden headache after lunch and said we'd have to do it another time. I wasn't sure if she was making up the headache as an excuse. Regardless, I didn't push the issue. Mom needed to take things at her own pace.

"I came here for a few reasons," Thea said. "I wanted to tell you I was sorry about Beth."

"Thank you. But there's no need. You expressed your condolences at the time."

"Not like I should have."

I didn't know what to say. What was it that bothered her conscience? "Teenage girls aren't exactly their best selves. Whatever petty jealousies there were between you and Beth don't matter now. You shouldn't give it another thought."

"You don't know what I did." Her eyes shone with emotion. Exactly which one, I wasn't sure. Guilt? Grief? Anger? "It's partly my fault she's dead."

My limbs tingled. Had Thea killed her over the head cheerleading position?

"Thea, what did you do?"

"I didn't kill her. Nothing like that. I mean, yeah, we competed over everything, but I've never done something like that."

"Then what?" My voice had hardened. What game was she playing here?

"You'll know soon enough. I can't tell you yet because I need to do something else first. Before it all comes out, I wanted to tell you how sorry I was."

"Comes out? What will come out?"

"I withheld information that I should've shared with the police. To save myself. My reputation." She blurted this out and seemed to immediately regret having done so.

I scooted both hands under the backs of my thighs. "Information about the killer?"

"I don't know." Her hand shook as she reached out for her drink. "I don't know if what I did has anything to do with the killing."

"You must think so, or why bring it up to me? Why not just tell the authorities what you know, even if it's thirty years late?" I couldn't keep the accusatory tone from my voice. What did this silly woman know? Was it enough to have found my sister's killer? "Why wouldn't you have done that in the first place?"

"I told you why. To save myself. Don't think for an instant that the whole decision hasn't ruined my life. I've regretted a lot of things, but none as much as what I did that summer." She looked past me with cloudy eyes. "I can trace it all back to the exact moment. The second that I decided to do something simply because your sister was, and I could never let her have anything I didn't have. I know that now. My actions were all because of jealousy. I was always second-best to Beth. The sweetheart of Logan Bend. Beth and her perfect family. Beth and Luke, the king and queen of the high school. And there I was. Not quite as pretty or as talented. I only had my mom who worked at the pancake house and barely made ends meet and grew more and more bitter as the years went by. I wanted what Beth had. Even when what she had didn't make sense for either of us, I took it anyway."

"I don't know what you're talking about." My head swam almost as fast as her rapid speech. "What did you do?"

She downed the rest of her drink, then lowered the glass back to the table as if she were afraid it might break. "What happened to me wasn't my fault. I've learned that in therapy. I was a child. Please remember that." She scooted out of the booth and practically ran for the door.

"Wait. Don't go." My pleas fell on deaf ears. Through the window, I saw her jogging toward her car. I hadn't thought it was possible, but I was more confused than when I'd walked into the place.

I rubbed my temples before taking another sip from my wine. What had just happened? Was this simply middle-aged guilt, or did she actually know something relevant? Had she seen Beth with Z? Was she the girl Beth referred to in her journal? Z's girlfriend? The one he couldn't leave because it would hurt her too much? Had Thea found out they were messing around together and killed her in a fit of rage? Or did Thea cover something up to save Z? Was that what she hadn't told the police?

I couldn't remember who Thea's boyfriend had been back then. I tried to recall seeing her anywhere that summer with a guy, but nothing came to mind. I'd been too involved in my own world in the months before Beth's murder. My job at the library and Cole had taken up all the space in my brain.

Thea was just a girl in Beth's cheer squad. Had she held the key to Beth's killer all this time? Or had she killed Beth in a jealous rage over some boy? Seventeen knife stabs? Personal. A crime of rage.

I needed to tell Ford what she'd said. Maybe he could bring her in for questioning? Yes, I thought. I needed to tell Ford and let him do his job. I was not a detective, even though I'd been acting like one. My mother didn't need a second daughter murdered.

I sat in Sheriff Ford's office, sharing what I'd learned from Thea. "And then she ran out," I said to the sheriff. "Leaving me totally confused."

Ford had listened without asking any questions or interrupting as I'd conveyed the conversation I'd had with Thea. I made sure to tell him every detail that I remembered. "In hindsight, I should have recorded her."

"Odd, isn't it?" Ford said.

"Which part?"

"The part about her being a child and that it wasn't her fault. Like she was about to seek revenge on the man who hurt her."

"Why do you think it was a man?"

"Isn't it always?" Ford asked.

My stomach hollowed as I realized what he meant. "Do you think she was molested? And if so, what does it have to do with Beth?"

"No idea. Maybe Beth knew something she shouldn't and had threatened to tell someone?"

"Which would mean it didn't have anything to do with Z at all," I said, thinking out loud. "Maybe I've been looking at this all wrong."

"You find anything interesting yet in the journal? Anything that could lead to the killer?"

"Not a thing. She's vague, obviously worried someone would

read what she wrote. Probably me. She knew I'd sneaked a peek at her diaries before."

"Sisters, right?" Ford asked.

"I thought I knew everything about Beth. I clearly didn't."

He tutted sympathetically. "Don't be hard on yourself. You were a kid."

As much as I appreciated his kindness, guilt clung to me. If only I'd known what was truly going on, maybe I could have prevented her murder. "Will you bring Thea in? She might tell you what she did that she thinks helped get Beth killed."

"I plan on it. Don't you worry. If she knows anything, I'll get it out of her."

I thanked him. "There's one other thing. A couple of nights ago, there was a man in Cole's yard. He'd left the gate open and the guy came in. Cole couldn't see him."

"How come you didn't tell me this when it happened?"

"I don't know. There wasn't much anyone could do. Cole didn't get a good look at him or his vehicle."

"Listen here. I understand you want answers, but you're not a detective." His voice had hardened with obvious worry. "You can't be running around town asking questions. I don't want you hurt, do you understand?"

"Yes, I know you're right. I told myself that very thing just now, which is why I came by."

"Promise me from now on, you tell me everything."

"Yes, I will. I promise."

"Good girl." He stood and came around his desk. "Come on, I'll walk you out. You tell Paisley to keep his darn gate locked."

14

COLE

I sat in the passenger seat of Joseph's truck as we bounced down a dirt road, dust swirling behind us. What a day. Wildflowers grew in bunches on the sides of the road. Natural grasses swayed in the slight breeze. A few puffy, lazy clouds drifted across an otherwise blue sky.

"Mountains look blue this time of day," Joseph said. "You can see how the mountain got its name."

A true statement. "For sure."

"This here's my secret spot," Joseph said as he parked his truck under the shade of a tall oak. "I don't want a bunch of tourists showing up, so I keep it to myself."

I didn't have the heart to tell him I was familiar with the North Fork of the Blue River. I'd fished here dozens of times. However, I preferred a spot on my own property where the waters were thick with rainbows and cutthroats, and no one fished there without my permission. If today went well, I'd invite him over to the house.

"You have good luck here?" I asked.

"Every time." He chuckled. "I should have blindfolded you so you couldn't find your way back."

"I'm honored." I grabbed my cowboy hat from the seat and tugged it onto my head.

He killed the engine and shot me a boyish grin. "This here is a good day, am I right?"

"Can't argue with that," I said.

We got our gear and a small cooler out of the back of the truck. I'd worn my hiking boots and was glad of it as we walked over uneven and rocky ground to the river's edge.

When we reached the water, I set the cooler and my fly box under a shrub. Several ducks bobbed in the currents but paid us no mind. Gentle rapids gurgled over rocks. I tugged my hat lower and put my sunglasses on to protect my eyes from the glare.

"You good?" Joseph asked.

"Right as rain."

"I'm going to wade out to the middle. It's shallow enough."

I nodded and reached into my bag for my waders. "Me too." I sat on a rock to tie a black woolly bugger onto my line before pulling the waders on over my boots. Despite the warmth of the afternoon, these waters ran cold if you stood in them for too long. Before I set out, I clipped my net to the back of my cargo shorts and grabbed my pole.

I traipsed out over the slippery and uneven rocks until I found a level spot.

"Mostly brownies here," Joseph said from a few feet away. "But we might get a rainbow or two if we're lucky."

For the next few minutes, we cast our lines in the arc of the fly fisherman. I had to admit that Joseph knew what he was doing. I'd expected him to be a city guy who thought he knew the ways of the Idaho river. However, his casting skills were artful and beautiful to watch.

A few minutes later, I pulled in a twelve-inch brownie. A fighter, he yanked my line into a C shape before I managed to get him close enough to capture him in the net. I held him gently as I tugged the fly from where it had caught in his lip. "He's a beauty."

"You got that right, young man." Joseph's eyes were bright under his Rangers cap.

I set the fish back into the water and watched as it swam away. "Have a good life, fighter," I said under my breath.

By the time we decided to take a break, Joseph had caught and released a rainbow and a cutthroat. I'd added another two brownies to my list.

"You hungry?" Joseph asked. "I got us some fat ol' sandwiches from that deli in town."

"Starved."

We set aside our poles and waders. I pointed out a nice spot in the shade of a maple and hauled the cooler over while Joseph went to get some folding chairs from the truck. I grabbed us both a sandwich and a beer.

The camping chairs were comfortable. We ate in compatible silence for a few minutes. The sandwiches were made on crusty rolls that melted in my mouth. The fish jumped at the bugs that flew near the surface, causing ripples in the water.

"Who taught you to fish?" I asked.

"My old man. We came to Idaho every summer from the time I was big enough to hold a pole."

"All the way from Oklahoma?"

"That's right. We drove here, too. Boy howdy, those were some good times. We had a bag of Fritos and a fat Coca-Cola and listened to his eight-track cassettes of Johnny Cash, Waylon, and Loretta Lynn over and over. My dad wasn't much of a talker but when he did, he said a lot."

"I bet that was nice."

"Yes sir, it was. I miss him every day." Joseph gestured toward heaven. "He's up there in the fly-fishing hole in the sky, though. We'll meet again." He went to the cooler and pulled out a bag of sliced carrots. "Loretta has me eating rabbit food these days."

"Let me know if you ever need any fresh veggies. I've got a garden bursting with them."

"I'll take you up on that. Carrot?"

I took a few from the bag.

"Who's your baseball team?" Joseph asked.

"Dodgers for life."

"And here I thought we could be friends. Rangers all the way."

"Football?" I asked.

"Houston, although people around these parts are crazy for those Seahawks."

"Including me," I said.

"You go to Dodgers games with your dad?" Joseph asked.

I made a scoffing noise at the back of my throat. "Never."

His brown eyes flickered. "Not a sports guy?"

"Not a father-and-son-outing kind of guy."

"How'd you learn to fish, then?"

"Self-taught. When I was a kid, my brothers and I fished at the spot on our property. Luke found a book at the library with instructions. When we needed to get out of the house, which was most of the time, we'd go down there and spend most of the day. During warm months, we swam and fished. In the winter, we fished and built a campfire."

"Is that why you wanted to come back here?"

"That and other things. Despite everything with my dad, we had a lot of good times."

"You're tight with your brothers?" Joseph asked.

"Yeah. I'm a twin, so that's part of the territory. And my older brother, Luke, always looked after us. Protected us from him."

"Your old man?"

"That's right." I stretched my legs out and dug my heels into the dirt.

"He still around?"

"Nah. Died five years ago." I told him how I'd bought the family property from my mom. "I always wanted to come back here, but it took me a while. Once I had the funds, I left LA and built a house and barn on the old property. I'd like my brothers to eventually join me, but I doubt it'll happen."

"Too much baggage?"

"Right. Because of how it all went down after Beth was killed, Luke doesn't exactly have fond memories of the place."

"People. Not the place."

"That's right. But you know how it goes. This place is poisoned for him." I took off my hat and wiped my brow with the paper napkin.

"Loretta says the same's true for Carlie. That she never came home much."

I nodded but didn't say anything.

"But you're hoping she stays for good this time?" Joseph asked.

"It's all I want. *She's* all I've ever wanted. Can you believe that? I've loved her since we were this high." I held my hand about three feet from the ground. "The two us are weird. Like there's just no bull, you know? We get each other. Always have. I could tell her anything and know she'd never hurt me with it."

"That's a rare thing to find."

"Agreed. But a lot of things here remind her of the way Beth died, not how she lived. She wants answers."

"Loretta too." He drew on his beer before setting it back in the chair's cup holder. "I wish I could give them to her. It would make things easier between us."

"How so?" I asked, curious.

"Loving a woman with that much sadness in her isn't always easy. She holds herself back from living. Like it's a betrayal to Beth if she's happy."

"Carlie's done the same." I took a swig from my beer and wiped my mouth with the back of my hand. "She used to sparkle. Now there's a sadness in her eyes that never goes away. When we were kids, she was one of those genuinely happy people. Always laughing or reading. She wore glasses and hated those things, but I always thought she looked as cute as a bug. My little bookworm."

"Loretta says she always loved you."

"Yeah. It went both ways. Didn't take but a moment for the feelings to come back."

He gazed out over the water. "When you know, you know, right?"

"Two weeks ago, I would've said I was unlucky in love and that the only girl truly made for me slipped out of my life when I was sixteen."

"I never thought it would be possible to love two women in one lifetime," Joseph said. "After my wife died, I figured I'd spend the rest of my days alone. Then along came Loretta. Life keeps on rolling by whether you decide to participate in it or not. I decided to participate instead of being a bystander."

"Life's full of surprises, that's for sure. I sometimes feel like I dreamed Carlie up. Like I've finally gone bonkers and started seeing someone who isn't really there, simply because I wanted her to be."

"I'm curious why you didn't contact Loretta when you moved back here."

I shrugged. "Couple of reasons. I wasn't sure she'd want to hear from me. Also, I didn't want to know that Carlie was married. If I got in touch with Loretta, I'd know for sure. It was nicer to have the fantasies to hold on to."

He laughed. "Same reason I hate going to the doctor."

"I did drive by her house a few times like a stalker," I said. "Speaking of the house." I told him my idea about taking it off Mrs. Webster's hands.

"Seems like a win for everyone. As far as that goes, the sooner she's out of the house the better. I want her to marry me and move into my place."

"Is that what she wants?"

"She's not yet convinced. She has it in her head that Carlie will be hurt if she remarries."

"Seems to me she thinks of you as an answer to a prayer."

"Good to know," Joseph said.

"Do you have kids?" He probably had adoring sons who loved spending time with their good-hearted dad.

"No, never had the luck with that. We wanted them, but God never blessed us that way."

"That's a shame."

"It was all right in the end. We did a lot of traveling, which turned out to be good seeing as Rae died at sixty. If we'd had kids, I wouldn't have been able to take her so many places. Not that I wouldn't have traded all that for a child. She would've too."

Nothing replaced family. Here I was without a father. I'd never had one, really. Here was Joseph without a son.

"Well, I'm around," I said. "If you ever want to fish or just hang out and watch a ball game."

"I'd like that." He gestured toward the river. "You want to fish some more, or should we call it a day?"

I glanced at my watch. It was nearing three. "I should get back. I told Carlie I'd be back around this time, and I still have a lot of chores to do before dinner."

"Yeah, looks like a storm's coming anyway."

I looked up at the sky where a black cloud seemed to be making its way over to us at a fairly rapid rate. "That came out of nowhere," I said.

"I bet we get some thunder and lightning later."

"All the more reason to get home. My animals don't do well with storms."

We stood at the same time. He gripped my shoulder in a quick squeeze. "Thanks for a great day, bud. It's good getting to know you."

I nodded, resisting the urge to hug him. "Same here. We'll do it again soon."

We gathered our things and headed to the car. "You deserved better than what you got from your dad. I'm real sorry, son."

"Yeah, well, you can't have it all in this life."

"No, but you darn sure can try. And you can fill in the gaps with family you find, if you know what I mean."

"I sure do." We exchanged a smile and then went back to being guys by loading our equipment into the truck without saying another word.

15

CARLIE

By the time I left the sheriff's office, the air had grown dense with moisture. A summer storm would come through before long. Angry clouds promised rain. Indeed, the first drop hit my windshield as I punched in the code to Cole's gate.

I drove through, and the gate closed behind me. I shivered at the thought of the intruder. The gate would keep them out, I reminded myself. Still, a sense of doom settled on my shoulders like a weighted cloak. How would I ever find the truth of what really happened to Beth that summer?

I sighed with relief at the sight of Cole, Moonshine, and Duke waiting on the porch. I parked in front of the garage. The rain had started in earnest now. The sound of thunder rattled my car windows. I grabbed my purse and ran down the paved walkway toward them, shivering in my sleeveless blouse. When I'd left the house earlier, the temperature had been warm. A sweater hadn't seemed necessary. I was completely drenched by the time I got to Cole.

"Hey there." He pulled me into his arms and kissed me.

"I'm all wet," I said against his mouth. "And a mess."

"I don't care." He drew away to give me a searching look. "You're later than I thought you'd be. I was getting worried."

"I'm sorry. After I met with Thea, I stopped to talk to Sheriff Ford." Hot tears leaked out of the corners of my eyes. I told him as briefly as I could what she'd said. "Then she ran out of the bar, leaving me with no answers, only questions. One more time." I started shaking, either from cold or anger.

He wrapped his hands around my bare upper arms. "Come inside. I'll get you something dry to change into and a cup of tea."

Duke whined, then licked my hand. Moonshine rubbed against my legs.

"These knuckleheads are worried about you." Cole motioned for the animals to go into the house. "Inside, guys. Let's get our girl dry."

They obediently did as he asked. He held the door for me to pass by, then followed. I heard him latch the door behind us as I walked down the hallway toward the kitchen.

"I have some shirts hanging in the laundry room," Cole said. "Let me grab one and you can change."

I thanked him and then wandered over to stand in front of the gas fireplace. My damp shirt and shorts clung to me. I hugged my arms around my middle. Moonshine and Duke sat on their haunches and looked at me with sympathy in their eyes. "I know, guys. But I'm all right, just sad. You don't need to worry." I patted Duke's head and scratched behind his ears.

Moonshine mewed. "Yes, you'll have a turn too." I combed my nails over the top of her head and down her back. "Aren't you a pretty girl?"

A streak of lightning lit up the sky, followed by a loud clap of thunder that made all three of us jump. Moonshine scrambled up to the couch and scooted under a pillow with just the tip of her pink nose showing. Duke lay beside the couch with his chin resting under his paws and gave me a worried glance. "The lightning can't get you."

"Was that thunder?" Cole asked as he returned with a towel, a T-shirt, and a pair of sweats.

"Yes, and it scared these guys. Me too. We never got much of this in Seattle."

"Nothing to worry about. You're all safe here with me."

"I'm not driving back to my mother's, so you're stuck with me," I said.

"Lucky me." He gestured toward the half bathroom. "You can change in the powder room."

I thanked him and scurried off, anxious to get out of my wet clothes. I tugged my damp clothes off and set them aside. I dried off with the towel, then pulled the sweats over my legs. They were too big around the waist but were warm, as if they'd just been taken from the dryer. I brought Cole's navy blue T-shirt to my nose. Would the cotton fabric smell of him? No, I caught only a pleasant whiff of fabric softener. Shivering, I slipped his T-shirt over my head, then glanced in the mirror. My mascara had smudged from all that silly crying and the rain. I tidied up using a tissue but didn't bother to reapply my makeup.

I pressed my fingers into my hips. What did he see when he looked at my figure? Did he remember how tiny I'd been and wish that my body had not filled out into womanly curves? *No, don't do that*, I told myself. Cole thought I was attractive. That much was obvious. There had always been an electricity between us, even back when we were kids. Now it seemed to have gathered speed and weight, like the storm outside.

I sat on the toilet seat for a moment to gather myself. Was I ready for all of this? Two nights in a row, I'd stayed over but we hadn't done anything but kiss and talk. If I stayed over tonight, we would not be able to resist. At least, I wouldn't be able to. A twinge of guilt hit me. Was it right to enjoy myself after the disconcerting conversation with Thea?

I couldn't do this and then walk away from him again. This could never be only a casual fling or a walk down memory lane to satisfy a fantasy. I'd known it when we were kids, and I knew it now. Cole Paisley was the one. He belonged here in Logan Bend. I belonged wherever he was.

All of the ugliness of my sister's murder could be pushed away for tonight. I'd been waiting for Cole to return to me my entire life. Too much of my life had been about tragedy. This night, with Cole, was just for me. No obligations. No guilt. No trying to compensate for Beth's loss by being the most devoted daughter in the history of all daughters.

He'd poured us both a glass of red wine by the time I returned with my wet clothes in my hands.

"Let me put those in the dryer for you." He directed me to sit on the couch and start on the wine. I did as he asked and curled up on one end of the couch. Moonshine had gotten over her fears and was now on the dog bed with Duke.

"You warming up?" Cole asked as he joined me on the couch.

"All but my feet."

He patted his thighs. "Give them here. I'll rub them."

I hesitated. On his lap? There was something so intimate about a man holding bare feet in his hands. Feet were almost as vulnerable as the spot between my legs. They told the story of a life. Would he feel the calluses and dry spots?

"Come on now," he said. "Your feet are pretty like the rest of you."

"How did you know what I was thinking?"

"Because I would never let you see my feet this close up."

"I'm sure they're fine." I swung my legs onto the couch and let him take my feet into his hands. He held them between his palms before pressing his thumb into my arch. I almost moaned with pleasure. Who knew that a foot rub could waken all the other parts of a body too?

"Ford's going to bring Thea in for questioning," I said. "Do you remember who she dated back then?"

He shook his head. "Honestly, I barely remember her."

"Never mind," I said. "I promised myself I wouldn't talk about all of this tonight. I want to focus on you."

His eyes were serious as he leaned closer and brushed his thumb across my bottom lip. "I like that idea."

Goose bumps traveled up my arms. "I'd like to stay tonight. Not to sleep."

His eyes darkened. He trailed a finger over the sensitive skin on the top of my foot and spoke softly. "I've been daydreaming about the future."

"And?"

"This is going to make me sound like a total sap, but I've been thinking about the holidays. Having everyone here for Christmas dinner. My brothers and nieces. Brooke and your mom and Joseph. The big family gatherings I always wanted."

"I want that too."

His forehead wrinkled as he reached for his glass of wine. "Staying here for me—is that the right reason?"

"What could be a better one?"

His mouth slowly curved into a smile. "Actually, I don't know."

"I want to be where you are. It's been long enough. Brooke loves to ski." I filled with joy at the thought of my daughter being here with us for Christmas. Us. I was already thinking about everything as an us.

"Do you think she'll like me?" Cole asked.

"How could she not?"

"What about me with you? Will she like that?"

"She wants me to be happy. You make me happy. End of story."

"If you say so," he said.

"Let's go upstairs. I'm ready."

"Before dinner?"

"Dinner can wait." I stood, tugging his T-shirt down over my hips.

He rose up from the couch. "Listen, you should know, I haven't done this for a while. And you're...so beautiful. The woman of my dreams. I'm not sure how much stamina I'll have."

Laughing, I put my arms around him. "Then we'll just have to work toward some stamina. Like exercise. We'll grow stronger over time. Daily practice is key."

"I always like daily exercise," he said.

"Lead the way." I followed him upstairs, enjoying the way his jeans hugged his backside. Moonshine and Duke followed behind. "Do they sleep in your room?"

"Yeah. They have a bed on the floor."

"Will we scar them for life?"

"I hope not. They haven't seen much action. Actually, no action. So we might."

When we reached the hallway to the second floor, he took my hand and drew me into the dark bedroom. The animals came too but went immediately to their bed.

Cole turned on one bedside lamp and the gas fireplace. I'd slept here with him the first night, but somehow the room seemed different to me. Decorated simply, the main objects of the room were a gorgeous four-poster bed made of dark walnut and a matching dresser. A vintage light blue quilt and white sheets covered the mattress. In the corner near the windows, an armchair and ottoman made a cozy reading nook.

He padded over to the large window that faced the mountain and started to pull the shade down, but I stopped him.

"I want to see the storm."

Cole chuckled as he turned back to me. "Whatever you want." He left the window and came to stand before me. "What now?"

"I don't know. I think we're supposed to kiss like crazy and then tear each other's clothes off."

He put his hands into the back pockets of his jeans and rocked back on his heels. "I didn't think I'd be this nervous."

"I haven't been with anyone since I was married." I'd only ever been with one man, my husband. Should I tell him that? I sank into the easy chair and clasped my hands together. "I'm not experienced, really." My husband had said my prudishness caused him to stray.

He knelt by the chair and placed his hands on my knees.

"Do we get undressed and get into bed together?" I giggled, nervous. "That's what married people do. We did, at least."

"Then by all means, let's not do that." He smoothed my hair away from my neck and kissed me under my earlobe. I shivered when his hands moved up my legs. He raised his head to look into my eyes. Another bolt of lightning streaked across the sky, followed by thunder. He scooted me closer to him, then wrapped my legs around his waist. The muscles in his thighs tensed against my own. "Do you know how many times I've dreamed of this moment?"

"I can imagine," I said.

He placed his hands on either side of my face. "The way I feel about you—I don't know how to say what's in my heart without sounding like an idiot."

"You could never sound like an idiot."

Another lightning bolt lit up the room. Suddenly, nerves got the best of me. My heart was beating so loud and fast I couldn't hear the thunder. I had to show him my imperfect body. The scar from my C-section, stretch marks on my butt, and the extra five pounds that lived on my belly. My breasts that sagged slightly from nursing a baby.

"What is it?" Cole asked gently. "Have you changed your mind? If so, that's perfectly fine. I'll wait however long you need."

"No, I'm ready. It's not that. My body isn't like it was when I was young."

"No, you're better." He stood and pulled me to my feet. "I'll go first." With quick movements, he took off his pants and shirt and stood before me wearing only boxers.

I giggled. "Are those cats on your shorts?"

"I have a pair with dogs too. Otherwise Duke would be jealous."

I swallowed as I took him in. God had done well, and Cole's active lifestyle had done his work justice. His wide shoulders and trim, muscular stomach were like the front of a man's underwear box. I ached with desire.

"Your turn," he said.

I lifted the shirt up over my head. Thank God for dim lighting, I thought, only to be thwarted by another streak of lightning. Too late now. The shirt was off.

He drew in a quick breath. "You're as beautiful as I imagined you were under those clothes. Come here. I want to show you exactly how beautiful I think you are."

Nerves forgotten, I did as he asked.

16

COLE

I woke to the sun shining through the windows. For a second, I wondered why I'd left the shades open, and then I remembered. Carlie. She was here in my bed. We'd been up a good portion of the night as the storm raged.

Feeling the weight of her in my bed, I turned over to look at her. Curled up on one side like Moonshine, she breathed steadily. Still asleep. I glanced at the clock. The hour was close to nine. I never slept this late. Duke and Moonshine had already risen and were probably downstairs wondering where their breakfast was.

As quietly as I could, I slipped from the bed and used the bathroom, then brushed my teeth. Carlie was still asleep, so I left her and went downstairs to care for my roommates and start a pot of coffee. Duke and Moonshine were sitting by their food dishes in the laundry room. Moonshine swayed slightly as if to demonstrate that she suffered from low blood sugar. I chuckled to myself and made a quick decision that today would be a wet food day.

"Since I'm so late," I said, "you can have a special treat."

I received a purr and a wag for my efforts.

A few minutes later, they were happily eating and the coffee was brewing. I took a quick glance at my email on the tablet I kept in the kitchen. There was nothing that couldn't wait until after Carlie left.

I went out and did my chores, including feeding the chickens and letting the horses out to the meadow. After collecting eggs, I headed back inside to fix breakfast.

I remembered Carlie's clothes were still in the dryer. She would want them for today. I grabbed them and hustled upstairs to leave them for her. As I opened the bedroom door, I heard the shower come on. I left the clothes on the top of the dresser and went back downstairs. She might not like me hanging around while she readied herself for the day. It has been so long since I lived with another person that I was out of practice.

Would it feel awkward in the morning light? After the intimacy of our time in the dark, I certainly hoped not. But this was all happening fast. I kept expecting her to run like a frightened colt. However, Carlie Webster did not frighten easily, and I loved her for it.

I'd feed her a good breakfast before she left for her mother's. From what she'd said last night, she had a long day of sorting and cleaning ahead of her.

The scent of coffee filled the kitchen. Moonshine and Duke appeared and went to the patio doors and sat stoically waiting until I came to let them out. Duke bounded out first, followed by Moonshine. Crazy cat preferred the outside to her litter box.

I whipped some eggs together for a scramble and cut up a zucchini and onion to go with them. The shower stopped. A few minutes later, I heard the hair dryer. I smiled to myself, pleased to think of her in my home doing normal, everyday activities.

I poured myself a cup of coffee and drank it at the island while perusing the morning news on my tablet. Nothing unusual on the national front, but when I turned to our local online paper, my mouth dropped open.

The headline read: Local Psychic Takes on Cold Case

Moonstone Phillips, the owner of the Peregrine Inn and self-proclaimed psychic, has come to the press in an attempt to find the family of a murder victim. The psychic, who goes simply by Moonstone, claims to have had a dream about the case and believes she has clues to what happened.

"I don't know what any of it means but suspect that anyone familiar with the case would," Moonstone said. "My dream told me the victim's name was Elizabeth and that she was murdered thirty years ago somewhere nearby. I have other information but don't want to share that in the paper until I can contact the family. My heart breaks for them, and I will do whatever I can to help. Thirty years is much too long to wait for answers."

If anyone has any information about this case, please contact Moonstone directly at MoonstonePsychic@Moonstone.com.

The article went on to describe Moonstone's involvement in several other cases, including the recent murder of a local Peregrine woman.

Shocked, I stared at the screen without moving a muscle. What would Carlie think? Would she want to reach out to this Moonstone? The photograph that accompanied the article was of a robust woman with a handsome face and honest if not a bit intense eyes. My gut told me she was legitimate. The article said she'd helped the Lanigan family solve several cases involving their family. The Lanigan siblings were the heirs to Lanigan Trucking and well known around these parts for their charitable work. In addition, Moonstone was the owner of a business, not some grifter off the street. And anyway, what could she possibly want to gain by coming forward? She hadn't asked for reward money or anything. Was it possible this woman really did know something that could help find the truth?

I'd heard about this kind of thing before. There were many incidents when the police force in various places had insisted a psychic helped them to solve murder or missing persons cases.

I jumped when my phone buzzed on the counter. The number wasn't one I recognized. Usually, I'd let those types of calls go to voice mail, but something compelled me to answer.

"This is Cole," I said.

"Cole?"

"Yes, that's me. Cole Paisley. Who's this?"

"My name's Moonstone."

Good God, was this really happening?

"I don't want to alarm you, but I believe I have information about Beth's murder. Does that name mean anything to you?"

"It does." I swallowed, suddenly nauseous. "How did you get my number?"

"The numbers came to me in a dream last night. But now I'm not sure if I have the right one. In my dream, the number was associated with a different name. Luke, not Cole, so maybe I don't have it right? Sometimes my wires get crossed, so to speak. Especially when it comes to math. I'm more of a bookish type." She had an airy quality to her voice that reminded me of an artist I'd dated back in my twenties. She'd called herself Star and lived at Venice Beach. Not the same woman, obviously, but the same type. A free spirit. One who believed in astrology and psychics. Star, however, had never claimed to be a psychic. She *had* claimed she had healing powers and had opened a business with rocks or crystals. I couldn't remember the exact details.

Moonstone's next question brought me back to the present. "Do you know a Luke? Is this his phone by any chance?"

"I know a Luke. He's my older brother."

She let out a long, satisfied sigh that came over the line loud and clear. "Ah, great. I'm relieved, I have to say. I hate when I'm wrong. Who was Beth? Was she your sister?"

What Moonstone lacked in grace, she made up for in details.

"No. Beth was Luke's girlfriend back when we were all in high school here in Logan Bend. Beth was murdered thirty years ago."

"You're in Logan Bend? How strange. I looked in the archives of the local papers and couldn't find anything about the murder of an Elizabeth. Nothing. Like it never happened. That's why I had to go to the papers."

"There wasn't anything in the archives?" That couldn't be right. I knew there was at least one. The one that had driven us out of town. "I remember an article from the local paper at the time."

"It's been erased, then. Which makes you wonder, doesn't it?"

"Does it?" Wonder what exactly?

"If there were people involved in a cover-up." She said this as if it were obvious and I needed to pay attention.

I pressed my fingers into my forehead, hoping to stop the spinning. "Listen, Moonstone, we're getting a little ahead of ourselves here. Beth has a sister and a mother. They're both very interested in solving this murder."

"How do you know?"

"Because Carlie's a good friend of mine. I was with her the night it happened. The paper falsely accused Luke of being the murderer. He wasn't. They had no evidence against him and he had a solid alibi. But whoever did this wrecked two families."

"I certainly didn't get that Luke was the murderer," Moonstone said. "In fact, part of my dream makes more sense now. I need to see Carlie. Can you help me?"

"She's here at my house right now, but listen, I need to talk to her about all this first. She may not be open to something like this."

"Do you think she'll say no?" She allowed no time for me to answer. "Tell her to read the *Logan Bend Tribune* this morning. I've helped solve cases before."

"I saw the article."

"You did? Why didn't you say so?" Again, she didn't wait for me to reply. "I'll meet you two somewhere but it has to be private. Whoever did this is still around, and he's dangerous."

"How do you know?"

She made an impatient grunt. "Do we have to go over this again? I'm psychic."

I ran my hand through my hair. This Moonstone might be

psychic and she might be able to help us, but she gave me a first-class headache. Then another thought came to me. One that made my stomach feel as if it dropped to the floor. "Aren't you worried whoever this guy is will see the paper this morning? What if he comes after you?"

"That's a possibility. But I can't worry about that kind of thing or I'll get kicked out of my witch club. We make an oath, you know, to serve selflessly."

"You...you have a club?"

"What else would we do? Anyhoo, where can we meet?"

"You could come out to my house. I have a locked gate, but I'll punch you in when you arrive. But again, let me talk to Carlie first. I'll call you back."

"Groovy. I'll be waiting."

I hung up just as Carlie appeared. "Cole? What's wrong?" She rushed over to me. "Are you ill? You're pale as a ghost."

I turned to face her. She put her hand to my forehead. "No fever."

"I'm not sick. I've just had a shock." I got up from the stool and guided her over to the couch. "I have something I need to tell you."

———

Moonstone wore a bright purple blouse over white jeans. An ample but attractive woman in her late forties, her auburn hair was cut in layers around her round face.

"Thanks for having me," Moonstone said as we all sat in my family room. She took the easy chair, and I sat next to Carlie on the couch.

"We're grateful you reached out." Carlie slipped her hand into mine. "What can you tell us?"

When I'd told Carlie about the exchange with Moonstone, she hadn't hesitated. We should at least hear what she had to say, even if it led nowhere. Now, as I stole a glance at Carlie, her hopeful expression made my chest ache. Was this a mistake to get her hopes up?

"Let me lay it out as best I can," Moonstone said. "I had a dream two nights ago where a pretty blonde in her teens came to me. She wore a cheerleading outfit with the name Elizabeth stitched into the fabric."

Carlie's grip on my hand tightened.

"She held a notebook in her hand." Moonstone's long earrings jangled as she sat forward in the chair. "A journal, I think."

"Yes, she had one of those," Carlie whispered. "I recently found it hidden. She wrote in it the summer she died."

Moonstone's eyes flickered. "Are there missing pages?"

Carlie nodded. "Yes. They were ripped out. I could see the remnants of three missing pages. The last entry is about a week before her death. I've felt they might hold important information."

"In my dream, Beth said as much. She told me her family needs to find them."

"Did she say where?" Carlie's voice had taken on a high-pitched, desperate tone.

Moonstone scooted to the edge of the chair. "She said they were in a book. Her favorite book."

"Oh, God," Carlie said. "I packed away all her books and took them to the used bookstore last week. I don't know if they'll have them or not."

"Let's go there now," Moonstone said. "It's unlikely they were sold."

We all stood at once.

"Do you have any idea what her favorite book was?" Moonstone asked as we headed toward the front door.

"There were two. One was a romance novel we read in secret," I said. "Our mom didn't approve of those kinds of books, so we had to sneak them home from the library. There was one she liked so much that she kept it and just paid the fine."

"What was the other favorite book?" I asked.

"*Black Beauty*. My parents gave it to her for Christmas one year. She always wanted a horse. But I kept that one. There's nothing in it. I don't think, anyway."

"It'll be in the romance book," Moonstone said. "I feel quite certain."

The secondhand bookstore smelled of dust and old books. When we went in, a clerk with stark white hair and thick glasses greeted us. I hadn't been in here since returning to Logan Bend. When I'd lived here back in the eighties, the building had housed a used record store. My brothers and I had frequented the place back then, pooling our money to buy Zeppelin, Springsteen, and Pink Floyd.

"Carlie, you're back," Martha said. "Do you have more books for me, or are you shopping this morning?"

"Actually, it's neither of those," Carlie said. "I'm wondering if you still have the books I brought last week."

"I most likely have all of them," Martha said. "It's been a slow few weeks."

"It was a romance book from the eighties. The cover had a—"

Martha cut Carlie off. "I know the exact one. A mostly naked man and a young redheaded woman. Had a good chuckle over that picture. I'd forgotten how delicious those old romance covers could be. Sucked you right in, didn't they?"

"Sure," Carlie said. "Do you still have it?"

"I didn't put it out for sale. I decided to keep it for myself."

Carlie let out a breath. "Oh, thank God. I need to take a look at it."

"Hang on. I'll get it from the office." Martha hobbled toward a closed door. The woman was ninety if she was a day.

In the meantime, Moonstone wandered over to a table of science fiction. Carlie glanced at me nervously. "I don't see how they could be in there. They would have fluttered out when I moved the book into the box. The trade paperback size is too small to hide sheets of paper."

Martha returned with a thin paperback and handed it to Carlie.

"You look," Carlie said to me. "I can't."

I took it from her outstretched hand. The pages were yellowed from age. A coffee cup stain marked the front. I flipped through it using the pad of my thumb. Nothing. I shook it but again nothing came out. Carlie slumped against the counter. "Just wait. I'm going through each page," I said as I opened it to the beginning. *Logan County Library* was stamped in black ink on the title page. One of those library slots where they used to put the return date cards had been glued to the back of the card stock front cover. It no longer held a checkout card. I ran my finger over the pocket. "It's too fat," I said. "There's something in there." I lifted the edge and peered under to see a piece of lined paper folded into a square. "The pages are in there." Using my thumb and fingernail, I managed to slide the square out of the pocket. "This has to be them." I set it in Carlie's hand.

"Oh my God," Carlie whispered. "How did I not see that?"

I felt Martha's eyes on us and turned toward her. "Thank you, Martha," I said.

Moonstone, who I'd completely forgotten was even here, brushed my elbow. "You might want to hold on to Carlie. She doesn't look too good."

Carlie looked as if she might faint. "Are you all right?" I asked gently.

"I need to sit somewhere to read these," Carlie said.

"Let's go outside and sit in the park," I said, suddenly craving the sunlight. This store was too dark for my taste.

"May I have the book back?" Carlie asked Martha. "Turns out I shouldn't have given it away in the first place."

"Of course, dear. I hope whatever it is that's in there gives you the answers you need."

We all went outside into the sunny morning. In silence, we walked toward the park. When we arrived, I led Carlie over to a bench under the shade of one of the old oaks. Moonstone hung back. "I'll just go for a walk around and leave you two for now. When you're ready, I'd like a chance to hold the papers. Depending on what's inside, I may or may not be able to give you more information."

Hunched over the tight square of papers, Carlie didn't respond.

"Thanks, Moonstone," I said. "We'll be right here."

After she walked away, I sat next to Carlie. "It's time. Unfold them and find out what they say."

17

CARLIE

I nodded, agreeing with Cole's sentiment that it was most certainly time to find out the truth. Yet I was scared. What if it were another dead end? Or, worse, what if it prompted only further questions?

I unfolded the square carefully, worried I'd tear the fragile paper. There were three pages. Every line on both sides had been written on. Shaking, I started to read.

August 21, 1989

I missed my period. It's been two weeks. I'm freaking out! I don't know what to do. I feel so alone. I can't even tell Carlie. And what about Z? If I'm pregnant, he'll kill me. I mean, not really. But he'll be so mad. Maybe I'm just late.

August 22, 1989

Thea told me there's a pregnancy test you can buy at the drugstore. You just have to pee on a stick and wait ten minutes. But how could I buy one without Mrs. Jones at the drugstore knowing and telling the whole town? I cried myself to sleep last night, and Carlie gave me a weird look this morning at breakfast. She knows something's wrong. I can see she wants to ask me about it, but I can't tell her. She'll be so disappointed in me. I've ruined my life. Mom and Dad will hate me if they find out what I've done. I don't know what to do.

August 23, 1989

I threw up this morning. There's no doubt now. I don't know what I'm going to do. If I tell Z then I have to have proof. I have a feeling he won't believe me. I have to get one of those pregnancy tests that Thea told me about.

August 24, 1989

I managed to buy a pregnancy test by driving down to Peregrine where no one knows me. When I got home, Carlie was in the bathroom trying to get her hair to curl. I paced back and forth in the hallway until I finally had to bang on the door and tell her to get out. She did as I asked, but I could tell I'd scared her. I'd never pounded on the door before, even when I needed to pee and she was taking forever. I didn't apologize, which I felt bad about later but all I could think about was the test.

It was the longest ten minutes of my life. But it was pink. I knew it already. My life is over.

August 25, 1989

Last night Carlie and I went to see the fireworks with Luke and his brothers. I swear Luke knows something. He kept looking at me when he thought I wasn't paying attention. Before the fireworks started we broke away to take a walk together. Carlie and Cole were doing their thing where they sit and talk for hours. I don't know how they could have that much to say. I can't ever think of a thing to talk to Luke about. Drew was making out with his latest girlfriend so he was busy too. Luke asked me if I was okay. I started crying and he held me and stroked my hair. He said whatever it was, even if it was that I didn't love him anymore, he understood. He didn't want me to be sad because of him. If he only knew what a terrible person I am. How I've lied and cheated on him. I told him how good he was and how much fun I'd had being his girlfriend and that I didn't want to break up. I said I was just going through some stuff that had nothing to do with him. I can't keep putting off telling everyone the truth. Eventually, everyone's going to know what I've done and what Z has done. I've ruined both our lives. I deserve to die.

August 26, 1989

My heart is broken. I went over to Z's house today, determined to tell him. I'd heard she was out of town for a few days so I thought it might be safe. I couldn't wait for our usual day. I just couldn't. There's a baby growing inside me. His baby. I walked over so no one would see my car in his driveway. I knocked on the door, but there was no answer. But I knew he was there. His car was there. He didn't want to see me. My last hope was that maybe he was in the backyard and didn't hear me knocking, so I went around the side of the house. That's when I saw the bike. I knew instantly. Thea. She was there. I knew only too well why. He's doing it with her too. I wanted to make up a reason, like maybe she needed help with something at school, but I know the truth. If he did it with me, why wouldn't he do it with another girl?

I'm devastated. I can't believe I was stupid enough to think I was the only one. That I was special. That what we had was special. Instead, I'm just sex to him. I hate myself. I hate him.

I'm going to have to tell the truth. I can't hide my pregnancy forever. Mom and Dad will assume it's Luke's. I've already ruined my life. I can't ruin his too, especially since he's been so good to me even thought I don't deserve it.

We're all supposed to go to the fair tomorrow night. Dad wants me to drive Carlie and me and meet the boys there. He's weird about us riding in cars with other teenagers. Which is pretty funny considering what I've been doing for the last six months. I'm going to pretend to be sick and leave Carlie there with the Paisley boys, then come back here to tell Z that I'm pregnant. I can't let Luke take the fall for this. After I tell Z, I'm going to tell Mom and Dad the truth. All of it. I have a plan. One that they'll agree to, I feel sure. I'm going ask them to send me to Aunt Sally's to have the baby. I can put it up for adoption and then finish high school in Aunt Sally's town. I can't ever come back here. Not with Z still here. I know Mom and Dad are going to be upset, but the only thing I care about at this point is making sure no one thinks the baby is Luke's. He has such a bright future. I know he's going to be a doctor and have a great life. After everything I've done, I have to protect him. As for Z— all I know is that I want him to understand what he's done and what my plans are and that I know who he really is now. A lying snake.

The only one I don't know how I can face is Carlie. She's obviously totally in love with Cole, and I don't know what this will do to them. The Paisley brothers stick together. I've messed everything up for myself and probably for my sister. When Luke knows that I'm a cheater and liar, there's no way he's going to want Cole to have anything to do with this family. I can only hope that Cole will be able to make his own decision.

Yet even as I write this, I know one thing for sure. Even though Mom and Dad and Carlie will be shocked and saddened by what I've done, they'll never abandon me or turn me away. I've screwed up, but they'll still love me. Over the last few days it's like I can see with new eyes how much they've done for me, how much they love me no matter what. I need to make sure they understand how much I love and appreciate them. We're the Websters, and even though I messed up, I'll be able to keep going because of them.

Please, God, watch over me tomorrow. Help me to be brave.

The words blurred from the tears that ran down my face. My Beth. My sweet sister. All alone in this decision.

My heart thudded fast and hard within my chest. Z had killed her to keep her quiet. There was absolutely no doubt in my mind. Who was he?

With trembling hands, I handed the pages to Cole. "You won't believe this."

I watched Cole as he took in the meaning of Beth's final words on what proved to be her final days. When finished, he folded them back into a square and hung his head. "Poor Beth."

"Beth wanted to protect Luke. She wanted to do the right thing even though she was in deep trouble. That's the Beth that I knew and loved." I drew in a ragged breath, fighting tears. Crying wasn't going to help me figure out the identity of her killer. "He did it. Whoever he is."

Cole nodded. "He must have decided keeping himself from being identified was worth killing her over. The violence of the crime tells us how enraged he was. As if he hadn't gotten her pregnant." His face went blank for a moment. "You realize something, though. Thea knows who he is. She may not have known at the time, but whoever she was with that day is the killer."

In my grief, I hadn't thought that through. "God, you're right. I wasn't thinking." I rubbed my face. "Wait a second." There was a "she" in her journal. But Beth was surprised by Thea. Publicly, he had a girlfriend, and then there were Beth and Thea, possibly more. "She's always referring to his girlfriend—the one who was out of town when Beth went to the house." I shook my head. "It doesn't make any sense, though. If he were a high school student, he didn't live with his girlfriend."

"I think she meant that he would normally be hanging out with her?"

"I don't know, Cole. The way she said it doesn't add up."

A horrible thought occurred to me. "Unless he was an adult. Maybe she was a wife, not a girlfriend."

Sweat dampened the palms of my hands. "A man? A married man? But she was seventeen years old. Who would sleep with a minor?"

"Men see seventeen-year-old girls who looked like your sister as a woman, not a girl. Especially if their morals aren't exactly virtuous in the first place."

"Beth and Thea were sleeping with an adult? A married man?" This idea had not occurred to me. Not once. Since finding the journal I'd assumed it was another one of our classmates. "This means any married man who lived here in 1989 could be the killer. Or even ones with a girlfriend they lived with."

"And Thea knows who he is," Cole said. "We should go see her. Ask her point-blank."

I nodded as I jerked to my feet. "I know where her mom lives. Right in town on the same street as the Catholic church."

Cole jerked to his feet. "Let's go."

We sprinted back to the truck.

I yanked open the passenger-side door. "Wait, what about Moonstone?"

She was on the other side of the park with her hands folded behind her back while looking into the water of a small pond.

"Text her that we'll meet up with her later," Cole said as he thrust his cell phone my way. "I want to do this now."

I agreed. For some reason, timing seemed of the essence. I'd waited thirty years for Thea to tell the truth. "It's about time she did what's right."

I sent a quick text to Moonstone that we had something urgent to do but that we'd come back and treat her to lunch at the pizza place if she would be so kind as to meet us there. She texted back right away that she'd see us around noon.

My mind couldn't exactly keep up with what was happening. We were going to know at last who he was. Then what? Would we even be able to find him? Was he alive still? He had to be. Unlikely he would still be in town. Thea would tell us. She would have to when I explained why we needed the information. Although maybe she knew who had killed Beth all along. Maybe that's why she felt so guilty. I seethed. If that were true, I would not be able to control my rage.

Cole drove through the downtown area of Logan Bend, then took a left off Logan Drive and another at Third Street. The Catholic church was a large brick building that took up an entire street block. "It's just a few houses down from here," I said. "Used to be light blue with white shutters." I leaned forward, my heart beating fast as we passed one house and then another. "There. That's the one." I recognized the metal fence, even though the house was now yellow with black shutters.

That's when I heard the sirens. I looked behind us to see an ambulance barreling down Third Street. I turned back to the front to see a cop car coming from the other direction. Cole pulled the truck over and parked behind a car on the street. The ambulance passed us and then pulled into Thea's mother's house.

"No, no. Cole, no." Thea was hurt or dead. The killer knew she was going to talk. *Please, please, don't be dead.* I knew it even as I told myself the opposite.

Cole cursed under his breath. "This can't be happening."

We sat in his truck watching as Thea's mother, wearing a pink housedress, came running out of the house waving her arms frantically. The paramedics ran into the house.

Cops got out of their parked car and sprinted across the driveway and into the house. A few minutes later, one paramedic came out of the front door and over to his ambulance. He pulled out a stretcher. "Oh God, Cole. He killed her. He knew she knew."

"Which means he's here somewhere."

"Do you think it was him the other night?" A cold dread chilled me to the core. "He wants me dead, too."

He didn't answer except to reach for my hand.

Paramedics came out of the house, carrying the stretcher. A blanket covered the body from head to foot. Z had killed Thea in her mother's home.

We waited until Ford came out of the house. The moment I spotted him, Cole and I jumped from his truck and ran toward him. He must have seen us, because he headed in our direction.

"What happened?" I asked, breathless.

"Sharpshooter took her out." Ford pointed to the church. "We think he or she was up on the roof of the church. Looks directly into the Moores' backyard. She was out there sunbathing. One shot in the head."

"I can't believe it," I said. "Just when we thought we'd caught a break."

"How so?" Ford asked.

I started to explain, but then pulled the journal entries out of my purse. "Read for yourself."

We waited for what seemed like days for him to finish.

"This is rough stuff," Ford said.

I vowed to myself not to cry. "Thea knew who killed Beth. I think she was going to come to you. She had something else to do first."

"Agreed. I'm sorry, Carlie." Sheriff Ford squeezed my shoulder. "This is a setback. But I'm going to talk to Mrs. Moore. She might know something that will help us."

Numb, I nodded. "Poor Thea."

"She had a hard life," Ford said. "That much was obvious. I feel real bad for her mother. Poor woman."

"Sheriff, we have a new theory," Cole said. "You see how she says there that she—his girlfriend—was out of town, implying they lived together."

"Which led us to thinking he might be older," I said. "An older, married man who lived with his wife."

"Holy cow, I didn't think of that," Ford said. "It's hard to believe, though, isn't it? A seventeen-old-girl with everything going for her to sleep with a married man? She's not the type."

"Type?" Cole asked.

"Sad. Lonely. Latchkey kid type without the family support Beth had. Those are the type of girls a man like that would prey on."

"Girls like Thea," I said.

"Exactly right."

"How will we ever find him?" I asked, voice breaking.

"You two go home and lock that gate. Stay low and out of sight. I don't want you anywhere that this monster could shoot you."

I shivered, suddenly aware of how exposed I was on the street.

"Come on," Cole said. "Let's get you back to my house."

Ford squeezed my shoulder again. "I'll pull records of every married man who lived here in 1989. Trust me, I'm not going to rest until I find this guy."

18

COLE

Thirty minutes later, we sat in my living room with Moonstone. I held Carlie's hand as Moonstone, sitting across from us, read through the last of the journal pages. We'd texted her to meet us back at the house instead of the pizza place.

"I'm sorry, Carlie," Moonstone said when she was done. "This must have been hard to read."

"Thank you," Carlie said. "And thank you for coming here and helping us. If it weren't for you, we would never have found these."

"Something else has happened?" Moonstone asked. "I can see it in your faces. Does it have anything to do with the sirens I heard?"

Carlie nodded. "Thea Moore was killed by a sharpshooter this morning. Right before we went to see her and ask her what she knew." Carlie gestured toward the pages spread out on the table. "That's why we hurried off this morning. We both felt an urgency to talk with her."

"We were too late," I said. "They pulled her out on a stretcher."

"This is terrible," Moonstone said. "I know how disappointed you must be."

Carlie told Moonstone about the conversation she'd had with Thea. "She must have gone to him and said she was going to expose him."

"And he put a stop to it," Moonstone said.

"We have a new theory. We think he was older," Carlie said. "A married man. An *adult* married man."

"Ford's going to pull records of all the married men in Logan Bend at the time," I said. "I can't figure how that'll lead to anything. There's too many, and how would we know who she had contact with?"

Moonstone's brow wrinkled. "I wish I could get something. I thought I might from the journal papers. Sometimes energies get left behind when people go. I thought Beth's might be in here."

"Was there anything else you can tell us from your dream?" Carlie asked. "Any clues to who Z is?"

"I'm afraid not," Moonstone said. "The message was clear. We were to look for the missing pages."

"But they don't really tell us anything, other than she was pregnant," I said. "We still have no idea who Z is."

"We know now that she was going to confront him," Moonstone said. "Which is an important piece of the puzzle. We can deduct that he knew she was pregnant and about her plan to tell your mother and father. He killed her to keep her from exposing him."

"Motive," I said.

Moonstone ran her hands over the sheets of thin paper as if they were a precious cloth she was about to sew.

"Why would she have hidden these pages in a separate place?" I asked. "Almost like she was planting evidence in case anything happened to her."

"Which would make sense," Carlie said. "If she actually wrote his name."

"Exactly. Why would she hide these separately? Also, when

did she do it?" I couldn't get my head around that particular move. Why would she hide the last entries in a different location if they didn't have any information in them? How were they different from the rest of the journal? Despite my pity for Beth, she also infuriated me. Why would she have played this game? If she knew he was dangerous, why hadn't she told someone? Especially Carlie? She'd lied to my brother and gotten herself in a dangerous position and left no real information about the identity of this mysterious, probably married man she'd been having sex with. "If she were nervous about his reaction, thinking him possibly dangerous, then why not spell it out?"

"I don't know," Carlie said, sounding exasperated. "I can hardly recognize the girl in this journal. All the secrets and lies."

"Love makes us do things we wouldn't normally consider," Moonstone said. "Your sister was young and vulnerable. Whoever this guy was, I'm sure he charmed the pants off her." She flushed. "I'm sorry. Poor choice of words."

Carlie mouth lifted in a sad smile. "It's okay. He quite literally did just that." Her eyes filled with tears. "As angry as all this makes me, I have to remember she was only seventeen. When I think of my daughter at that age, it all makes sense. Beth was a child who had been taken advantage of by an adult."

"We can only hope that I'll get something," Moonstone said. "Perhaps from the list the sheriff comes up with? Sometimes words will jump off a page. Speaking of which, do you have the rest of the journal with you?"

Carlie nodded and reached into her purse. She placed the ratty journal on the tabletop. "Here. Do you want to read it? I can tell you I've read it through several times and there's nothing in there that even hints at the guy's age."

"I'd like to touch it, if I may?" Moonstone's gaze was fixed on the notebook a bit like a person wary of a rabid cat.

"Be my guest," Carlie said.

Moonstone took the journal into both hands and held it

against her ample chest. Without warning, her eyes fluttered and rolled back in her head.

We stared at her as the muscles in her face twitched and her mouth moved without making any sounds. I squeezed Carlie's knee under the table. At least ten seconds went by.

As fast as it had come, she just as quickly changed back to normal. She blinked, as if she weren't sure we were really there. "Z was in his twenties."

"How do you know?" Carlie asked.

"Beth told me."

That afternoon, the temperatures reached the mideighties. Hot and mentally exhausted after the day's events, Carlie asked if we could go down to the river for a cleansing swim. I put some cold drinks in a backpack and called to Moonshine and Duke. The four of us walked past the garden and down to the river's edge.

We swam for a few minutes until the chill of the water forced us onto the large rock that jutted out of the water like a small island. Four people could easily sit on it, and as kids we'd often done so. Time and water had worn holes and dips, making it nature's best chair.

Carlie closed her eyes and tilted her face toward the sky. Slim and toned, the woman did not look a day over thirty. I didn't care what she thought or saw when she looked in the mirror. Her sky-blue bathing suit brought out her eyes and contrasted with her alabaster skin. A layer of slick sunscreen beaded on her skin.

I traced my thumb down the arch of one of her feet.

She giggled and snatched her foot away. "Tickles."

"Good to know." I did the same to her other foot.

"Stop that." She yanked that one away and wrapped her arms around bent knees. I scrambled up and plopped down next to her. Water cascaded from my body and soaked into the hot surface of the gray rock. I kissed a shoulder, then nibbled at her neck. Her skin was cold from the chilly water, but soon we would become too warm and need another dip.

"God, I love it here," I said. On the other side of the river a thicket of trees grew tall, sheltering the spot from wind. Not that there was any today. This was the perfect summer day. Not too hot but hot enough to swim. The water so clear I could see straight down to the rocky bottom.

A blue dragonfly hovered nearby before darting away. From the shore, Duke barked at us.

"Lie down, boy," I shouted to him.

He wagged his tail, then shook his coat dry before collapsing next to Moonshine, exhausted from his swim.

"Isn't it weird that we now know a Moonshine and Moonstone?" Carlie asked in a lazy voice. In mere minutes, the sun and river had done its magic on us. The horrific morning couldn't be believed here next to the green water and the blue sky and the scent of moss drying on rocks.

She buried her face against my shoulder. "I need my sunhat and sunglasses."

"I'll get the backpack. I want a beer anyway."

Before she could stop me, I dived back in and swam to shore. I put her hat on my head and held the backpack in one hand and swam with my free arm and legs back to the rock.

"I'm impressed, Mr. Paisley. Swimming with one arm in the air like you're still a kid."

"It's only a few feet," I said as I followed the backpack onto the rock.

She snatched her hat from my head. "I'll take that before I decide you look better in it than I do." Straw and wide-brimmed, it sufficiently shadowed her face.

I dug both our sunglasses out of the backpack and tossed hers over to her.

"Bless you," she said. "As much as I love the sun, it hurts my light eyes."

"Beautiful eyes." I leaned close to peck her mouth before settling across from her.

She moved to a dip in the surface of the rock that was almost like one of those low beach chairs. "It's so nice here. I always loved your swimming hole. Those were some of the happiest times of my life."

"For me too," I said. "I'm so grateful my mom kept the property. This land is worth much more than I could have ever bought it for on the open market. She sold it to me for what they'd paid back in the late seventies."

"She wanted you to have it."

"Yeah. She knew how happy I was here."

"What was it like for you after you left here? High school in LA seems scary."

"It was all right. Bigger but pretty much the same. Cliques. Popular kids. Bullied kids. Ones like me that kind of flew under the radar."

"True enough," she said.

"I missed you and this." I waved toward the water. "Being in the country where I belonged. But I played sports every quarter, and that brought the positive kind of attention that I needed to get friends."

"Did you have any girlfriends down there?"

I chuckled. "No way. I had this plan to find my way back to you."

She flicked my thigh. "You're such a liar."

"No, for real. I compared everyone to you. All the girls were so fake down there. Drew hated it and was always trying to fix me up with a friend of whomever he was dating at the time."

"He was always such a lady killer."

"When we were little, I always figured you'd go for him. He was so much more outgoing."

She shook her head, smiling over at me from underneath the brim of her latticed hat. "It was always you. From day one."

"I can't wait to tell him that." I laughed as I reached into the backpack for a beer. "You want one?"

"Why not?"

She took the can I offered. I put a cap on to shield my eyes and settled next to her. Our shoulders touched as we sat looking out over the water. Nearing four in the afternoon, the sun was still high and shedding light and heat.

"Mom wondered if we wanted to attend a fundraiser for Richards," she said after a few minutes passed. "We'd have to get dressed up."

"Would you like to go?"

"I wanted to go to prom with you." Her eyes twinkled at me. "This would be sort of like that."

"I'd have loved to take you to prom." My chest ached as I looked into her eyes. "So much was taken from us, wasn't it?"

She glanced away and rested her hand on my knee. "Too much."

"Did you go to prom?"

"No. I didn't want to go. Not without you. Not without Beth. She and I had been super excited about junior and senior year because we'd both be able to go to prom. We had this whole plan about double dating with you and Luke. I swear, we talked about it a hundred times. She had all the details figured out. Where we would eat beforehand and what color dresses we would have. A soft pink for her and a baby blue for me. And we'd ask you guys to wear ties that matched. I don't know why we thought you two would just do whatever we wanted."

"We would have. I would've rocked a baby-blue tie."

I expected her to laugh, but instead she played with the can's pop top as she gazed out over the water. "I should've known something was wrong between her and Luke. But it never occurred to me. Maybe because I was so wrapped up in you. Sometime in the spring, Beth stopped talking about anything in the future. In the spring right before prom—the one you and I weren't old enough for—I brought up how fun next year would be, and she snapped. She said something about who knew where we'd be in a year."

"God, Carlie, that's so incredibly sad."

"For all of us."

We were quiet for a few minutes. A fish did a silver somersault out of the water. Ripples on the water were the only proof he'd been there.

"We're not that old," Carlie said, out of the blue.

"For what?"

"Getting the most out of the rest of our lives. Together, I mean. We can do all the stuff we missed. There's no one stopping us now. No one can ruin this for us. Right?"

I lifted the brim of her hat to get a better view of her eyes but also as an excuse to draw nearer. "No one will ruin this for us. Why are you asking me that?"

"I don't know. I started thinking this afternoon that maybe you'll grow tired of this whole thing. I'm obsessed with finding my sister's killer. I can't think that's sexy."

I brushed her shoulder with my thumb. "Everything about you is sexy. Caring about your family happens to be at the top of a long list of things I love about you." I picked up her hand and placed it on my bare chest. "Do you feel that? My heartbeat?"

"Yes."

"It beats for you. It's always beaten for you, even when I didn't know where you were. We spent too long without each other. Nothing and no one will take you away from me a second time. All right?"

She nodded as a tear slipped from one eye. "I'm sorry I cry so much."

"You don't ever have to be sorry. I want the real you. Whatever you're feeling—share it with me. I'll do my best to listen and not try to fix it." I smiled. "My ex-wife said I did that too much."

"You being here is enough." She touched my face with her hand.

The look of love in her eyes was enough to heal any ailment. All the years of pain and loneliness seemed far away. "I want to spend as much time together as possible, doing all that we missed out on."

"Agreed. And we'll start with going to this fancy shindig for Richards. When is it?"

"Tomorrow night. I'll have to find a dress in town. I don't have anything to wear. Do you have a suit?"

"I have several suits, so not to worry. I clean up real good. And I happen to have ties in a variety of colors, so don't feel like you have to pick a baby-blue one."

"I'll keep that in mind." She laughed. "I don't know where Beth came up with baby blue in the first place."

"I know why. She wanted the dress to match your eyes."

She looked down at her lap. "She did say that once. I'd forgotten." Her face tilted upward, but she didn't meet my eyes, looking out across the water instead. "I wish we could go back to the summer before she died. The one where she and Luke were smitten and you and I were having water fights and eating peanut butter sandwiches. Just one more day where all of us were still innocent. When Beth still believed in puppy love. When I still believed that no one I loved would ever leave me. When I was convinced that most people were good." Her voice broke. "Whoever he was, he took that from all of us the day he convinced Beth to get involved."

"I know. I know he did. We can't bring Beth back or the innocent children we were. But Beth wouldn't want what happened to her to change your big heart or the belief that most people are good."

"I can feel it, Cole. We're so close to figuring out who he is. He's out there, and we're going to find him. Ford's a good cop. Moonstone's the real thing, which is so weird but true. Once we do, I think I can finally let this go. I can start truly living."

"When are you going to tell your mom about what you've found?"

She sighed. "Tomorrow morning. I can't wait any longer. She'll want to know, even if it brings the whole thing up for her."

"All right. That's decided. What do you say we spend the rest of the day having fun? Making a new memory at this swimming hole."

"I say that's a great idea."

19

CARLIE

The next morning, after Cole insisted on driving me back to my mother's, I found her in her usual place in the family room eating her bowl of oatmeal and watching the morning news.

"Hello, honey." She didn't look away from the television.

"Mom, I need to talk to you." This was a conversation I didn't want to have, but she needed to know everything I knew. However, having experienced the crushing blow of the truth myself, I knew how much it was going to hurt.

She clicked the television off and set aside her oatmeal. "I already saw it on the news. That poor girl. I remember her from cheerleading. Beth never liked her much. She said she was always bragging about herself. I've just been sitting here thinking how strange that they were both murdered." My mother sounded almost manic. "It's just a coincidence, right? Thirty years is a long time. Surely they're not connected."

"Mom, hang on. I have something to tell you that's going to be hard to hear, so I need you to be brave, okay?"

Her eyes widened. "You're scaring me."

Not wanting to torture her, I didn't hesitate. "We think the two murders might be connected. I need you to listen carefully, all right?"

Mom tented her hands under her chin. "I will. Please tell me."

"I found a journal of Beth's when I was cleaning out her closet. A hidden journal under the bookshelf. It's written the spring and summer before she died."

Her eyes widened as she brought a shaking hand to her mouth and spoke with her knuckles pressed into her upper lip. "Does it tell us anything?"

"Quite a bit. She was seeing someone other than Luke. She was sleeping with him." I blushed, mortified to have to tell her that her teenage daughter had been having sex.

"Sleeping?"

"Sex."

"No. Can't be." She shook her head so violently that I was afraid she'd give herself whiplash.

"The journal's full of entries about him. She thought she was in love with him."

"Who? Who is it?"

"She never said his name—just called him Z."

"You're thinking he could be her killer?" She reached for my hand. "Is that what you're saying?"

"It's a possibility."

"But why would he do such a thing?" She made a guttural noise in the back of her throat. "Do you think he was one of those controlling types who couldn't bear her to be with someone else and killed her because she wanted to break up? I've seen those on the news."

"I don't think that was it." I let out a long breath before telling her the next part. "She was pregnant."

She froze and stared at me. "What?"

"The last entry says she's going to tell Z first and then you and Dad. She wanted to go to Aunt Sally's and have the baby, then give it up for adoption."

"Pregnant?" A sob like a wounded animal rose from my mother's chest. She covered her mouth with her hands as if to keep from screaming. "Wait, no. That's impossible. The autopsy would have shown that."

I flinched as if she'd smacked me across the face. That had never occurred to me. "You're right. Why didn't Dr. Lancaster find that?"

Cole said Moonstone thought there was a possible cover-up. No newspaper articles about the case at the library archives. The town doctor, newspaper, and sheriff. Brothers? In on it together. But they'd been in their forties and fifties back then. Surely Beth hadn't been sleeping with one of them? I thought I might be sick, but I pushed through.

"Mom, think about it for a second. The Lancaster brothers ran this town back then."

"Are you saying they were in it together?" Mom asked. "But why?"

"We think the man she referred to in the journal as Z was older and probably married."

"No, Carlie. No. They were like old men back then. She couldn't have possibly been involved with one of them."

"There's evidence that she's involved with a married man in the journal," I said. "We could be wrong, but I don't think so. But Moonstone thinks the man was in his twenties."

"Who's Moonstone?"

"A psychic." Just then, as if I'd conjured her, my phone rang. I glanced down to see that it was Moonstone. "I'm sorry, Mom, but I have to get this."

She waved a hand in my direction as she continued to stare out the window with a faraway look in her eyes.

I went out to the patio to talk without my mother being able to hear. "What's up?" I asked.

"I had another vision. From what I can tell, the man was a prominent citizen and I kept getting the words: 'There were others.'"

"Others? What does that mean?"

"I'm assuming that whoever this guy was, he was sleeping with more than just Beth."

"Thea, for one."

"Right. Be brave," Moonstone said. "You're going to figure this out and finally get you and your mother some closure."

I returned to my mother. She was sitting in the same spot I'd left her. "Carlie, I think I know who Z is."

"You do?"

"Z is Thom Richards. The three men were his uncles. That's what they have in common. A man in his twenties. Thom Richards was in his early twenties back then. Handsome and muscular. Someone Beth would have fallen for if he'd seduced her."

I went hot, then cold, before I stumbled over to the couch. I tried the theory out by saying it out loud. "Thom Richards killed Beth when she told him she was pregnant. Then his uncles covered it up." *A prominent citizen.*

"It makes sense," Mom said, sounding remarkably calm suddenly. "Town hero sleeping with a high school student. He was a teacher. If anyone had found out, he would have lost everything. All hopes for a political future, perhaps even been cut off from his family."

I sank onto the couch. My stomach and head churned as I thought through this idea. Most of the girls at school had talked about how cute Coach Richards was. Now, with this new clue from Moonstone, it all fell together. Richards, handsome coach and teacher, with access to hundreds of students, seduced high school girls. Thea had said she wanted what Beth had. She'd offered herself to him. There were others, too. How many? My sister hadn't known of others. Thea had been a shock to her. But she wouldn't have seen it, believing herself to be in love with the lying cheater. "Mom, it makes sense. How could this have never occurred to us?" The walls of the small room seemed to draw closer. I fought to catch my breath.

"Because he's got us all fooled into thinking he's a good man. I've worked on his campaign for a year. Not once did he flinch as he looked into the eyes of the mother whose daughter he killed."

"But what if we're wrong?"

She looked up at me. "We're not wrong. I feel it in my gut."

"He had Thea killed."

Mom reached for my hand. "I'm scared, honey. What if he comes after you?"

"I'll go to Ford and tell him what we think. His team can protect us."

"From someone as powerful as Thom Richards? I have my doubts," Mom said.

I looked out the window. Were we vulnerable at this very moment? No, not yet. He didn't know that we suspected him. I still had a chance to trap him into telling me the truth. "Screw it, Mom. I'm not going to hide away in here. I'm going to that fundraiser. I want to look him in the eye when I tell him I know what he did."

"Carlie, no. Just stay away from him. Go to Ford."

For the first time since I'd lied about sneaking romances up to my room, I lied to my mother. "You're right, Mom. But he doesn't know we suspect him. I'll keep it that way." I patted her hand.

The bell rang overhead as I walked into the nicest dress shop in town. An attractive woman around my age dressed impeccably greeted me as the door closed behind me. "I'm the Judy in Judy's Threads." She smiled at me at the same time she was searching my face as if she knew me. "Are you Carlie Webster?"

"I am. Do we know each other?"

"You probably don't remember me. I was a few years behind you in school. Judy Dierks."

"I'm sorry, I don't remember you. Please don't take it personally. I have trouble recalling much of the last years of high school."

"Understandable, considering what your family went through."

I decided to leave that alone and get right to the point of my visit. "I'm attending the fundraiser for Thom Richards this evening. I know it's short notice, but I hoped you might have an appropriate dress for the occasion?"

She nodded. "Yes, yes, I've had several customers come in for the very same fundraiser. As a matter of fact, I had a feeling Richards would be fundraising in his hometown and bought more than my usual inventory of dresses just in case. I don't have much left, but I do have a few I think would do nicely with your creamy complexion and fair hair."

"I'm a six or an eight, depending on the brand," I said.

She gave me an indulgent smile. "I wouldn't be worth my salt if I didn't know your size by looking at you."

"Do you think a cocktail dress will be fancy enough?"

"For the country club patio in the summer? Yes. You'll want something light but with a pashmina for when the evening cools."

I thought of my classic black cocktail dress that was currently hanging in the closet of my Seattle home. I'd worn it to several business events when I'd been married. If only I'd thought to bring it. I hated to spend money on a dress I might never wear again.

However, I was on a mission tonight. One in which I would inspect every move Thom Richards made. If possible, I was going to get him alone and ask him questions, see if I could see any cracks in his armor. I just needed something to go to Ford with.

"I know what you're thinking," Judy said. "You don't want a dress you can only wear once. Don't worry, I have several classics that you could wear to weddings or graduations."

I smiled. "You're good at your job. That's exactly what I was thinking."

She smiled back at me, clearly pleased by my compliment. "I do my best. Now let's get you settled in my best dressing room. Get undressed and I'll bring them to you. What kind of bra do you have on?"

"The normal kind?"

"I'll bring you a strapless one to use while you're trying these on."

"I'm a thirty-four C."

"I know."

"Right." I laughed and then docilely obeyed her instructions, stripping down to my bra and panties in the large dressing room. With mirrors covering three walls, there was no escaping my reflection. The usual heinous glow of fluorescent lighting revealed every dimple and stretch mark on my middle-aged body.

I hadn't been in a dressing room in years. After my ex-husband's confession, I'd been filled with self-doubt and loathing. Plagued with insecurity, I hadn't wanted to look at myself in the mirror. Many nights I'd lain awake wondering if I'd been this or that or the other, would he have had the need to hire prostitutes? It was only after a year of therapy that I had been able to understand that his actions had little to do with me and mostly all to do with his addiction to risky behavior. His tolerance for risk had been both his triumph and demise. The same personality that had chanced it all for a start-up in the technology sector had also been responsible for his interest in dangerous sex.

Judy called out from outside the dressing room door. "I have three for you. Hopefully one of them will work, because I don't have much else in your size."

I opened the door and took them from her outstretched hand and hung them on the rack to get a better look. None were outrageously priced like the higher-end shops in Seattle, reminding me again of the practical reasons for moving back to Logan Bend. One was a classic fit-and-flare style in a dark blue color; one a sheath in light green with a lace overlay; the last a baby-pink chiffon sheath with a pattern of faded flowers and ruching on one side and a flouncy ruffled hem. I was immediately drawn to the last one. Romantic and feminine. The perfect dress for a summer's evening.

I tried on the other two first. The green lace was tight-fitting and clung to me like plastic wrap to the side of its box. Definitely no. The traditional one was nice and actually flattering. But I didn't want to wear such a dark color to a summer outside event. I might buy it for some other time, I thought, as I slipped into the pink, having already forgotten my previous misgivings about buying something new.

The chiffon was as flirty and romantic as I'd thought it would be and felt smooth and light against my skin. I could imagine dancing with Cole in it and feeling like a girl in the spirit of our missed homecoming and prom dances. I almost did a little twirl in front of the mirror.

I'd buy them both, I decided. There was no reason to think I might not need the blue dress some other time, like for a cocktail party this fall or winter. Or maybe for a nice dinner out some-where with Cole. The strapless bra I could definitely use again. I'd get that too. Should I? Would I really use the bra again? Or the dress? When was the last time I'd bought anything nice for myself?

I sat on the bench in the dressing room with a thud. Beth's face floated before me. I could almost hear her telling me to buy them both. *Live a little. Treat yourself, you've been through a lot.* For too long, I'd chosen a life that would make up for Beth's lack of one. I'd lived like I shouldn't have been here when Beth couldn't be. So many choices had been that way. Teaching literature but abandoning my writing. A husband I knew deep down wasn't capable of loving me as I deserved to be. Perhaps even the choice to have only one child could be traced back to my survivor's guilt.

I stood up from the bench and took a final look at myself in the soft, sensuous dress. *If I have my way, Beth, we're going to nail the devil.* Whether it was tonight or next year, I'd never give up.

I paid for the dresses and walked to my car. For hours I'd debated myself. To tell Cole my intentions for the evening or not? If he knew what I suspected, he wouldn't let me get anywhere near the man. No, I'd keep it to myself for now. I needed to look Richards in the eyes. I had to believe I'd be able to see the truth. If I got anything tonight, even a vibe or a hint of guilt in the eyes of Thom Richards, I'd tell Cole on the way home. After that, I could go to Ford.

20

COLE

The country club and golf course were north of town and had views of both Logan and Blue Mountains. We were seated next to an elderly couple name Ruth and Charles Cassis. They were white-haired and blue-blooded, having told us almost immediately that their families went back a hundred years in Logan Bend. I vaguely recalled them from Sunday school back when I was a kid. Mrs. Cassis had been our teacher when we first moved here. She hadn't been a fan of Drew, and by connection of me. If I recalled correctly, neither my brother nor I had been impressive when it came to memorizing verses. Although the conversation had remained benign throughout the meal, Mrs. Cassis sent curious glances Carlie's way. They obviously wanted to ask Carlie questions about the murder. I understood now how being defined as the murdered girl's sister was burdensome. For the first time, doubt crept into my thoughts. Was it wrong to ask Carlie to live here? Should I tell her that I'd go with her wherever she wanted to go?

We'd been served a meal of dry chicken, limp asparagus, and mashed potatoes the consistency of glue. I'd eaten it because I was hungry, but Carlie had picked at hers. Fortunately, the wine was a red blend from Walla Walla and quite good. She had barely sipped hers.

The servers were now bringing chocolate cake with a raspberry swirl, indicating that the speech portion of the night was about to start. I braced myself for a boring speech and nodded yes when the server asked if I wanted a refill on my wine. Carlie agreed to another as well.

Sharon Richards walked up to the lectern, dressed in an expensive-looking black dress and a pair of those pointy-type shoes I could never figure how a woman's foot fit in. With a mushroom of white-blond hair that wouldn't move in a windstorm as well as bright red lipstick, she was the epitome of the politician's wife. She smiled out at the room full of tables as all gazes turned in her direction.

"First, thank you all for being here and supporting the next governor of Idaho, Thom Richards."

She paused as the crowd clapped. "I thought it might be fun to share with you a little about the Thom Richards I know and have loved for over thirty years."

Here we go, I thought, yearning suddenly for an evening on the patio with Duke and Moonshine. Politicians loved to hear themselves talk.

"We met at the University of Idaho—go Vandals—and I knew instantly he was the one. It took him a little longer, but he finally got there and we married right after graduation. He brought me back here to his hometown of Logan Bend. I was a city girl and unfamiliar with the wild ways of the Richards and Lancaster families. But soon I acclimated and could skin a deer as well as the next girl."

Laughter erupted around the room. I wasn't sure what part of skinning a deer was funny, but I kept that to myself.

She went on for a few more minutes about how they hadn't been able to have children, but that it had turned out to be a blessing in disguise because it fueled Thom's desire to devote his life to the children of Logan Bend. "In the early days of our marriage, he found his calling as a coach and teacher at the local high school. That was the beginning of a life of service."

More clapping from the crowd.

"All right, that's enough from his wife and biggest fan." She gave her best dazzling smile, making sure to look around the room before fixing her gaze back on her husband. "May I introduce you to Thom Richards, the next governor of Idaho."

Richards got up from the front table and loped up to the lectern. He and his wife exchanged a kiss that went a second too long. They wanted to make sure we all knew what a healthy and wholesome marriage they had. I hated politicians.

He stood before the microphone. His once-brown hair was now more salt than pepper, but his face had aged remarkably well. Thom Richards was a man who had been born with it all: money, looks, intelligence. No wonder he wanted to be in politics. It was either this or Hollywood. Except in politics you could buy your way in. Hollywood didn't care about where you came from, only what you looked like in front of the camera.

"Well, shoot, if I'm not a lucky man, I don't what I am," Richards said. "Thank you to my beautiful wife for that introduction. But listen, folks, don't be fooled. That woman right there is the reason I'm the man I am today. She brought out the best in me from the first day I met her, and I've been learning from her ever since." He paused for a moment as he tilted his head. "I'd also like to acknowledge my mother and thank her for all her work on my behalf. Mother, stand please."

A tall woman with silver hair stood and waved at the room. Although she was in her eighties now, she was still straight-backed with wide, muscular shoulders. Always a strong ox of a woman, she hadn't been pretty, exactly, but handsome. Fierce, arrogant, and never one to keep her opinions to herself, she'd frightened my mother the few times they'd exchanged words at one of our games. What had Mrs. Webster said about her the other day? Shelley Lancaster had held the keys to everything back in the day. She must be thrilled her son was about to become governor. Would she urge him on to the presidency next? I had the feeling the women in Thom Richards's life had a lot to do with where he was now.

"All right, my friends, let's talk policy," Richards said from the lectern. "That's why we're really here. This isn't about me or you. This is about the kids. Just as it's been. Let me lay out to you what I plan to do if I'm blessed enough to be your governor. I'm a simple guy with a simple plan. Everything we do should be about the kids. Education, health care, and making sure every child has the proper nutrition to succeed. The future of our state and our country is our youth. We must do right by them."

He then yammered on about some of the specifics. I only half listened. As hard as I tried, I couldn't really muster up any passion for politics, and especially politicians. This was just another example of a rich guy running for office. Why was Loretta so taken in by him?

Finally, he finished his speech. The entirety of the room rose to their feet and clapped for him. I did the same, not wanting to stand out. I glanced over at Carlie. She watched Richards with squinted eyes, as if she wanted to see inside his brain.

When we all sat back down, dessert had been cleared. We made small talk with the Cassis couple. I stifled several yawns.

"Come on," Carlie said. "I promised my mom I'd get a photo with him."

We waited as the people before us posed for pictures and promised their campaign dollars. After a few minutes, it was our turn. One of Richards's well-groomed eyebrows raised as he looked from one of us to the other. "You're both looking nice tonight."

Carlie stuck out her hand and introduced herself as they shook. "My mom sends her best. She wasn't feeling well and asked if we'd come in her place."

"Your mother's been a godsend," Richards said. "What a gem."

"Thanks. She truly believes in you."

He turned to me next. "Thanks for being here tonight. Sure makes me swell with pride seeing how great you kids turned out."

There was no arguing this man was as charismatic as they came. He'd devoted his life to service of others even though his family was filthy rich. I supposed that said something about the guy. Still, I didn't completely trust him. I hadn't back in high school either. He always struck me as disingenuous. The question was, why? What was I picking up on? Or was it simply that I loathed politicians?

A memory came to me. One day after football practice my brothers and I had limped across the parking lot to Luke's old truck. "Don't you wish Coach Richards could be our dad?" Luke had sounded so wistful and sad that it made me mad.

Drew had rolled his eyes. "No way. He's too pretty to be related to us."

Me? What had I thought? What had I said about him?

"He's a phony." I'd said it as I crawled into the bed of the truck. Back then I was in the full throes of my Holden Caulfield phase. I'd grabbed on to the *phony* description and run with it in addition to creating another category in my head. Salt of the earth. I had put everyone in either one category or the other. Coach Richards, phony. Mrs. Little, our hippie English teacher, salt of the earth.

Carlie had fallen in the salt of the earth slot for sure. She was the only girl I ever knew who didn't try to be something she wasn't. She didn't care if she fit in or if she was part of the popular crowd. She'd always had her nose in a book and didn't care who said what about her. I'd found that such an unusual quality in a girl. My poor mom always worried about what everyone thought of her. Of us. Of my dad. I couldn't count and probably didn't even know the full extent of the half-truths and downright lies she told her friends and coworkers about what our life was truly like. All the long sleeves and turtlenecks. The excuses about why he didn't have a job. She sacrificed her own safety and that of her boys just to save face. She dug in even when she knew she should get us out of there. Pride was an ugly thing. It had taken Beth's murder to get us out of here and ultimately away from my dad.

"Do you remember my sister?" Carlie asked Richards.

I looked at her, surprised. She never asked anyone that question. Now she was staring at him as though she'd like to bore a hole into his skull and discover all his secrets.

"I do, sure," Richards said. "May she rest in peace."

Carlie seemed to consider saying more, but instead she took my hand. "We wish you all the luck with the election."

"Thank you both. That means a lot," Richards said. "Carlie, your sister was very special. Her death shaped a lot things for me, including keeping our kids safe."

"Yes, she was special," Carlie said. "And didn't deserve to go out the way she did. Anyway, we have to go."

We said our goodbyes and turned to go. Carlie seemed on fire suddenly. She practically pulled me out the door of the banquet hall.

"What's gotten into you?" I asked Carlie. "You're acting kind of manic."

"I'll tell you in the car."

As sad as Luke's wish had been, there had been no way Richards could have been our father. He was closer to our age than Dad's.

Carlie led me out of the banquet space and down the hall. That's when it struck me. She was saying something about a glass of wine at home when I stopped dead in my tracks. Richards was probably twenty-two when he first started teaching here.

Moonstone had said the killer was a man in his twenties. *A married man in his early twenties.* Someone Beth would have had contact with. A person with deep ties and influence in the community. Why hadn't we thought of him before? Thom Richards fit the profile exactly.

I felt sick, as if that awful dinner might come up. Had he been sleeping with Beth? Had he killed her to keep her quiet? And now Thea? Had he seduced underage girls and ruined their lives? Were there others?

Everybody said what a genuinely nice man he was. He'd devoted himself to teaching and coaching. But what if there was a sinister side no one saw? If there were two girls, there were likely to be more. How long did it go on? My mind buzzed with all of the possibilities. Had Thea come back to tell people what he'd done to her and he'd had her killed, too?

I kept my face stoic so as not to give away the fact that I was panicked. If I went to Ford with this, what would happen? There would still be no evidence. *God, give me a sign if I'm onto something here. Tell me what to do next.*

We were almost to the double doors when a woman's voice called out to us. We both turned to see Shelley Lancaster striding toward us. I remembered that same determined gait as she sprinted up and down the field shouting instructions to the players. What did she want?

"Carlie, is that you?" Shelley asked.

Carlie gave her a stiff smile. "Hello, Ms. Lancaster. This is Cole Paisley. I don't know if you two have met?"

"Right. One of the Paisley twins. You've moved back, I heard." A brisk, assertive voice from a woman used to getting what she wanted. Had she raised a killer?

"That's right, ma'am."

"You built out on your parents' old property? Do I have that right?" She fixed her hazel eyes on me. Loretta had mentioned what a great athlete she'd always been. It was no surprise, given how tall and imposing she was. I couldn't help but notice what large hands and feet she had.

"Yes, correct," I said.

"Where is your mother?" Shelley asked. "Wasn't she supposed to join us tonight?"

"She didn't feel well this evening," Carlie said. "We've come in her place."

"She was fine this morning on the green," Shelley said. "The woman is a worthy golf opponent."

"She says the same about you," Carlie said. "Although she does go on sometimes about how she's never able to beat you."

"Well, that's never going to happen." Shelley barked out a laugh. "Just kidding. My son tells me I'm too competitive for my own good."

"I admire how active you and my mom have stayed," Carlie said. "Now that she was finally accepted into the country club."

A dig, I thought. Go Carlie.

My hands were damp with sweat by the time we reached the bar. Carlie looked over at me with a concerned expression. "Are you all right? You look weird."

"Can we go home?" I asked. "I'm not feeling too great."

"Of course. Do you want me to drive?"

"I think that would be a good idea."

Darkness had fallen and the lights that ran the length of the patio twinkled as we descended onto the grass and crossed over to the parking lot.

By the time we reached my truck I was breathing a little easier. Still, I loosened my tie and shirt the minute I was inside the truck.

We didn't talk until she reached Holland Loop Road.

"I'm sorry," I said. "You're all dressed up and probably wanted to extend the evening."

"Don't be sorry. We can do that any time. Is it your stomach?"

I shook my head. "No, it's nothing physical. I'll explain when we get home." There was no way I was telling her my theory while she was driving.

"All right." She reached over and patted my knee. "Whatever it is, we can talk it through, okay?"

"I know, baby." I closed my eyes. Would she think I was crazy? I really hoped I was. Because if it was the state's beloved Thom Richards who had killed Beth and Thea, then we were in deep, deep trouble.

I took off my tie and collapsed onto the couch while Carlie fetched me a glass of water from the kitchen.

"Here, drink this and then tell me all about whatever happened back there," she said.

I took a grateful sip from the glass. Laying out my theory would be a relief, but at the same time I knew that it would affect Carlie as deeply as it did me. After I set the glass aside, I folded my hands together and turned to look at her. "This might sound insane, and it probably is, but I thought of something tonight."

"Go ahead."

"It's about Beth." I reiterated what Moonstone had said about Z's age and that it had occurred to me tonight that Thom Richards would have been in his early twenties at the time of the murder. "He was married and certainly had access to Beth. They would have crossed paths a lot that year since she was the head cheerleader and he was the football coach."

She brought her hands to her cheeks and took in a deep breath. "Mom and I came to this exact same conclusion this morning. Also, Moonstone called. She thinks there were others. Other girls."

"Like Thea?" I asked. "He had her killed because she was going to tell the truth. Made even more dangerous if there were more women who might come forward."

"It adds up that it could be him," Carlie said. "But it's hard to believe, isn't it? Seeing him in action tonight...I don't know. We could be wrong."

"There's definite motive. He has a lot to lose. Even back then, he had a lot to lose. His career would've ended."

"Unless he was sloppy with Thea, how would we ever prove it to be true?" Carlie wrung her hands. "A thirty-year-old case. The two women who could accuse him are dead. That's what Thea was talking about the other night. She said she didn't tell the cops something she should have. Something that would have led to the killer. Instead, she ran away from here and him too."

"Maybe she was afraid of what he'd do," I said. "After she saw that Beth had been killed, she must have been scared to say anything. How many more girls do you think there were? And do you think we could figure out a way to get them to talk?"

"If we could even find them," Carlie said. "Is it odd he only taught for three years? Maybe his wife found out what he was doing and made him quit. I can remember my senior year he abruptly announced he was moving on to something else. They left town after that. Next I heard of him, he was running for a state representative spot."

"If he had a pattern of this behavior, it wouldn't have stopped just because he quit being a teacher. There are young aides and interns. If that's his thing."

"What do we do now?" Carlie got up and started to pace back and forth in front of my fireplace.

"Should we go to Ford? At least tell him our theory?"

She put up her hands in a helpless gesture. "We have no evidence. Not a bit."

"Maybe Ford could find some."

Carlie sat in the chair as she pressed her fingertips against her forehead. "He's a powerful man. Without evidence, we have no leverage with Ford. He's not going to call Richards in for questioning."

It occurred to me then that Thea's mom might know something. Even if she didn't think she did at the time, looking back, the truth might come to her. "We could see if Thea's mom will talk to us," I said. "Maybe she knows something."

"Ford said he was going to talk to her. If she knew something, he'd have told us."

"Let's go see her anyway," I said. "We should pay our respects."

Just maybe, Mrs. Moore would lead us to Richards. And we could all move on, once and for all.

21

CARLIE

The next morning, I rang Mrs. Moore's doorbell promptly at 9:00 a.m. When I'd called her at eight, she'd agreed to see us and said to give her an hour. A minute or so later, the door opened. "Carlie?" Mrs. Moore asked.

"That's right. And this is Cole Paisley."

Her tired blue eyes flickered to him. "Come on in. Both of you."

We stepped inside the house and followed her into the front room. She wore a cotton housedress similar to the one my grandmother had worn when cleaning or doing laundry. Overweight, she shuffled slowly across the yellow shag rug and was nearly breathless by the time she sat in a faded easy chair. The room smelled faintly of cigarette smoke, although I didn't spot any ashtrays.

"Have a seat there." Mrs. Moore pointed to a plaid couch. "I don't have any coffee or I'd offer you a cup. So expensive I had to give it up."

"No problem, we're fine," I said. "Thank you for agreeing to see us. I'm so sorry about Thea. I just saw her a few nights ago."

"Thank you. She mentioned she was meeting you." Mrs.

Moore's voice had the rasp of a smoker. If she wasn't currently smoking, she'd done enough damage that it sounded as if she still were. "I hadn't seen her much over the years. Then, a week ago, she showed up on my doorstep with a suitcase." She touched a hand to her white hair, so thin her pink scalp showed. "We hadn't had the best relationship. After she left here, she only called if she needed money."

"That must have been hard," I said.

"Can't say I blame her. I never had much to offer her growing up. I was always working to keep us afloat. After her dad left us, well, you know, it was hard to raise a little girl alone. She never had the things the rest of you girls did. I think it made her mean. You know, always wanting what others have hardens you. That was my Thea. Hard as nails." She twisted her gnarled hands together on her lap. "She left right after your sister was killed. I don't know if you remember that?"

"I don't. I don't remember much of anything. The year was a blur."

She dipped her head. "I expect it was."

I spoke as calmly as I could despite my rapid pulse. "The night I saw Thea, she told me she was going to do something to finally face what had happened to her here. Do you know what that was?"

"Whatever it was—I believe it got her killed." Mrs. Moore dabbed at the corners of her eyes. "Do you think it had something to do with your sister's murder? Is that why you're here?"

"We found a connection that might indicate that's so," I said. "I found Beth's journal from the summer she died. In it, she describes having an affair with a married man but she calls him only Z. One of the last entries describes seeing Thea with the exact same man. We have reason to believe he was under twenty-five. Do you have any idea who that might have been?"

Mrs. Moore visibly trembled. "She was sleeping with a married man? An adult? I don't think so. She had a crush on Luke Paisley." She turned toward Cole. "But he was in love with

Beth and told Thea he wanted nothing to do with her." Her gaze turned toward the window as she spoke. "One night she came home and told me she'd made a fool of herself. She'd tried to get Luke's interest, and he shut her down. When I suggested that she give up on him and focus on a boy who was available, she slammed her bedroom door in my face. Then I heard her crying. I don't think there was much she wouldn't have done to beat Beth at something. Which is why when she ran away, I thought she must have been the one to hurt Beth. Why else would you leave town so unexpectedly with nothing but a small suitcase? She was seventeen years old."

"Did you think she was guilty all these years?" Cole's eyebrows rose.

"No, just at first," Mrs. Moore said.

"But you never went to the police. Why?" Even as I asked the question, I knew the answer. I had a daughter too. One that I would do anything for, even if I suspected she'd murdered her frenemy.

"I did. I did go to the police," Mrs. Moore said. "It about killed me, but I went in and told them what I knew."

"Was this before or after the article in the paper?" Cole asked. "The one that accused my brother."

"It was the day after she was found," Mrs. Moore said. "Before the article."

"But why wouldn't they have investigated her?" I asked. "Especially since she skipped town. That makes a person look guilty, doesn't it?"

"I'd have thought so," Mrs. Moore said. "But they dismissed my worries about Thea. Told me she was just acting like a teenager. Her best friend had just been stabbed to death and what did I expect? They said she'd be back home in a few days. They were wrong about that. As it turned out, Thea had an alibi. I found out later she'd been with two of the other cheerleaders at the fair during the night in question. A lot of people had seen her. She was wearing a bright pink top. Very memorable."

I shut my eyes as a memory flooded my thoughts. I'd seen Thea on the fairgrounds from the top of the Ferris wheel. She'd had on white jeans and a pink top. Her hair had been pulled back into a ponytail. "Mrs. Moore, did it ever occur to you that Thea might have been asked to leave town? That maybe she knew something about the murderer and they made a deal with her?"

"Or maybe she left on her own because she was scared," Cole said. "Either way, there was a reason."

"Because she'd been with the same man?" Mrs. Moore asked. "The same one who killed Beth?"

"That's right," Cole said.

"Did Thea ever mention anything about Thom Richards?" I asked.

Mrs. Moore visibly flinched. "Why do you ask about him?"

"We have a hunch that the man Beth referred to as Z might be him." I spoke slowly as if that would help the message be less harsh. "It's possible he killed Beth because she was pregnant. In her last journal entry, she says she's going to tell my parents the truth. After she tells Z."

Mrs. Moore's face had whitened to the color of bread dough rising in a bowl. "You think Z is Thom Richards?"

"We don't know for sure, but there's a strong possibility." I explained as much as we knew, including our theory about the man Beth referred to Z as someone she would have had to have close proximity to, like a teacher.

"Do you know who he's related to?" Mrs. Moore asked.

"We do. They had the power to make all of it disappear for their nephew." I hugged my purse to my chest.

"Are you saying you think Thom Richards killed your sister and Thea?" Mrs. Moore's old eyes seemed to leak tears. "And his uncles covered it up?"

"That's exactly what we're saying," I said.

"This whole town knew the cops were dirty," Mrs. Moore

said. "Payoffs and the like. They even got confessions from inno-cent men."

I turned back the reel of time, seeing the three men who had questioned me in the days following Beth's death. Ford, much younger, his cheeks still rosy from youth and without the mustache. Sheriff Lancaster's bald head had shone under the lights, beads of perspiration evident on his forehead. Detective Wright was the younger of the two but still seemed old to me. He wore a cheap polyester suit the color of Silly Putty. His brown hair was cut into the mullet style, so popular with the high school boys. That style had seemed odd on him, especially because his hair had thinned on top. Only Ford had been young and kind. The room had been hot, and he'd brought me a cola.

Time and time again, they'd come back to the Paisley boys. Around in a circle like the Ferris wheel, trying to trap me into saying something that contradicted what I'd already said.

"Deep ties ran through this town. They protected their own," I said, thinking out loud.

"But we're about to put a stop to that," Cole said. "Mrs. Moore, I hope that will bring you some comfort."

"Is there anything else you can think of?" I asked.

"The night before she died, she came home late," Mrs. Moore said. "I asked her where she'd been and she wouldn't say and told me to mind own business. We got into a fight. I thought she'd gone to see some man, and I shamed her for it. Now I feel pretty sure she must have gone out to confront whoever it was who killed her."

"The next day she was killed," I said. "It has to be connected to wherever she went that night."

"To who she went to that night," Cole said.

Mrs. Moore pressed a tissue to her mouth. "All my life I've had to take scraps and act like I was grateful when the Lancasters and Richardses pranced around this town. If Richards did this, I want to know. I have to know. And I want him punished."

Cole jerked to his feet. "I just thought of something. Mrs. Moore, do you have Thea's cell phone? Maybe she has one of those tracker things where you can tell where people were."

"Sheriff Ford already took it," Mrs. Moore said. "He said it was evidence or something."

Ford already had the phone. They would have examined everything already. If they had anything on Richards, he would have already seen it. Texts, calls, and wherever she went in the days before her death would all be on there. He obviously hadn't found anything or he would have told us. Once again we were without any leads.

"You think it was Richards?" Ford asked as he sank into his office chair. "Are you kidding me?"

"We could be wrong." I instinctively put my hand on Cole's knee. We were sitting side by side, and I suddenly felt as if we were in the principal's office. "But we wanted to tell you what we thought of and how it all fits together."

"A cover-up?" Ford asked. "It seems completely implausible to me. No one has that much power."

"They might have thirty years ago," Cole said. "It would explain why they wanted to pin it on Luke."

"Listen, guys, I understand where you're coming from, but we don't have a trace of evidence. Hell, we don't even know if he was the married man Beth talked about in her journal. We can't just implode a guy's life because you two have a hunch."

"Can't you bring him in?" I asked. "At least question him."

"On what grounds?" Ford asked. "Anyway, I think you guys are mistaken about this. I was friends with his wife, Sharon, back in the day. We went to high school together in Boise. Those two were madly in love. Richards isn't our guy."

"You were friends with Sharon?" I asked. This development

210

had me reeling. Did this mean he would never be able to accuse Richards? He'd be blind to his guilt perhaps? Or—and this thought made me sweat—had he helped the rest of them cover it up and was merely putting up with my questions to keep himself out of trouble? How deep did this go? Had they involved Ford?

I exchanged a look with Cole. I could tell by his heightened color that he was wondering the same thing I was. Had we been misled by Ford all along?

I studied Ford, trying to see some crack in his conviction. Did he simply not want to interfere in Richards's life and turn out to be wrong? But his expression was as open as always, looking back at me with the same compassionate eyes I remembered from thirty years ago.

"I want to solve this as much as you two," Ford said. "But I can't just go around accusing people. Especially not ones who have as much to lose as he does."

As much to lose. That was exactly why we thought it was him. A teacher with the ambition to become governor and maybe even president someday doesn't pair well with a pregnant teenager.

We'd just arrived back at Cole's when his phone buzzed. He looked at the screen and then back at me. "You won't believe who's at my gate." Before I could guess, he said, "Sharon Richards."

"Sharon Richards is here." What was she doing? Had she noticed me poking around town and gotten worried I was going to figure it out? Did she even know I was here? Or was she here to talk to Cole?

"Should I let her through?" Cole asked.

"I think we have to," I said. "But we better make sure we've got one of our phones on record the entire time."

He gave me a worried look before punching the code into the app on his phone.

"Do you think she knows anything? Like has she been protecting him all these years?" I asked after he put his phone back in his pocket.

"No idea," he said. "But I have a feeling we might be about to find out."

A few minutes later, Sharon Richards was sitting on Cole's couch. She wore an impeccable summer suit in light gray with a pink silk blouse. Her perfectly made-up blue eyes were fixed on me. Apparently, she wasn't one who needed to blink much.

"What can we do for you, Mrs. Richards?" Cole asked.

"Please, call me Sharon. I apologize for barging in on you like this. But I saw you at the fundraiser and wanted to thank you for coming in your mother's place. She's been extremely generous with her time and talents."

"It was our pleasure," I said. "My mother thinks the world of your husband."

"How kind of you to say." Sharon peered at me. "Did you have glasses when you were younger?"

"Unfortunately, yes." I tucked my hair behind my ears, a habit I had when I was nervous. "I have contacts now."

"You look wonderful," Sharon said. "Loretta must be very proud of you."

"Thanks, she is."

Sharon turned toward Cole. "And you had a twin. Isn't that right? He was always in trouble? I recall my husband complaining about him missing practice because he was in detention."

"That's right. Drew was the unruly one of the three of us. Luke and I were more the walk-the-line types."

"The football team was never the same after we lost the three Paisley boys," Sharon said.

Cole studied his hands.

"What a terrible time that was for our town," Sharon said. "Your poor families. I couldn't imagine how tough that must have been. Thom was beside himself, losing one of his favorite students and watching your family be run out of town. All of that mess was one of the reasons we ended up leaving a few years later. He's such a sensitive man. The whole thing didn't sit well with him."

"In what way?" I asked.

"He's a man who believes in justice," Sharon said. "It disturbed him to see his uncle bumble the investigation and then there was that ridiculous article in the paper. He didn't speak to either of them for years."

Was that true? I studied Sharon Richards as carefully as I could without being obvious. She was either a really good actress or she was telling the truth as she knew it.

"Your brother and Carlie here were Luke's alibi," Sharon said.

I twitched, shocked, and crossed one leg over the other. "That's right."

"I always thought that was awfully convenient," Sharon said.

"Convenient?" Cole asked. "What's that mean?"

"The clerk saw all three of the boys, as did several customers," I said. "Convenience has nothing to do with it." Why did we have to defend Luke to this woman? He was innocent then, and he was innocent thirty years later.

"Yes, of course," Sharon said. "I simply meant it was good or they'd have convicted Luke. It's almost always the boyfriend in cases like this. Between you and me, my uncle-in-law wasn't the brightest man who ever served as sheriff. I never thought they looked carefully enough for Beth's killer."

"It's too late now," I said. "My mom and I just want to move on. We'll never know what really happened to her, and we have to learn to live with it."

"Your sweet mom. How I feel for her. If there's anything that ever comes up about the case, don't hesitate to contact Thom. If and when he's governor, he'll have the power to look into the case again if he feels like there's new evidence."

"What new evidence would there be?" I asked.

"I've no idea. This psychic you're working with, does she have any ideas?"

Instincts kicked that made me say, "No, she's a fraud. She gave us nothing."

"I'm so sorry to hear that. I really hoped she could help. I've heard of it before. On television anyway."

"Yeah, wasn't the case here," Cole said, following my lead.

"I've come to ask you a favor," Sharon said. "I'm having a small dinner party while we're here and wondered if you two would like to join us."

Cole and I exchanged a look. Why would this woman want us at a dinner party unless she wanted to do us harm? I had visions of every horror film I'd ever seen. Cole and I would go into the house and never come out.

"Why us?" I asked, not caring if I sounded rude or blunt.

She studied me for a moment. "I thought it might be a kick in the pants for my husband to spend a little leisure time with some of his old students. Seeing successful adults from the ramshackle children he once knew cheers him to no end. The campaign trail's been arduous. He often needs a reminder about why he's doing what he's doing."

Ramshackle? Is that how she'd seen us?

"That would be lovely," I said.

"Wonderful. I've invited Sheriff Ford as well. You're friendly with him lately, are you not?"

A jolt hit my chest as if someone had punched me. Was that a threat to him or us? What was she doing? Did she want us all out there to charm us into silence? Did she know what we suspected? My head was swimming.

"The sheriff's not a friend," I said. "I've been by to see him about my sister's cold case."

"But nothing new?" Sharon asked. "What a shame. Be sure and give your mother my best."

"How do you know Sheriff Ford, Sharon?" Cole asked.

A satisfied smile, like that of a fat cat, curved her mouth upward. "We go way back. In fact, we went to high school together in Boise. By coincidence, we all ended up here in Logan Bend in the late eighties."

"He was there the night they brought us all in for questioning," I said.

There was only one way to get to the bottom of this. We had to go to that dinner party. I had to get Richards to confess. If it was the last thing I ever did, I'd get him to tell me what really happened that night. Somehow.

2 2

COLE

"A re you sure this is a good idea?" I asked Carlie as we came to a stop in the circular driveway of the Richardses' enormous house. Perched above the valley of Logan Bend, the home was built in a clearing on the mountain. Stucco exterior and precision landscaping.

"This is where they live only part of the time?"

"I've never been up here before. It's well hidden from below."

The house was built in a Mediterranean style with a grand design of sweeping staircases and forty-foot ceilings, expensive furnishings, and shiny wood floors covered with oriental rugs. We were greeted by a maid in a black uniform and white apron and followed her across the marble foyer and into a formal living room. Ford had already arrived and stood in front of a large window with Sharon.

Thom Richards was seated talking to an attractive woman with sleek black hair and dark eyes. Ford's wife, I assumed. He rose to greet us as we approached, shaking both our hands with a politician's vigor. Ford and Mrs. Richards joined us.

Ford slapped me on the back and squeezed Carlie's shoulder, then introduced us to his wife.

"It's a pleasure to meet you," Mrs. Ford said. "Call me Lily, please."

"Nice to meet you too," I said.

We'd debated at length about how to handle tonight and had finally agreed to see how things went. If the opportunity arose, we'd decided to bluff our way into a confession. Carlie was prepared to say she'd heard from some of the other women that Richards had taken advantage of in phone calls and emails. This wasn't true, of course, but he wouldn't know that.

The maid served flutes of champagne and we all sat around an ornate square coffee table. I made sure to sit close to Carlie. I didn't want her out of my sight tonight. This might look like a friendly dinner party, but I suspected there were enough dirty secrets in this room to bury us all alive.

"Nice to see you somewhere other than my office," Ford said to Carlie and me.

"You too, man." As I looked over at his earnest face, I questioned myself again. Was Ford part of the deception? If so, how far into the mud had he gone with these two?

"Tell me, Carlie, how's your mother feeling?" Richards asked.

Right. Her mother was supposed to be sick. Would Carlie remember the ruse?

"Much better. We think it was a touch of food poisoning," Carlie said without missing a beat.

"Please give her our best," Sharon said. "I sent a get-well basket over to her earlier today with soup from that wonderful deli in town and some French bread."

"That was thoughtful of you," Carlie said. "She'll enjoy not having to cook."

"I saw a gentleman picking her up the other day from campaign headquarters," Richards said, eyes twinkling. "Does your mother have a boyfriend?"

"Yes. His name's Joseph Marley. They're pretty serious." Carlie smiled over at me. "Love's in the air here in Logan Bend."

"My husband tells me you two dated in high school," Lily said.

"That's right," Carlie said. "But we were torn apart by fate." She said the last part in a theatrical voice. As if it weren't actually true. Probably orchestrated by the very people in this room.

"What do you mean?" Lily asked.

"Cole had to move away when we were sixteen," Carlie said. "After his brother Luke was falsely accused of murder."

"I remember, yes." Lily looked at Carlie, then me. "The gossipmongers were strong back then."

"We didn't think so," Carlie said. "Until my sister's murder, I always thought Logan Bend was a close-knit community. But after what they did, I could see that perception was false."

"It never made any sense why the paper ran that story," Lily said. "Thom, it was your uncle who owned the paper, right?" Lily asked.

"Yes, he did. As a matter of fact," Richards said, "we had a falling-out over it. One that lasted for years."

"He wrote the article," Sharon said. "We were both deeply troubled by it. Logan Bend was a different place back then."

"It was all too easy to assume the boyfriend did it, I suppose?" Lily asked. "People are sheep even in the face of facts."

"We think the boyfriend might have done it, after all," Carlie said. "While cleaning out my mother's house, I found Beth's journal. She had another boyfriend. A married one. An older, married boyfriend."

"No, really?" Lily's eyes gleamed with interest. "Honey, have you finally got a lead on the case?"

"No, it's been a bust," Ford said. "She doesn't say who it is."

"Yes. We're no closer than we've ever been." Carlie paused, possibly for dramatic effect. My girl could think on her feet. "But we know she was pregnant."

"What? That's new information, isn't it?" Richards asked. I

had to give him credit. The man looked merely curious, not guilty.

"She wasn't sleeping with Luke," Carlie said. "So whoever this guy was—had gotten her pregnant and probably killed her to keep her quiet."

I watched Richards. A muscle in his jaw twitched.

"That's awful," Lily said. "Do you think you'll ever know who did it?"

"Your husband says no," Carlie said. "But I still have hope. I have to."

"Listen, babe, they don't want to talk about this stuff." Ford plucked at the collar of his shirt as if the room were too warm, when in fact the air conditioner made it too cold. "Anyway, the details of the investigation are confidential." He turned to Carlie and me. "My wife was trained as a reporter. I'm afraid her curiosity is getting the better of her."

"You're right. I'm sorry," Lily said. "I had my reporter hat on there for a minute. I'm like a cat, much too curious. It must be terrible not to know. Your poor mother."

"It's been hard on her. My father went to his deathbed not knowing what really happened to his girl," Carlie said. "The carnage that's left behind has been hard on two families. But don't apologize for being interested. I like to tell Beth's story to as many people as will listen."

"But again, we need to keep our investigation quiet," Ford said. "It's not appropriate to talk about at a dinner party."

"Why?" I asked. As if I didn't know.

"We don't want anything leaking to the real press," Ford said. "God forbid another innocent man has his reputation ruined because of speculation. As much as the three of us want this solved, we've got as little to go on as we ever have." He shot Carlie a sympathetic look. "I'm sorry to say."

Lily turned to me. "What happened after your family left town?"

I summarized the turn of events for the Paisley clan, making sure to tell them Luke had become a doctor. "So all in all, we're all fine."

"That's a relief," Lily said.

The housekeeper came in then to announce that dinner was now ready, cutting off any further discussion that might lead us to evidence that we were correct about Richards. My questions remained unanswered. I didn't know if Sharon Richards knew about the affairs, but my instinct was telling me she didn't. She seemed like the devoted, content wife of a powerful man. Her invitation might have been purely innocent. As far as Richards went, I thought I'd detected an uneasiness when Carlie had spoken about Beth but I couldn't be certain. Ford, on the other hand, was acting jumpy and definitely had tried to steer the conversation away from Beth's murder. Had he been hiding the truth all these years? Hiding the truth to save his friend? If so, what had he gotten out of it?

"What are you two up to?" Ford asked through gritted teeth.

He and Carlie and I were all out on the back patio, having a brief moment alone. The other women had gone down to look at the roses and Richards had said he needed to make a quick call, leaving us alone with Ford.

"We accepted a dinner party invitation," Carlie said. "How could we say no when we found out how far back you three go?"

"Jesus, Carlie." Ford spat out the words. For the first time, I saw a hint of temper and darkness. "I already told you this is ridiculous. Thom is the finest man I've ever known. You're stirring up trouble for no reason."

"No reason? I'd say two dead bodies justify a reason," Carlie said. "Why are you so protective of them? Were you in on it?"

"In on what?" Ford asked.

"The cover-up. Along with Richards's uncles," I said. "Did you cover it up to protect your golden boy?"

"Are you kidding me?" Ford drew closer to me. "You have no idea what you're talking about. This psychic you're talking to has your head filled with nonsense."

Carlie was shaking her head. "To think I thought you were a good guy. On our side. You're one of them."

"Hold on now." Ford turned to her, the back of his neck as red as a fire engine. "I'm not on their side or anyone's side but the law."

"Then why won't you look into him?" I asked. "You have to admit that between the paper, the town's doctor, and a sheriff, they could certainly pull off protecting their nephew from going to jail."

The door to the kitchen swung open and Richards walked out. "What's going on out here? Do we need another drink?"

Out of the corner of my eye, I saw the ladies coming up the stairs. Inside, the staff scurried around the kitchen cleaning up the dishes from dinner. As the ladies reached the top, Carlie lunged toward Richards. "I know you did it. You were sleeping with my sister and Thea and you killed them both."

Richards staggered backward as if Carlie had shoved him. "What are you talking about? That's ludicrous."

Carlie's voice rose in decibel and pitch. "I know you were sleeping with Beth the spring and summer she died. She was pregnant with your child. You, you stabbed her to death, you son of a bitch. If it's the last thing I do, I'll prove it."

"Thom," Sharon said. "What's she talking about?"

Sheriff Ford held up a hand, much like a traffic cop, and spoke in a dismissive tone. "These two amateur sleuths have been listening to a lunatic psychic and are imagining things that aren't true. We should all call it a night."

"A psychic told you Thom was sleeping with your sister?" Sharon asked Carlie.

"That's right," Carlie said. "Did you know, Sharon? It wasn't just Beth, either. There were others. We've talked to them. We know."

If I hadn't known she was bluffing, I would have believed her.

"Thea was one of them, wasn't she?" Carlie asked. "And you killed her for it. Just like you killed my sister."

"You're insane," Richards said, exploding. "This is outrageous. I didn't kill anyone."

"My husband doesn't have affairs," Sharon said. "Especially not with underage girls. His life is about service to others."

"These were high school girls he slept with when he was a teacher. God only knows how many more there are from later years. We only know about the ones from here. I'm not sure how many there were total." Carlie pulled out her phone and spat out another bluff like a professional. "But two of them answered my email and another two emailed me. And there was Thea. We have proof of that too. My sister saw her at your house. It's in the journal. When she came to you and said she was going public, you had her killed."

"You're lying," Richards said. "I didn't even remember Thea."

"No, this can't be true." Sharon turned to her husband, her eyes pleading with him to tell her we were wrong. "Thom, please, say something."

"Who are they?" Richards asked. "I want their names. They probably want money. That's all this is. They're taking advantage of my wealth and know I'm vulnerable because of the governor race."

I stepped closer to Richards, hoping my bulk would intimidate him. "No, they're telling the truth and are prepared to testify in court." If Carlie could bluff, so could I. "None of them came forward back when Beth was murdered because they were embarrassed and scared. We know you killed her because she was pregnant and threatening to go to her parents with the truth. It's all in the journal entries."

Richards shook his head vigorously. "No, I never knew about a baby. She never told me. The night she was killed, we were supposed to meet but she didn't show."

"Oh my God." Sharon collapsed against Lily, almost knocking the small woman over. "Did you kill Beth?"

Richards looked from one of the women to the other, his face ashen. "No, I didn't kill Beth. Yes, we were sleeping together. But as God is my witness, I would never have killed her. I loved her. I didn't care who knew it, either. She was all I ever wanted. There were no other girls. I don't know what you're doing, but there was no one but Beth."

Sharon let out a wail. "Love? You loved her? You pervert. She was a child."

"I was twenty-two," Richards said. "Later on in life, a five-year age gap wouldn't have made any difference. I know it's no excuse, but I fell for her. I didn't want to. Sharon, truly, I didn't mean for it to happen. There was simply something about us together that defied all logic. I couldn't stay away from her. She couldn't stay away from me. I'm sorry. I am." He turned to Carlie. "But I would never have hurt her. If she'd come to me, I would've taken her away somewhere new so we could start fresh. When she turned eighteen, we could have married and had the child even without your parents' permission. Eventually, your parents would have had to accept it."

"What about me?" Sharon's voice was cold and eerily quiet as she separated from Lily to move closer to her husband. "How were you going to explain this ill-fated love affair to your young wife who was trying desperately to have a child?"

"I didn't have a plan," Richards said. "I didn't know what to do. I was stuck."

"Stuck with me?" Sharon asked.

"Yes," Richards whispered. "Stuck in a marriage that I never wanted in the first place. You know it was my mother who arranged it all and forced me into marrying you or be cut off."

"How dare you," Sharon said. "After everything I've done for you."

"What about all the other girls?" Carlie asked. "Did you love them too?"

"What? No, there were no others," Richards said. "Just Beth. I don't know who these women are, but they're lying. I swear on my father's grave."

"Beth saw you and Thea together." Carlie's voice shook as she pulled the papers from the journal and shook them in the air. "August 26, 1989. She saw Thea's bike in your backyard. You had her in there with you."

"It wasn't me," Richards said. "There's no way it was me. I wasn't even in town that day. I had to leave town unexpectedly that morning because my father had a heart attack. I didn't have a chance to tell Beth I was leaving town, so she didn't know. My dad died just after I got there. The hospital records would show that I'm the one who signed his death certificate. We buried him a few days later. There were a hundred witnesses. All members of his church. You can check the obituary in the Boise paper along with the date of the funeral. Sharon, tell them."

"You expect my help now?" Mrs. Richards asked. "I don't think so."

Lily had gone rigid, her gaze fixed on Ford. "I remember that weekend. Sharon and Thom asked us to stay at their house and look after their new puppy. We spent four days there while they were in Boise taking care of funeral arrangements and all that. It was a Saturday. The afternoon of my sister's bridal shower. I was at my mother's house all day helping her with the preparations. You were at the house alone taking care of the puppy. It was you with Thea." She covered her face with her hands. "How could you? A man of the law?"

My limbs tingled. Ford was at the Richards house that weekend? He'd been sleeping with Thea? Moonstone had said it was a prominent member in town but hadn't gotten Richards's name directly. What she'd really gotten was Ford. They were scared to come forward because they were sleeping with a sheriff's deputy. Now, a sheriff.

"It was you?" Carlie asked. "You with all those girls?"

Ford hung his head. "Yes, it was me. Thea and a few others. It was nothing but a young man making bad decisions. Logan Bend was a really small town back then, and the deputy was appealing to the ladies. Lily, they meant nothing to me."

My stomach churned. How could it be? The man was unrecognizable to me now. How had we thought of him as good and righteous? He'd been lying to us the entire time.

"Nothing to you? How many? How long?" Lily was now clinging to Mrs. Richards. They both looked as if buckets of water had just been thrown in their face.

"It was all a long time ago," Ford said.

"But we were married," Lily said. "And you were sleeping with high school girls. Children."

"They threw themselves at me," Ford said.

"Did you kill Beth?" Richards lunged at Ford and grabbed him by the collar.

"God, that's rich." Ford wrapped his hands around Richards's shoulders in an attempt to get away. "Trying to pin it on me when everyone and God knows it was you."

Richards tightened his grip and thrust Ford against the wall. "Why? Why would you do it? She was just an innocent girl."

"Jesus, Thom, we all knew you did it." Ford shoved into his chest, knocking Richards backward. "This is just like you to try to make the whole thing seem like my fault. Isn't that how we always did it? You were the golden boy and Sharon and I cleaned up all your messes?"

"What are you talking about? Cleaned up my messes?" Richards looked over at Sharon. "What does he mean?"

"You know perfectly well what he means." Her eyes glittered. "You killed Beth. I knew it at the time. I knew everything."

"We all knew it was you," Ford said. "We both knew you'd been sleeping with Beth and the moment I heard she was dead, I knew as sure as I knew my own name that you'd done it. You threw a tantrum and killed her because she wouldn't give you your way. Your uncles and your mother and Sharon—we covered it up for you. To save your reputation and your political aspirations."

"You covered what up?" Richards asked. "There was nothing *to* cover up. I'd been prepared to tell her I was ready to leave town if that's what she wanted. Now or later. Whatever she wanted. I was through with all of it. The pressure from my family and my wife. All I ever wanted was a simple life. I didn't care about any of that. Honestly, I wanted to be left alone with Beth." His jaw clicked as he jerked his head around to look at his wife. "Wait a minute. Sharon, you knew about Beth and me?"

"Of course I did." Sharon bit out the words. "I'm the brains of this marriage. Don't you know that by now? We covered it up to save you from prison."

"I didn't kill her. I loved her more than I'd ever loved anyone or anything. I didn't know she was pregnant until tonight." Richards said this quietly and with such grief in his voice I almost pitied him. Tears filled his eyes as he raked a hand through his hair. "Oh God, Sharon. You weren't home when I called the house the night she was killed. Sharon, no. You didn't. You couldn't have? Please tell me you didn't kill her."

"This little act won't work any longer, dear," Sharon said. "Soon enough, everyone will know the truth about who you really are. A rapist and murderer."

"You killed her. Oh my God." Richards stared at her as if he were seeing a monster for the first time. "Where were you all those hours? Were you cleaning up at my mother's? Ridding yourself of Beth's blood? My God, you stabbed her seventeen times. What kind of sicko does that to an innocent girl?" He placed his fist against his mouth as a look of horror took the place of confusion. "Why did you have to do it? If you wanted a career in politics, you could have just run yourself. You didn't have to kill the woman I loved."

"You've lost your mind or you're one heck of a gaslighter," Sharon said as she turned to Carlie and me. "Can't you see what he's doing?"

"Sharon, how did you know my sister was pregnant?" Carlie asked.

"Nothing in this town happened without me or my mother-in-law knowing it," Sharon said.

"My mother? What did she know?" Richards asked.

"She knew everything," Sharon said. "In fact, she's the one who came to me after she saw that little idiot buying a pregnancy test. By then, we already knew about your secret hiding spot that wasn't so secret. You never understood that the two most important women in your life were much smarter than you. If you'd followed directions, none of this would've happened."

"Directions?" Richards asked. "Was it in my mother's directions to kill Beth?"

Mrs. Richards shook her finger at him. "Just stop all this nonsense and tell the truth. I'm not big enough to hurt anyone with an ice pick."

Carlie rose to her full height. "How did you know it was an ice pick? That was never released to the public."

Sharon's face transformed into a hundred contorted shapes. She stepped backward, holding her arms out in front of her as if she were being attacked. "That fact was released. I read about it. You're wrong."

"No, it wasn't," Carlie said. "I know every detail. Real-life nightmares are like that. You killed my sister out of jealousy. You'd discovered the affair and that she was pregnant. Beth was going to have a baby. Something you could never give him."

"You have quite the imagination," Sharon said, having returned to her usual composure. "It wasn't me." She looked over at her husband. "Your mother killed her. She couldn't stand the thought of that little girl ruining everything."

"My mother?" Richards asked. "But...how?"

"She's strong as an ox. Always has been," Sharon said.

"Did she kill Thea too?" Carlie asked. "Because she knew?"

How could Shelley Lancaster have shot a gun so precisely from the church that it hit Thea in the exact right spot to kill her instantly? Like a sudden spark from a match, the truth came to me. The two murders didn't have anything to do with each other. She'd been killed by a professional, a sharpshooter. Ford had been trained to shoot for his work. He'd shot Thea.

"No, it was Ford," I said. "Wasn't it? You killed the girl you raped to keep her quiet. She threatened to dismantle your whole life."

Lily gasped, then whispered, "Please, Don, tell me it's not true."

"No one can prove it," Ford said. "All these girls—it was consensual. They came to me."

Carlie gasped. "Oh my God, you were the sharpshooter who killed Thea. Trained to protect, not to kill. I trusted you."

"She was just a junkie slut." Ford's voice had turned nasty and sharp. "How dare she come to me and threaten to expose me? I'm Sheriff Ford."

"You killed her to keep her quiet," Carlie said.

"No one will miss her like they will me," Ford said. "This town needs me."

"Her mother cares, you son of a bitch," I said.

"Don, how many were there?" Lily asked.

"It doesn't matter," Ford said.

"What about the girls? Why, Don?" Tears streamed from Richards's eyes. "Just to keep up with me? You knew about Beth and me and just had to have one of your own?"

"Shut up, you fat face," Ford said. "Not everything's about you, okay? I saw an opportunity and I took it. Those girls were all over me. They loved a man in uniform, what can I say? How could I resist them?"

"How many?" Lily asked again.

Ford shrugged. "I don't know. More than a half dozen

maybe. Over a few years' time. What does it matter? The statute of limitations is up anyway."

"I should kill you." Lily reached under the back of her shirt. Did she have a gun? "And rid the world of a parasite."

Ford reached inside his jacket pocket. For his gun, I realized. Before I knew what was happening, a gunshot rang out. Ford fell to the floor screaming and clutching his left thigh. "She shot me. My own wife shot me."

Lily had a small revolver pointed at Ford. "I'll shoot you again if I have to. Reach into your coat and toss us your gun. Nice and steady. You know what kind of shot I am."

Ford did as she asked. I stooped to pick the revolver up from the ground. Out of the corner of my eye, I saw the housekeeper pop up over the kitchen sink, as if she'd hit the floor at the sound of the bullet firing. "Cole, do you know how to use that thing?" Lily's voice was surprisingly steady.

"Yep." A lie, but no one needed to know that.

"Keep it on Don. If he makes a move, shoot him." Lily turned her gun toward Sharon, who seemed frozen. "Stay where you are or I'll shoot you too."

"Lily, don't be silly." Sharon put up her hands and moved slowly toward Lily. "It was my mother-in-law. Not me."

"Back up," Lily said. "Or I shoot."

Sharon walked backward to the edge of the patio. At this point, we all knew the kind of shot Lily was. "Carlie, tell the housekeeper to call 911. We need an ambulance and the police."

"I am the police," Ford yelled, holding on to his leg, which was now spilling blood all over the floorboards of the patio.

"Not anymore you're not." I pointed the revolver at him. "And Carlie, tell them to send a car to Shelley Lancaster's."

Carlie slipped her phone into my pocket. Knowing she must have hit record at some point, I simply nodded. They would use the phone inside the house to call for help.

Sharon lurched toward the stairs. Richards grabbed her and twisted her arms behind her back. "Not so fast."

He pressed his body against her and yanked his tie off with one hand. "Cole, tie her up."

"Get off me." Sharon struggled but she was no match for her tall, athletic husband.

"You're going to tell the police everything you know."

I did as he asked, tying her up with my best Boy Scout hand-cuff knot.

Carlie returned to the patio. "They're on their way."

"You'll be sorry for this," Sharon said. "All of you. We could have just left well enough alone."

"Your mother looks my mother in the eye every day on the golf course. One mother to another. How could she take away someone's child and look her in the face?"

"She was stabbed seventeen times," Lily said. "Your mother-in-law must've been very angry.

"Once for every time the little slut gave it to my husband. Shelley made sure they hurt, too." She glared at Carlie with cold, dead eyes. "I'd like to tell you she didn't suffer, but that wouldn't be true."

"Or was it you, Sharon?" Lily asked. "You killed your husband's lover, didn't you? Tell the truth for the first time in your life."

"Shut up," Sharon snapped. "I already told you who did it."

"Give me the gun," Carlie said to me.

Frightened by the look in her eyes and against my better judgment, I handed it to her. "Carlie, stay cool," I whispered.

Carlie crossed over to Sharon and pressed the barrel of the revolver against her chest. "You're a vile human being. I'd kill you but I don't want to go to jail. I have no interest in being your roommate. Because I'm positive you're going to be locked up for being a conspirator to murder for a very long time. After that, the devil will welcome you downstairs for all eternity. I'd like to say it won't hurt but I'd be lying. Or is Lily right and you did it and are now trying to pin it on your mother-in-law? I want the truth. Did you kill my sister?"

Sharon yelped as Carlie pushed the barrel of the revolver harder into her chest. "Shelley did it. For you, Thom. So you could have the life you were supposed to have. It was all her."

"You just helped her clean up afterward?" Richards said. "And then tried to pin it on a kid?"

"As if you have any moral grounds to judge me," Sharon said.

"You're going to pay for what you did," Richards said.

"It's what you did, dear," Sharon said. "You did this by screwing a teenage girl."

"You're going to jail," Carlie said to her. "If it's the last thing I ever do."

"They'll have to prove it first," Sharon said.

"You couldn't let her get away with sleeping with your husband, could you?" Lily asked. "She had to pay for what she'd done. Or did you really have someone else do your dirty work? Were you too chicken to do it?"

"Of course not," Sharon snapped. "All I needed Shelley for was to hold her down. Stabbing was the easy part. She was such a stupid little bitch. Never saw us coming. And I loved every second of it." Sharon glared at Carlie. "I'd do it again."

"You're going to rot in a jail cell." Carlie gave her one more shove before handing the gun back to me.

"As for you, the statute of limitations may have run out on raping minors, but you're going to pay for killing Thea Moore. You know how they feel about cops in prison." Lily kicked her husband in the spot of his gunshot wound, causing him to howl in pain.

"You did it together?" Richards had collapsed to the floor of the patio. "My wife and my mother murdered the woman I loved."

"She was a girl," Carlie said. "No matter how you've twisted it in your mind, Richards, she was seventeen and your student and you seduced her."

"It was love," he whispered.

"I never thought I'd say this, but I almost feel sorry for you," Carlie said. "Even though Sharon's right. Your actions got a beautiful girl killed by two psychopaths. You're pathetic."

"I know. And I'm sorry," Richards said. "But I did love her. I know it was wrong, but I cherished her."

"Stop, please," Carlie said. "I don't want to hear one more thing from you about my sister."

"My life's over. It was the moment she died. I might as well be dead too." With that, he lunged toward Lily and yanked the gun from her hand. Then he put it to his head and pulled the trigger.

Carlie and Lily screamed as Richards fell to the floor. I went to my knees but there was no need. Richards was dead.

And then the sound of sirens came from the road below us. The sound of justice.

23

CARLIE

Cole and I spent the rest of the night answering questions from Ford's deputies. We told them everything we knew, including handing over the journal and the recordings from Carlie's phone. Because Idaho was a one-party state and I was there and aware of the recording, they were admissible. I felt confident that both women were going to jail for a very long time.

The hour neared midnight by the time we stumbled inside to two very anxious animals. I worried that poor Duke would have had an accident but darned if that silly dog hadn't used the litter box.

Exhausted and utterly emotionally spent, we fell into bed and slept until the next morning, when I awoke to a call from my mother. Apparently, the story had been in the morning paper. I silently cursed, angry at myself. I should have gone home last night and told her everything so that she didn't have to read it in the paper.

She was crying so hard I could barely make out the words. "Is it true? Richards? Sharon? Shelley Lancaster?"

"Yes, Mom."

"Sharon and Shelley confessed," Mom said. "And Richards is

dead." More sobbing from the other end of the phone. "It's over. She can finally rest in peace."

"I know." I started to cry, remembering all over again what Sharon had said about how Beth had suffered at the end. I wouldn't tell my mother.

"The paper says Ford claims he's innocent. There will be a trial, I suppose. You'll have to testify."

"It'll be my pleasure. Mom, come out to Cole's. We'll have breakfast."

"Thank you, sweetie, but I need some time alone today."

"All right, whatever you want. I'll call you later, all right?"

"Yes, that would be nice."

Later that afternoon, I called out to my mother as I came in through the kitchen door.

"I'm in here," Mom said.

I walked through the kitchen to the living room. Mom was on the couch. Several photograph albums were open on the coffee table.

"Mom, are you all right?"

"Yes, I'm fine." She wiped under her eyes. "Looking at old photographs. Would you like to join me?"

I sat down next to her.

She pointed at the album labeled "1989." "That's the last photograph your father ever took in June of that year. After that, your father stopped taking pictures. Nothing but blank pages after this. And I was sitting here thinking about how much we wronged you. You were still here. There were proms and events that happened and there are no photographs of any of it. Did you even go to prom?"

"No, but I didn't want to."

"I'm sorry, honey, that we couldn't do better."

I rested my head against her shoulder. She smelled of lilacs.

The scent of my mom. "We all just got through, Mom. You don't have to apologize."

"Joseph wants me to marry him."

I blinked, surprised. "Do you want to?"

"Very much. Are you mad?" Mom asked.

"No, not at all. I want you to be happy. That's all I care about."

"We were such a happy family." Mom brought the open album onto her lap. "Weren't we? Until they took her from us?"

"Yes. We were happy."

"And now everything's different. It was just you and me. Now there's Joseph. He's so insistent that we spend the rest of our time left on earth together."

"Do you love him?" I asked.

"I do. Not the way I loved your dad. Our love formed when we were young and passionate. We raised a family together. With Joseph it's less intense but not in a bad way."

"You're comfortable with him."

"Yes, he's such a good friend to me," Mom said. "We laugh and laugh."

"Is there something besides me that's keeping you from saying yes?"

"I worry that I'll forget what it was like back before Beth was killed. How happy we were. That I was Mrs. Benjamin Webster."

"Mom, just because you love Joseph doesn't take away from the past. You don't have to hold back out of some strange sense of duty to Dad. Or to Beth. And definitely not to me."

"I've been doing that, haven't I?"

"I think so. Moving forward is a good thing. Wasting away in this house out of a sense of duty does not honor Dad or Beth. They want us to live while we can. Later, when we're all together again, none of the trappings of earth will matter. You'll be free of all the pain."

"But what happens in heaven? Whose wife will I be there? And what about Joseph's other wife? It's very confusing."

I chuckled. "I think God has it all worked out. I doubt there are duels in heaven. Right now, enjoy your time with a wonderful man."

"All right, if you say so."

I looked down at a photo of Beth and me in front of the lake. Wearing our matching polka-dot bikinis, we had our arms wrapped around each other and grinned at the camera. My two front teeth were missing. Beth's light hair glistened under the sun. I touched the plastic that covered the photograph. "I miss her so much. There's not a day I don't wish I could pick up the phone and call her to tell her some little thing that happened. Or big thing."

"Me too. Your father and I adored you girls. We adored each other. I used to worry about getting sick and dying and leaving you girls without a mother. If only I'd been able to be the one and not Beth."

The lump in the back of my throat prevented me from answering.

As if she heard my question, she answered, "We carried on. For you. But we were never the same."

"I know, Mom."

"I'm sorry for all the times you probably wished it could be only about your life instead of Beth's death."

"Mom, I knew how much you loved me because you kept going. That was enough. You've been the most wonderful mother to me. I don't want you to worry about that ever again."

"What about you and Cole?"

I smiled. "Cole's my prize at the end of an arduous journey. I plan on basking in every moment."

"You're moving here, really?"

"Really."

"Oh, Carlie, that makes me so happy."

"Cole wants big holiday dinners with all of us. Doesn't that sound fun?"

"As long as I don't have to cook, I'm in."

We laughed and then hugged, holding on to each other as if we'd been parted for many years.

On a warm August morning, I knelt beside our family plot where my father and Beth rested. I placed roses I'd cut from Mom's garden into the vases that hung from the headstones.

These were the last of the roses. Cole and his team had already gutted the home we'd occupied for decades and were about to overhaul the landscaping as well. Soon, the house would be newly renovated and he would sell it to a young family who would make happy memories.

As for Mom and me, we were moving on to the next season of our lives. Mom had already moved in with Joseph. On a whim, they'd flown to Vegas and gotten married just last week. She'd already happily adjusted to living with her new husband in their home near the golf course.

"Hey, Beth, it's me." I brushed dust from the stone and traced my finger over the engraving of her name. *Elizabeth Mary Webster. Beloved daughter and sister.*

"I'm sorry I haven't come around much. I guess I was waiting until I had good news. I finally have some. We know now what happened. The monsters who did this to you are going to jail for the rest of their lives." I paused as tears welled in my eyes. "I can't stop thinking about how scared you must have been at the end, knowing you would have to leave this world. It hurts so much to think of you that way. I hope you thought of us. Of how much we loved you. I hope that was your last thought on this earth."

I sat and drew my knees to my chest and let the tears flow. And then, a great weight lifted from my shoulders. I was light and free. "Beth, are you free now?" I whispered.

A soft breeze as warm as a caress ruffled my hair. That breeze was my Beth, setting *me* free. "You've been free all along, haven't you? It was me and Mom. But we know now what happened and can move forward." I smiled as I brushed the tears from under my eyes. "I miss you every day. But I hear you." The time to live without the burdens of the past was now.

I twisted to look at my dad's grave. "Daddy, I wish you were here to walk me down the right aisle this time." I looked down at the diamond engagement ring sparkling under the sun. There wouldn't be any aisle for this wedding. Cole and I were going down to the courthouse later today to get married, with Joseph and Mom as our witnesses.

"I know you'll be there in spirit. Both of you. Now I have to go get married."

I got to my feet and brushed grass from my jeans, then walked down the path toward the parking lot where Cole was waiting for me.

24

CARLIE

O n the twentieth of December, I yanked open the door to see my beautiful daughter standing on the porch. She wore a thick white jacket and knit hat in a baby blue that matched her eyes.

"Mom." She held out her arms, and I brought her to me.

"Did you have any trouble on the road? I've been pacing." Her small SUV was parked near the garage, muddy from the journey.

"Not at all. It was nice, actually. I listened to music and daydreamed."

"I used to be a first-class dreamer."

"Well, I must have gotten it from you then." She wiped her boots on the mat before coming inside the house.

"Here, let me hang that for you," I said as she shrugged out of her coat.

"Mom, the house looks great."

"This was all Cole." He'd gotten his wish. Christmas was happening and happening big. We'd spent days decorating the house with garland and twinkling lights. "He's like a kid. I had to keep him from buying another box of lights."

Brooke sniffed the air. "It smells like heaven in here. Did you make apple pie?"

"I just took it out of the oven." Our tree was yet to be decorated but was in its stand in the great room. "We waited for you to do the tree."

"You did?" Her face lit up, and for a moment I saw the child she'd once been. My chest ached for a second, remembering how magical she'd made the holidays. But she was here now, I reminded myself. A wonderful grown-up woman. I'd done my job.

"I look forward to doing it with you every year. I guess this one is different, though, isn't it?"

"Yes. How do you feel about that?"

"I'm happy when you're happy."

"I'm happy," I said.

"Plus, I love Cole." When she'd come to visit last September for a week, she and Cole had eased into a comfortable friendship. I knew Cole was holding himself back from acting fatherly. Seeing him with her had made me realize how much he'd wanted a child.

Brooke glanced toward the kitchen. "Where's Cole?"

"He went into town for some supplies. We're supposed to get more snow tonight. I'm relieved you got here when you did."

"I am so excited to be here. You can't imagine how much."

"I think I can," I said. "I've missed you and have been counting the days."

"Me too."

I inspected her closely for any damage since I'd last seen her in September. She looked no worse for wear. Her skin glowed pink from the cold. Her exquisite cheekbones might be a little more prominent. She had on a pair of jeans that seemed a little loose. "You look gorgeous," I said, "if not a little thinner. Are you eating?"

"Yes, Mom. I've been running a lot. That's all." A shy smile crept over her face. "And I have a new special someone in my life."

"You do?"

"I'm in love."

"All right, well, I want to hear everything." I shivered and gestured toward the great room. "It's cold. Let's go sit in front of the fire. I'll put the kettle on." In love? I didn't know if I liked this. She was too young. Her heart might get broken.

"Yes, about that—Steven—that's his name. He's British and loves his tea." She tugged off her hat and held it in front of her like a peace offering. "Mom, here's the thing…he's kind of like driving here right now."

What? Had I heard her correctly? "You invited him for Christmas?"

"We couldn't stand the thought of being apart for two whole weeks. You don't mind, do you?" She clasped her hands together. "I should've asked, but I got carried away last night and told him to just drive out here and join us. Please say it's all right."

"It's all right. I'm just surprised." I smiled to hide my alarm and held out my hand to take her hat. "Give me that. I'll put it with your coat."

We headed toward the kitchen. I set the kettle on the stove. British. What if he had to go back to England and took my little girl with him? "Is he an exchange student?"

"Yes." She sat at the island and seemed to take great interest in the pattern of the granite. "But don't worry. I won't move to England. He loves America."

"But won't he have to go back at the end of the semester?"

"Not if we get married."

Light-headed, I placed both hands on the island. "Married?"

She grinned and tossed her hair behind her shoulders. "Don't worry, Mom. Everything's going to be all right."

Famous last words.

On Christmas Eve, Cole grinned as he looked up from carving the roast. "My mouth's watering. This is cooked perfectly."

I smiled back at him. "For what it cost, it would have been a shame had I overcooked it." I was across the island from him putting the last dab of butter on our mashed potatoes.

"You did good," Joseph said to me. Dressed in an ugly Christmas sweater with penguins on the front, he opened a bottle of wine from the other end of the kitchen. "This is a mighty fine meal if I ever did see one."

"Thanks for bringing the wine, man," Cole said to Joseph.

"Son, it was the least I could do," Joseph said.

I smiled to myself, knowing what a thrill it gave Cole every time Joseph called him son. Over the last six months, they'd grown close. I guess it doesn't matter how old one gets. We always want the approval and love of a parent.

My mother and Brooke were in the dining room putting out the rest of the side dishes. I could hear the murmur of their voices as they discussed where to put what.

Joseph pulled the cork out of a bottle of cabernet, then headed to the dining room. The scent of the rich wine mixed with butter and garlic filled my nose as he passed by me.

Next to me, Steven plucked hot homemade rolls from a baking dish into a basket. I had to admit, the boy was beautiful. Dark-skinned with even features and startling green eyes, he had only to look Brooke's direction to make her smile. I'd never seen her smitten like this, and I wasn't sure if I liked it. My baby was all grown up and probably going to end up in England with this special young man.

He'd told us his father and mother had been an interracial couple who died when he was small. After that, he was shipped off to a grandmother who did her best to raise a spirited little boy in the English countryside. Perhaps sensing my gaze, he glanced over at me. "Am I doing it right, Mrs. Paisley?" The English accent only added to his charm.

Mrs. Paisley. I still did a double take when anyone called me by my new name. Yes, it had taken thirty years before the doodles on my school folder had come true, but here I was at last. Mrs. Paisley. "Looks good to me."

"Again, thanks for letting me stay," he said to Cole and me. "I couldn't face the holidays without my mam."

He'd also shared with us that he'd lost his grandmother last year. "I'm officially an orphan," he'd said that first night at dinner. He'd smiled, but I could see the sadness in his eyes. Like my Cole, he craved family.

"We're glad you're here," Cole said.

"Brooke told me you're worried I'm going to take her back to England," Steven said. "But there's nothing for me there. She's all I want."

"I worry," I said. "That's what mothers do."

"I'm kind of in love with Logan Bend too," Steven said. "We were talking last night about maybe coming to live here after we graduate. If you gave your permission for us to marry, that is."

"You don't need our permission," I said.

"Although it's nice you asked," Cole said. "And if you two want to move here, we've got room right here on the property. We could build you a house."

Steven shook his head. "I can't believe you can make a house. Thank you for your kind offer, but I might need to find my own way. I'm not much for charity."

"Well, you don't have to decide now," I said lightly even as I said a silent prayer. *Please, God, send them here to us.*

"Yes, ma'am," Steven said. The way he said *ma'am* sounded like *mom.* I liked it.

"Let's eat before everything gets cold," Mom said from the doorway. She wore a red dress that flattered her figure.

Her eyes sparkled as Joseph appeared behind her with mistletoe. "Caught you," Joseph said.

She tilted her head for a kiss before pushing him back into the dining room.

We all grabbed a dish and joined the others at the table. Brooke had set the table with twinkling strands of tiny white lights interwoven between candles and sprigs of holly.

Cole and I sat on either end of the rectangular table as Brooke and Mom sat next to their loves.

I fought tears as I looked around the table at the people I loved best. "Who would like to say grace?" I asked.

"If you'd allow me, I'd be honored," Steven said.

I nodded. "By all means."

We all bowed our heads.

"Dear Lord, thank you for this feast," Steven said. "Thank you for my gracious hosts and most of all for Brooke, who makes me very happy. Amen."

I wiped under my eyes as we all echoed his "amen."

"Mom, we should toast," Brooke said as she raised her wineglass. "Last year, it was just you, Grammie, and me, and now we have three more."

"We do," I said. "For which I'm grateful."

"Last year it was just me," Cole said. "And now look at me. I have a family gathered around my table. This was all I ever wanted. Thank you all for being here."

"Same," Joseph said heartily. "A family. What could be better?"

"Joseph, you're too loud," Mom said. "We're all right here."

"I want God and Santa to know how thankful I am," Joseph said, in the same volume.

Mom rolled her eyes, but I could tell she was tickled. Joseph sprinkled fun dust wherever he went.

We all dug into the food, talking and laughing as we enjoyed the bounty of the holiday. After stuffing ourselves, we were just discussing when we should eat Mom's pies when Cole's phone buzzed from the buffet announcing that someone was at the gate.

Cole reached out for his phone to see who would be here on Christmas Eve. "Holy cow. It's my brother. Drew."

"What?" I asked. "Here?"

Cole nodded and punched the code in to let his twin drive through the gate.

"You guys wait here," I said. "We'll go answer the door."

I followed Cole down the hallway to the front. He opened the door and there stood Drew. I hadn't seen him since we were kids, but like his brother, I would have known him anywhere. They still looked remarkably identical, other than Drew was in need of a shave and perhaps a good night's sleep, given his red eyes.

"Drew?" Cole asked. "Am I seeing things?"

"Hey, brother," Drew said as he gave us a lopsided smile.

I shivered from the cold air blowing in from outside. "Come in. It's freezing out there." We stepped back to let him inside.

"Hey, lovebirds," Drew said. "Surprise."

"Drew Paisley," I said. "It's about time."

He pulled me into a hug. "You're gorgeous. I still can't believe you chose this loser over me."

"What are you doing here?" Cole asked as they exchanged a quick embrace. "It's Christmas Eve. Did you drive here from LA?"

"Yeah, sorry I didn't call first, but it was kind of a last-minute decision and I didn't want to give you the chance to say no."

"I'd have never said no." Cole narrowed his eyes. "Are you in some kind of trouble?"

"You could say so," Drew said. "I'm in a bit of a scrape and need a place to crash until things settle down."

"Things?" Cole asked.

"Listen, I didn't know she was married." Drew took off his fleece-lined denim jacket and peered down the hallway. "Nice place, man. Quite an upgrade from our trailer."

"Wait a minute, back up," Cole said. "Married? Who?"

Drew shrugged. "It's a long story that I'll save for tomorrow. I'm starving. You got any grub?"

"Are you in danger?" Cole asked.

"I might be, yeah." Drew winked at me. "But let's put all that aside for now. I want to meet Brooke and see your mom."

"Come on, then," I said. "We've got roast beef and all the fixings."

"I always knew you were the perfect woman," Drew said.

We showed him into the dining room and introduced him to Joseph and Steven. I brought him a clean plate from the kitchen. Brooke pulled another chair to the table. Joseph poured him a glass of wine.

I had a feeling Drew was in more trouble than he let on, but for now, I'd simply enjoy seeing him again. Whatever tomorrow brought, we'd get through it together. That's what families do, after all.

"Did you know your stepdad and I used to wrestle over who would get to marry your mom?" Drew asked Brooke.

"Really?" Brooke's eyes sparkled. "Tell me more stories about when you guys were kids."

"It all started when these two knuckleheads tripped into second grade," I said. "And I fell in love with Cole Paisley."

"You hurt me," Drew said with mock tragedy in his voice.

"I told him he never had a chance," Cole said.

As the night grew nearer and nearer to the time of Santa's arrival, we reminisced about the happy times of our childhood. Many of our stories included my sister. Most of my memories of growing up had Beth in them. She was my sister. My first friend. We'd shared so much. My sister. I caught a glimpse of myself in the window and for a second I imagined it was Beth staring back at me. What would she have been like now? I'd never know. Part of me would always feel the missing part of my heart that was her. Yet she was with me too. I could imagine her at the table smiling at me, maybe telling me she liked my outfit tonight.

My gaze found Cole next. He met mine with a look of concern. No one could ever read me like Cole Paisley.

I nodded to reassure him I was fine. "Just missing Beth," I said.

"Me too," Mom said. "But I'm at peace now. Knowing."

I glanced back at my reflection, and a deep peace came to me then too. *Everything is all right*, Beth whispered in my ear. *Enjoy this sweet world while you can. The best is yet to come.*

I took her advice and went to the kitchen to get the apple pie. Upon my return, Brooke was laughing so hard tears streamed down her face. I stood in the doorway for a moment, taking in the happy faces around our table and the way Cole's curls kissed his collar. A sweet life. My sweet life. Even after all we'd been through, here we were. Together. Loving one another as fiercely as we could, doing our best to make the most of the lives we'd been granted.

The End.

MORE BLUE MOUNTAIN

Have you read the other Blue Mountain novels? Start with Blue Midnight for meet Moonstone for the very first time.

Sign up for newsletter and never miss a release at tess-writes.com. You'll also get a free ebook copy of The Santa Trial.

ALSO BY TESS THOMPSON

CLIFFSIDE BAY

Traded: Brody and Kara

Deleted: Jackson and Maggie

Jaded: Zane and Honor

Marred: Kyle and Violet

Tainted: Lance and Mary

Cliffside Bay Christmas, The Season of Cats and Babies (Cliffside Bay Novella to be read after Tainted)

Missed: Rafael and Lisa

Cliffside Bay Christmas Wedding (Cliffside Bay Novella to be read after Missed)

Healed: Stone and Pepper

Chateau Wedding (Cliffside Bay Novella to be read after Healed)

Scarred: Trey and Autumn

Jilted: Nico and Sophie

Kissed (Cliffside Bay Novella to be read after Jilted)

Departed: David and Sara

Cliffside Bay Bundle, Books 1,2,3

BLUE MOUNTAIN SERIES

Blue Mountain Bundle, Books 1,2,3

Blue Midnight

Blue Moon

Blue Ink

Blue String

EMERSON PASS

The School Mistress of Emerson Pass

The Sugar Queen of Emerson Pass

RIVER VALLEY

Riversong

Riverbend

Riverstar

Riversnow

Riverstorm

Tommy's Wish

River Valley Bundle, Books 1-4

LEGLEY BAY

Caramel and Magnolias

Tea and Primroses

STANDALONES

The Santa Trial

Duet for Three Hands

Miller's Secret

ABOUT THE AUTHOR

Tess Thompson

HOMETOWNS
and HEARTSTRINGS

Tess Thompson Romance...hometowns and heartstrings.

USA Today Bestselling author Tess Thompson writes small-town romances and historical romance. She started her writing career in fourth grade when she wrote a story about an orphan who opened a pizza restaurant. Oddly enough, her first novel, "Riversong" is about an adult orphan who opens a restaurant. Clearly, she's been obsessed with food and words for a long time now.

With a degree from the University of Southern California in theatre, she's spent her adult life studying story, word craft, and character. Since 2011, she's published 24 novels and 5 novellas. Most days she spends at her desk chasing her daily word count or rewriting a terrible first draft.

She currently lives in a suburb of Seattle, Washington with her husband, the hero of her own love story, and their Brady Bunch clan of two sons, two daughters and five cats. Yes, that's four kids and five cats.

Tess loves to hear from you. Drop her a line at tess@

tthompsonwrites.com or visit her website at https://tesswrites.com/

Made in the USA
Las Vegas, NV
13 May 2021